The chin across the captured humans, passed on, then suddenly swept back as the general riveted his full attention on Davidson.

For a long instant the two were frozen, their gazes locked as surely as any duel. Then the chimp's eyes widened in outraged surprise. He threw up one long arm and pointed a stiff, quivering finger at Davidson.

"Attar, this one looked at me!" the chimpanzee general roared, turning to glare at the dark-pelted gorilla commander.

"He won't do it again!" Attar snarled.

Davidson reacted in reflexive shock. He grabbed Attar's wrists and stared at him in disbelief.

"You talk . . ." he said, amazed at an ape speaking a recognizably human tongue.

The black gorilla commander pulled back angrily. *"Take your stinking hands off me, you damn, dirty human!"*

He smashed Davidson's chin with stunning force, sending him spinning away into unconsciousness.

Also published by HarperEntertainment

Planet of the Apes
a novelization for young readers
by John Whitman

Planet of the Apes: Leo's Logbook—
A Captain's Days in Captivity
by Benjamin Athens

PLANET OF THE APES ™

OF THE

By William T. Quick
Based on the Motion Picture Screenplay
By William Broyles, Jr., and
Lawrence Konner & Mark D. Rosenthal

HarperEntertainment
An Imprint of HarperCollinsPublishers

HARPERENTERTAINMENT
An Imprint of HarperCollins*Publishers*
10 East 53rd Street
New York, New York 10022-5299

ISBN: 0-06-107635-X

First HarperEntertainment paperback printing: August 2001

Printed in the United States of America

Visit HarperEntertainment on the World Wide Web at
http://www.harpercollins.com.

Visit Planet of the Apes at www.planetoftheapes.com.

10 9 8 7 6 5 4 3 2 1

1

Deep space.

A blizzard of stars rushed in, vast beyond comprehension, pouring from the cup of time into the eye of eternity. Falling forward, falling onward, faster and faster—

Suddenly the perspective shifted, tossing the endless heavens across the grid of vision like a plate of thrown diamonds. And something . . . appeared.

Something glowing. A curl of luminescence, a lick of light, a rolling wave of electromagnetic pressure against the eye: a vacancy in space, a hole, a doorway?

Perhaps a doorway. A doorway in a star-streaked frame. The frame set above a control panel that glittered in Christmas tree profusion: winking, blinking lights, gleaming switches, enigmatic buttons.

Across the buttons . . . a long, hairy finger! Tap. Tap-tap. Tappity-tappity-tap! Digital patterns, a web, a path across the stars. Tap-*tap*!

The chimpanzee, his expression as he worked far more intelligent and aware than that of any normal monkey, wore a monitoring vest and helmet as he sat and watched his fingers leap and gavotte across the control panel. His brown eyes peered intently from beneath a bony shelf of brow, watching the panel, watching the screen, watching the panorama of stars wheel and swirl across the screen. His eyes widened as a sharp red light suddenly flashed with cruel clarity, limning his bulging features in a throbbing crimson glow.

Beeeeeeep! The piercing wail sharp as a razor, startling; the chimp jerked at the lash of sound. His fingers clutched, scrabbled at the buttons on the panel. *Beeeeeeep!* Panic now, a frenzy of fingers, spastic jitters. Heart pounding, breath whooshing, brown eyes wide, twitching and darting.

Faster and faster, negative feedback, loss of control . . .

BEEEEEE . . .

Black screen.

Shiny as a black mirror. In the mirror a reflection: slowly rising up, a face appeared. Captain Leo Davidson, a sturdy, dark-haired man in his twenties, reached over the chimp's shoulder and punched off the red light. The beeper stopped screaming.

Silence.

"You lose," Davidson said.

The chimp twisted in his harness, looked around the interior of the flight simulator, looked at Davidson. He opened his mouth, rubbery lips twisting around a confusion of chimp sounds.

Davidson nodded. "Surprised? I changed your flight sequence."

The chimp made more quizzical noises and turned back to the control panel. He tapped the dead keys, glanced at Davidson.

Davidson grinned at the chimp. "I know you can hit the fastball . . . but what about the curve?"

The chimp grimaced in puzzlement and banged harder at the unresponsive keyboard. When nothing happened, he looked at Davidson again.

"That's enough, Pericles."

The chimp twisted away, banged hard with both hairy fists on the control panel, the equivalent of a human five-year-old's temper tantrum.

"Stop it!" Davidson said, more sharply now.

Pericles ignored the order and continued to take out his frustration on the control board.

No response. Davidson fired his big gun.

"Or no treat!"

Pericles couldn't have ended his eruptions any faster if Davidson had stuck a live electrical cord in his furry ear. His long, flexible fingers stopped moving. He peered at Davidson anxiously.

"How well do I know you?" Davidson said, his tone rich with benign triumph. Evidently Pericles thought so, too, as he eyed Davidson silently and waited for his treat . . .

The huge craft coasted silently along, protecting the tender, delicate bits of life so carefully nurtured within, a metal shield against the cold and vacuum of space.

Davidson and Pericles walked hand-in-hand, with Pericles looking like a trusting five-year-old out for a walk with Daddy. As they passed by, Davidson glanced at a large representation of the *Oberon*'s ship identification icon on one wall: a stylized inverted triangle containing red and white stars and bars on a blue background above the name of the ship itself.

Beyond this was the entry to the animal living quarters. As always, the whoosh of warm, damp air and thunderously sharp animal smells that billowed into his face when he came through the door reminded him of pleasant childhood days at the zoo. The sounds came next, all the various grunts and hacks and sighs and snuffles that caged animals could make. To his human nose it smelled like long-forgotten excursions to see the lions and tigers and monkeys, but to Pericles, it smelled like home.

The first thing they saw as they entered was a large sign that read.

CAUTION: LIVE ANIMALS.
SECURITY ACCESS ONLY.

They strolled past dozens of cages, some empty, most occupied. The occupants of each cage were identified by square tags on the cage fronts with serial numbers and nicknames etched into the metal.

Davidson thought what he always thought when he came to visit this place: *Welcome to the Monkey House . . .*

There sure as hell were enough monkeys around. An orangutan, hump-shouldered, hairy as a giant Pekinese, watched them solemnly with a saggy-chinned old-man expression. A gibbon with his distinctive solid black face surrounded by a flaring muff picked his nose as they went past. And a gorilla, wide as an ox and about as lively, snorted phlegmatically over a belly like a kettledrum at Pericles, though he ignored Davidson entirely.

Most of the cages were filled with chimpanzees, however, a loud, noisy, and sometimes irritable crew, most of them now screaming raucous greetings at Pericles's return. Pericles eyed them with haughty disdain. He was a pilot, and he knew it.

In the background, medical techs had a few of the apes out of their cages, exercising them, checking them out, or just playing with them. One of the techs, with a chimp watching intently, picked out the tune of a simple melody on an electric keyboard; Davidson had heard it a million times, but never could remember its name. After he finished, the tech made way for the chimp, who leaned forward, placed his finger on the keyboard, and mimicked the tune exactly. All of these monkeys, Davidson knew, required a lot of human contact to stay in good mental shape. Which only made sense. Thanks to the marvels of gengineering, these were some of the smartest apes that had ever existed.

Up ahead the chief medical officer, Lieutenant Colonel Grace Alexander, turned and saw them coming. As soon as he spotted her, Pericles dropped Davidson's hand like a boiled potato and went loping down the hall toward the woman, who spread her arms wide in welcome, then staggered slightly as Pericles heedlessly leaped into her embrace.

She got him settled, looked down, saw how upset the chimp still was. "Was the *Homo sapiens* mean to you again?" she cooed into Pericles's ear. She looked up at Davidson. "We all know it's just rocket envy."

Ouch, Davidson thought. He didn't want to think about how right Colonel Alexander was, or how pathetic it was for him to be jealous of a monkey. But he managed a smile as he gestured at Pericles's passionate hug. "Ever consider an actual boyfriend?" he asked her.

"You mean, do I *enjoy* being miserable?" She snorted. "I'll stick with my chimps."

Pericles, growing bored with the human byplay, suddenly jumped away from Colonel Alexander's arms, bounced, and landed on the stainless steel counter nearby. He reared up, grabbed the latch of an overhead cabinet, and pulled open the door. Behind the door was a huge bag of treats, which the monk stared at wistfully. Leo watched a second, then went over, reached into the bag, and pulled out a biscuit. Pericles's alert brown gaze followed him every inch of the way. Grinning, Davidson put the hand holding the treat behind his back, then held out both hands, fisted, for Pericles's inspection.

Pericles eyed first one hand, then the other, his hairy visage solemn as a judge. He chose Davidson's left fist. Davidson uncurled his fingers to reveal an empty palm. Pericles's forehead wrinkled. Immediately, he indicated Davidson's right hand. Davidson opened it. Empty again!

Pericles's eyes opened wide. He let out a sound that was halfway between a screech and a whine, a clamor of pure frustration.

"Another curveball," Davidson agreed. He reached into his back pocket, pulled out the treat, and gave it to Pericles, who swallowed it in a single gulp.

Colonel Alexander's lips quirked in disapproval. "You weren't authorized to change his flight training," she said.

"I'm teaching him."

"You're teasing him."

Davidson watched Pericles glowering at him. The chimp didn't look exactly happy . . .

"He's gene spliced, chromosome enhanced . . . state-of-the-art. He can take it."

Alexander eyed him dubiously.

"When you frustrate them, they lose focus. Get confused, even violent."

Suddenly the sounds of a nearby disturbance distracted both the humans and the monkey. Inside a large cage, a chimpanzee was raising a ruckus, jumping, slapping at the bars, whining insistently. Alexander led Pericles over to the caged chimp.

"Congratulations, Pericles," she said. "You're going to be a daddy."

Pericles stood before the cage, peering at the female on the other side of the door as she flung herself with even greater vigor at the bars. He looked faintly puzzled, as if he couldn't figure out what the uproar was all about.

Davidson knew the feeling. He suspected it was a common emotion, shared by all males in the presence of the females of their species in full-tilt upset mode. He glanced at Alexander. "I thought I saw a smirk on his face."

The two of them stared at Pericles's erstwhile mate, who was now reaching a crescendo of emotional clamor. Her fervor almost frightened Davidson. He wondered what Pericles thought about it.

"Actually," Alexander said dryly, "the female was the aggressive one." She looked directly at Davidson.

No kidding, Davidson thought with a small inward

shudder. He'd known a few of *those* in his life, too. Maybe even this one right in front of him. *Is she coming on to me?*

"Aggressive works for me," he said, and thought he detected more than a flicker of response as he stared boldly into Alexander's eyes.

Their minor flirting was interrupted by a young tech who walked up to Davidson, grinned, and said, "Hey, Leo. You got a postcard."

Davidson nodded his thanks and took the small wireless screen the tech handed to him. The screen was blank, except for the date blinking in one corner: 02–07–2029. He glanced at Alexander, then wandered off to find a quiet corner so he could read his mail.

He got himself settled in, out of the general busyness, and clicked the screen. Immediately he was looking at a full-motion video shot of the front of his house back home. Squeezed together in a small crowd were his mom and dad, his sister, his younger brother, and a small posse of other assorted relatives. They were all smiling and waving madly. One little boy was waving a toy model of the *Oberon* itself, the ship where Davidson was now reading his video mail.

Davidson's mother, looking flustered, which only made her seem even more like the woman in the cookie commercials, glanced at somebody offscreen and said, "Now?" Davidson couldn't hear the answer, but his mom turned back to face him, gathered herself, took a breath, and said, "Okay. Hi, honey . . . It's me, your mom."

Hi, Mom, he mouthed silently.

In the close-up shot, he could see she was wearing a tiny pin in the shape of the *Oberon* on her chest. The camera jittered a moment and swung away, revealing the run-down airstrip in the background, a primitive wind sock dangling limply, and several small planes in front of a sagging, paint-scoured hangar.

Davidson smiled softly. This was the place where he'd first discovered his dreams of becoming a pilot. What a great leap, from that place to where he was now!

The camera's focus returned to his mother as she said, "I have so much to tell you . . ."

But Davidson's father good-naturedly elbowed in, grinning. "But she won't," he said. "'Cause this is costing me a fortune." His smile widened. "Hi, son. The TV showed some pictures of you from space."

A sudden burst of static distorted the picture. Davidson looked up, two vertical creases suddenly appearing above the bridge of his nose. *That's weird . . .*

Then the video returned. "We're all real proud of you," his father was saying.

And over his dad's shoulder, his mom added, "We just want you to come home to us safely . . ." Then she choked up, couldn't go on.

Davidson felt himself choking up a little, too.

Abruptly, the video of his family vanished entirely from the screen. More static, then a total blank, followed by the message: YOUR SERVICE HAS BEEN INTERRUPTED.

He shook the little screen, then banged on it, but nothing happened.

Except that *all* the lights in the room around him went out. In the darkness, he could hear the panicked animals going nuts, screaming, hooting, howling, banging on their cage bars.

The lights flared back up to normal brightness. *What the hell . . . ?* Davidson wondered. He glanced at

Alexander, who looked equally puzzled, then turned and dashed from the room.

Davidson jogged up to the security door that guarded entry to the *Oberon*'s bridge. Next to the wide, thick barrier made of shatterproof, mono-steel reinforced superglass was a handprint identification reader that was monitored and operated by a central security computer. Davidson placed his palm on the surface plate of the reader, then waited while the computer read the unique whorls and lines of not just his fingerprints, but his entire palm as well. Finally the telltale flashed green and the security door slid ponderously open; he pushed hurriedly on through to the bridge.

The lighting had been somewhat dimmed in the control room of the vessel, the better to see the large digital data screen that dominated the area. At the moment, the screen didn't seem to be showing anything—just a swirling, twisting rush of visual noise patterns, rich in colors and motion, but devoid of any coherent information—a computer-generated light show.

Davidson glanced at Frank Santos and Maria Cooper, a pair of air force majors standing next to him, then turned back toward the screen, where he finally noticed Karl Vasich, the fortyish commander who ruled the *Oberon* and everybody aboard with an iron hand. Vasich was working on the control panel with a young specialist whose name, Davidson vaguely recalled, was Hansen.

"We found it," Frank said.

Maria shook her head. "It found us."

Davidson looked at the screen. The formless colors had resolved into the starry black of deep space. But something was growing there, rushing toward them. A twisting, boiling cloud of energy. He'd never seen anything like it before. It was *huge* . . .

"It's moving like a storm," Hansen said, sounding impressed, and not a little frightened.

Vasich nodded curtly. "That's what it is. An electromagnetic storm."

"This is what's causing the blackouts on Earth," Frank added.

Maria watched the thing growing, growing. "It's . . . beautiful." She sighed.

Vasich gave her a look that might have been scornful. "So's the sun, till you get too close."

"This is weird," Hansen interrupted, as he worked his own controls. "I'm picking up frequency patterns."

Vasich looked over his shoulder. "Tune them in," he ordered.

The shifting wash of light across the screen twitched, then suddenly resolved into a flickering series of momentary images—like somebody channel-surfing at warp speed. The process was so rapid Davidson knew he wasn't catching everything, but in quick succession he made out an ancient set of television color bars, a nearly forgotten sight from the dark ages of broadcasting; a quick glimpse of something from the TV Ur-Western *Bonanza*; grainy figures kicking at a soccer ball, along with a recognizable scrap of noise as the announcer called the action in Arabic; oddly dressed teenagers dancing forgotten steps to unknown pop tunes in front of the *American Bandstand* logo; some kind of quiz show; the reassuring, hound-dog visage of Walter Cronkite, telling the world how it was on that long-vanished day; an earnest chef laboring over a cluttered cabinet topped with plates, dishes, cooking utensils; a senseless fragment from some vanished *Tom and Jerry* cartoon; a forest of sawing violins and a frantically pumping conductor leading a BBC symphony presentation; Fidel Castro, dark-bearded and long-haired, looking about twenty years old, waving his arms as he spoke passionately about something or other; Ally McBeal, thin as a stick, expression rapidly changing; a flash of posterboard Spanish, some indecipherable public service message; what looked like a million Chinese troops wheeling rigidly past a reviewing stand on which a smiling Mao Zedong waved cheerfully . . .

What made the experience even more surreal was that the soundtrack, with only a few accidental exceptions, had nothing to do with the images. As he watched the visual stew, Davidson heard an urgent, desperate-sounding radio announcement in what he thought was Korean; choppy electronic blurts from long-disconnected cell phone conversations; equally fragmentary bits from a time when airplanes were guided by men who sat in towers and actually spoke with pilots, which segued jerkily into a ten-second slice of some PBS program about the history of communication.

And a hundred more. It was as if every sound and image from the entire history of human broadcasting had been compressed into one infinite blurt of information. It made Davidson's head spin. He grasped for reality, finally found it by reading the date running along the bottom of the screen: 02–07–2029. Today's date. The real time in the real world . . .

Hansen stared at the screen. "It's sucking up satellite relays, cell phone conversations, TV broadcasts, every electronic communication from Earth . . . from all time."

Hansen sounded a little awed at the notion, Davidson thought. Well, why not? It *was* a little awesome. It was also a little weird and funny, and as usual, he couldn't keep his mouth shut about that, either. "Ten billion channels and nothing to watch," Davidson said.

What he was seeing on the screen and the aural scraps he was hearing didn't really do justice to the overwhelming wash of electronically frozen data that was assaulting the *Oberon*. But there were electronic counters on the sides of the digital screen, far faster and more sensitive than anything a human possessed naturally, and they were going crazy in their own digital version of polynomial overload; occasionally the readouts would pause just long enough for Davidson to see a number that looked impossibly large—until the next pause, and an even larger number.

The ship *shuddered*, as if some giant invisible hand had picked it up and shaken it. The huge screen went dark for an instant, then flickered back on as everybody caught his balance. Davidson realized his heart was thundering, and from looking at the expressions on others' faces, he knew he wasn't the only one.

Major Cooper said nervously, "It sure knows how to get your attention."

For himself, Davidson was giving some seriously concentrated thought to what sort of forces it took to boot a ship as big as the *Oberon* around like a hockey puck made of Silly Putty . . . and not liking much what he was coming up with.

Commander Vasich didn't look any happier with his own thoughts than Davidson felt with his, but at least

Vasich seemed to have made up his mind. The commander looked at Davidson and said, "Let's get to work. We'll start with a pass through the core. Take initial radiation and gamma ray readings."

Davidson raised his head, but before he could open his mouth to speak, Vasich brusquely cut him off. "Get your monkey ready," he said.

Davidson wanted to tell him that the order sounded like the tagline to a dirty joke, but decided that probably wouldn't help his case any. Instead, he said, "Sir, this is a waste of time."

Vasich eyed him coldly. "We have standard procedures."

Davidson overrode him. "And by the time you go through all of them, it could be gone."

But Vasich was no dummy. He could read Davidson's mind—at least on this issue—just about as well as Davidson could himself. Not that he liked the message he found there . . .

"*No manned flights!*" he said, shaking his head. "First we send out an ape, then if it's safe we send a pilot. *In that order!*"

"Let me do my job," Davidson replied heatedly. "You need somebody out there who can *think*, remember that?"

Vasich's sour expression showed what he thought about that recommendation.

Undeterred, Davidson plowed on: "You *need* me."

"The monkey's the canary," Vasich replied. He gestured at the maelstrom on the big screen. "That's the coal mine. Alpha pod deploys at sixteen hundred hours."

Which pretty much ended the discussion, whether

Davidson liked it or not. As a matter of fact, he didn't like it at all . . .

The *Oberon*'s pod launch platform was a busy place. Colonel Alexander and her crew scurried about, providing backup and support to Davidson as he worked to secure Pericles in the Alpha pod. Despite working hard to conceal his own misgivings, Davidson could see, from the way the chimp's large brown eyes darted nervously back and forth, that Pericles was picking up on his own bad vibes. He gave Pericles's flight suit one last careful inspection, hoping the extra attention would reassure the chimp and calm him down. It was bad enough sending a monkey out to do a man's job; far worse to send out a monkey too upset to function as well as he was able. The prospect of that made Davidson think uncomfortably of murdering a blameless animal, though Pericles was far more than any normal animal. At the bottom of things, Davidson was just plain *worried* about Pericles.

"Just follow your sequence and then come home," he urged the chimp. He leaned closer, looked deep into the monkey's eyes, and said with subdued emphasis: "You understand? *Home* . . ."

He could see that Pericles was picking up on his own unease, but the chimp was gutsy as hell, in his own simian way. Nevertheless, as the crew finished up and pulled back from the pod, Pericles looked up at Davidson and let out a long, plaintive sound—he couldn't speak in any human tongue, but to someone who knew him well—like Davidson—the meaning was plain.

Davidson stepped back from the pod, grinned reassuringly at Pericles, then slowly, firmly, gave him the thumbs-up sign. Pericles stared at the gesture, then looked down at his own elongated fingers, deep in thought. Finally he touched his own thumb, uttered another plaintive sound, and raised it to Davidson.

Then they shut the pod door on him, and that was the last Davidson saw of him.

Good luck, you poor sonofabitch, he thought. *Good luck . . .*

The flight control deck thrummed with tension. Davidson was huddled with his boss, Commander Vasich. Gathered around Colonel Alexander and Major Santos, the rest of the team conversed in hushed tones as everybody kept an eye on the telltales, the readouts, and the big digital screen overhead. Davidson was plugged into his own headset, listening to an aural soup of technobabble, data that even he barely listened to anymore. Above him a stomach-churning wash of color ebbed and flowed across the screen.

Commander Vasich turned, looked up at the board, suddenly went rigid with concentration. Davidson followed the direction of his gaze just in time to see the course of Pericles's Alpha pod tracing a path across the maelstrom, a scribble of bright color against a stormy digital sea. The pod itself was a gleaming point of light heading toward the darkly burning heart of the energy fields. Davidson watched the mote crawl deeper and deeper into the info-cluster, remembering how Pericles had been in the training pods—and how a few curveballs during the mission mockup had confused him, frustrated him, finally disabled him. And then he thought about Pericles replaying exactly the same thing, except *this* time it was for real, and Davidson knew even *he* wouldn't be able to anticipate all the curveballs likely to come whizzing his way, aimed right at his head.

Damn it, I'm the one who should be out there . . .

Just as the thought seared his mind, the screen punched in closer and the Alpha pod began to flicker. Davidson was afraid he knew what that meant, but before he could say anything, Colonel Alexander, her own worries plain on her face, leaned forward and said, "What's wrong?"

"He's off course," Davidson replied, and watched her face change.

But not Vasich. His face might as well have been carved from the same block of ice as his voice, as calm and without emotion as a winter snowbank.

"Lock on him," Vasich said.

Davidson reached across his control board, found a red lever, pushed it forward. By now everybody knew that things were no longer going according to the script, but nobody yet had any hint just how bad things could get. Davidson was starting to get an idea, though. He looked over at Vasich.

"He's not responding."

Colonel Alexander, in full alarm mode, was now personally monitoring her own team's boards. "Surge in the heart rate," she rapped out. "He's scared."

All her monitor lights flashed bright, then went dead. Everybody stared.

Oh Jesus, Pericles . . . Davidson thought.

"Light him up again," Vasich barked.

Davidson punched a rapid series of keys on his board, did it again. Nothing. "I can't . . ."

The command deck exploded in frantic activity as everybody struggled to learn what had happened, to regain contact with Pericles. Everybody was so busy that only a few happened to be looking at the big screen at precisely the moment that the flickering dot representing the location of Pericles's pod vanished.

"Jesus . . . he's gone," Davidson said, shocked.

Alexander looked up, glared. "He's trained to come back to the *Oberon*."

"If he's alive . . ." Santos added.

The knowledge was in all their faces. Vasich was unnaturally calm, Alexander trying to keep her worry under control, Santos and the others tightly wrapped but looking as if their fear might break loose at any second.

Davidson gritted his teeth. *If they'd sent me in the first place, none of this would be happening.* He turned toward Commander Vasich. "I'm waiting for orders, sir."

If Vasich could hear the contempt lurking just beneath the surface of Davidson's words, he gave no sign. "We'll just sit tight for now. And wait."

No, Davidson thought. He was so angry, so frustrated, that he barely trusted himself to speak. He slid from his seat, stood, looked at Vasich, and said, "I'm going to run some sequences in Delta pod. See if I can figure out what he did wrong." *What we did wrong, that's the real question.*

Vasich didn't say anything. He just watched Davidson stalk off the deck, then turned back to his own board, a patient, quiet, cold man, suddenly in far over his head.

* * *

Back on the launch deck, Davidson, in full flight uniform and helmet, slid into the command seat of the Delta pod, settled himself, and waited until the pounding ache in his chest began to lessen a little. As the pressure in his skull subsided, he began to listen to the scratchy, half-panicked chatter running across the flight deck control network that was plugged into his speakers.

He closed his eyes, then opened them and stared out through the pod's hatch at the immensity of space that surrounded the *Oberon*. By human standards, the vessel was huge. But here, spinning slowly in the diamond-velvet darkness, it was a speck, a mote, an insignificant afterthought in the consciousness of the universe.

I wonder, Davidson thought slowly as he stared at the stars, *if there's really that much of a difference between Pericles and me. On the galactic scale of things . . .*

He pushed the thought away. Mysticism had never been his strong suit. He was a man, Pericles was a monkey, and he had a job to do. The question would be whether Commander Vasich, with his by-the-book devotion to orders, would let him get that job done.

He switched on all the pod's systems, waited until the main screen lit up, and then began to run a series of flight simulations, variations on all the possible courses Pericles's Alpha pod might have somehow blundered into. The more he worked, the more depressed he grew. Vasich and the others might be worrying about the monkey wandering off course, but Davidson knew in his bones that wasn't what had happened. Something out there, something from the vast-

ness of the universe that neither monkey nor man knew
about, had jumped out of the shadows and *taken* the
chimp. He didn't know how he knew this, but he did.
The problem would be convincing Vasich, and also
convincing the tight-assed commander to let him do
something about it. For an instant, he felt an overwhelming flash of worry about Pericles. In his own
way, he loved the chimp as much as he would any fellow human pilot.

Just as he began to muse about what he might actually *do* about the situation, Vasich's voice cut through
the babble washing into his ears.

"Okay . . ." Vasich said. "That's it. We lost him."

Not yet, we haven't, Davidson thought. He took a
deep breath, then began to run his fingers across the
pod's control panel as he watched the telltales light up
in response.

Frank Santos's voice interrupted: "Want to send another chimp?"

Davidson's fingers stopped moving for a moment
as he waited for Vasich's reply. It came an instant
later.

"No, it's too dangerous. Shut it down."

About what I expected out of you . . .

Davidson took another deep breath, and lifted his
hands from the controls. He swung his pilot's chair
into the command position, felt it lock in with a solid
metallic clunk.

Now for the tricky part.

He reached over, groped for Delta pod's door lock,
found it. Punched LOCK. Slowly, hissing, the door
swung shut. Davidson checked his flight helmet, then
keyed up the pod's control panel to full active-launch

status. He closed his eyes, leaned back in the pilot's chair, gathered himself.

Hang on, Pericles. I'm coming . . .

With the gloom of Commander Vasich's last words ordering the abandonment of their mission still hanging in the silent air, the command deck was a depressing place. Only Vasich seemed to be concentrating on what was left of the mission. The others stared blankly at nothing, or busied themselves with useless maintenance tasks, anything to take their minds off the meaning of their failure. Of Pericles's failure.

So it was Vasich who noticed the anomaly first. He stared at the main screen, at the readouts, and at first he couldn't believe his own eyes. Equipment malfunction? No, there was confirmation coming in. There was no way that *all* the systems could be whacking out at the same time.

Hansen blinked, turned, astonished. "*Sir*! Delta pod has launched," he said.

They all clustered together, pretending that the launch was a huge mystery, while Vasich ran the controls like a robot. But it was no mystery. They all knew.

What they didn't know was *why* Davidson had done it. Or what to do next.

Davidson knew. He just didn't know how it would turn out. As he was now realizing while he pulled on his flight gloves and then continued entering the codes and courses he knew so well into the pod's control panel. Outside the pod, the vast, gleaming bulk of the *Oberon* slid slowly past, his minnow gliding past the hulking whale.

It'll take old iron-ass about thirty seconds to figure out I actually disobeyed him, and then . . .

He grinned as Vasich's voice suddenly grated in his ears.

"Delta pod, your flight is not authorized. Repeat, your flight is not authorized."

No shit, Sherlock.

Davidson made a few final adjustments to the controls, and watched as Delta pod began to track a wide, elliptical trajectory away from the *Oberon* toward the roiling heart of the vast electronic cloud that had swallowed Pericles and the Alpha pod. He knew that *Oberon*'s bridge could track him as easily as he could himself. They knew what he was doing. Nonetheless, he couldn't stop himself from telling Vasich what he'd been thinking all along: "Never send a monkey to do a man's job," he replied.

Vasich's voice sounded like he'd just swallowed a road grader. "I swear you'll never fly again."

Davidson shrugged. "But I'm sure as hell flying now."

Put that in your tailpipe and smoke it . . .

On the *Oberon*'s flight deck, Vasich listened to Davidson's sally with the expression of a man who'd just discovered his toilet paper was made out of steel wool.

Specialist Hansen, the only one who still seemed to be keeping up with the standard operations routines, checked the big screen and swallowed hard.

Vasich looked at Hansen, then up at the screen. Something blinking there . . .

Hansen said, "I'm getting a Mayday, sir. Jesus! It's on our secure channel!"

"Alpha pod?" Frank Santos cut in.

Hansen looked at the screen, then at his controls and

readouts, then back at the screen. Obviously flummoxed, he said, "I . . . don't know. But it's coming on strong."

Vasich could see that for himself. But without knowing *which* pod had activated its beacon, he had no way to evaluate the situation, let alone decide on a proper course of action.

"Put it up," he told Hansen brusquely. They had the capability to parse the beacon's entire data stream and put the digitized result on the main screen. Maybe that would tell him something.

Hansen complied immediately. The screen jittered, shifted, then adjusted to the new data flows and abruptly cleared of static. They saw bits and pieces, flashes of faces and shapes, but so fogged by visual interference it was impossible to make out exactly who, or what, they were.

But the sound was like everything else they'd heard from the heart of the digital cloud: unsynchronized, scratched with static, nearly random. A babble. A tower of digital Babel.

"Help us . . . Massive turbulence. Request instructions . . ."

Vasich stared, bug-eyed with shock. He looked slowly about the bridge, saw the same incomprehension smeared on every other face.

Vasich lunged for the radio controls, slammed open a link, and shouted, "Delta pod! *Abort mission!* Repeat, Delta pod. Return to ship!"

No answer, just hissing static.

Vasich listened hopelessly to the sound of his words emptying into the vast, whispering silence of the universe.

* * *

In the cramped command module of Delta pod, David-son was no longer paying attention to anything coming from Vasich or the *Oberon*. He had his own problems.

On his screen, he'd thrown up the last course Peri-cles had followed in Alpha pod, at least the best ap-proximation of that course his computer could come up with and was trying to match it with seat-of-the-pants flying. It was no easy task, not with the interfer-ence he was getting.

Vasich's final cry vanished into a rising tide of static. Concentrating on his own screens, he had only a fragment of attention left over for the larger region through which he flew. But he was a pilot, and pos-sessed the sixth sense all pilots had when it came to danger and his own safety.

A tsunami of light came roaring out of the cloud, a blazing visual overload that slammed into his tiny ship with the same force it slammed into his over-amped vision.

What?

It was like being tossed in a champagne glass full of burning light-bubbles, and it overwhelmed everything else, left his brain screaming for mercy and his heart climbing into his throat.

He fought the controls as the monstrous wave broke over him, pounding breakers of energy that tossed his tiny vessel about like a kernel of popcorn in a microwave.

Sweat bloomed on his brow, ran down into his eyes, further blinding him. A great crescendo of sound bat-tered at his ears. He bared his teeth and hung on until, just when he thought he couldn't take it any longer, the vast, frightening wall of energy rushed on past, vanishing as quickly and mysteriously as it had come.

In the strange, ringing silence, he looked out on a swath of once-again peaceful space, and saw, distant and glimmering, the flicker of Pericles's beacon. Hope filled his chest like a breath of cold, clean mountain air. He scrabbled for the comm switch, adjusted it, saw he had a clean link to the *Oberon* again.

"*Oberon*! I've got a visual on Alpha pod. Over!"

He couldn't tell if the energy wall had damaged his craft, Alpha pod, the *Oberon*, or even all of them. But it didn't matter, because the result was the same: another wash of static across his screens and from his headset. Nothing like a reply. For all intents and purposes, the *Oberon* had vanished, and he was alone.

Not a good feeling.

I've still got a mission, he told himself as he locked his course once again on Alpha pod. For a fleeting moment he wondered if Pericles was still alive. Had the monkey been battered by the same light wave that had pulverized him? What would Pericles have done?

Probably panicked and tried to hide under his chair . . .

Poor little monkey.

Another wave of light came billowing up from the cloud, roiling and boiling, and when it had passed, the disaster was complete. Out in the dark and the black, where Alpha pod had been at least a flickering, beckoning dot of hopeful light, Davidson now saw nothing. The pod was gone.

How can it be gone?

Didn't matter. It was.

"*Oberon*? Come back . . . ?"

Nothing but ominous silence.

"*Oberon* . . . ? Come back . . ."

He might as well have been a mouse, squeaking into a hurricane.

No Alpha pod. No *Oberon*.

And now, to his horror, yet another tidal wave of energy roaring in, bigger, thicker, like light somehow turned into superheated honey . . .

He fought the controls, but knew it was no use.

The wave hit . . .

2

The wave of force slammed into Delta pod like a hammer made of frozen light. Davidson felt it first as a slow heaving that lifted his craft, then began to shake it like a wolf with a rabbit in its teeth.

The shuddering vibrations surged and tore at him. He could feel the muscles in his back stretching, threatening to rip away from his spine. He closed his eyes, gritted his teeth, hung on . . .

Then it stopped. Just like that, nothing . . .

Davidson opened his eyes just in time to see everything on his control systems go dark. The blank, black monitor gleamed at him, as empty as the eye of a corpse. The silence stunned him. Then, as he realized what it really meant, panic clawed through his brain.

No sound. No engine noise. No hum of powerful heaters protecting him against the endless, killing cold of space. No whisper of air, cool, filtered air, whooshing into the compartment. Into his lungs . . .

His throat locked on a scream. He pounded on the controls with all the force he could muster, hoping that something had shorted out, that maybe he could slam it back, reestablish connections, make everything work again.

Then, out of the corner of his eye, he saw a sight that chilled him to the marrow of his bones: on the cockpit window, a single crystal of ice appeared, glittering like a flawless diamond. For an instant the crystal simply hung there. Then, spreading out from it, appeared tiny, glassy tendrils, like a spiderweb weaving itself across the window at hyper-speed. He stared at the ice web in horror; outside Delta pod, the ambient temperature approached absolute zero, minus 454 degrees Fahrenheit; without his heaters working, it wouldn't be long before the interior of the pod matched that chill. Cold enough to freeze human flesh to the consistency and brittleness of glass in a few seconds.

The thickening web of frost reached the edge of the cockpit window and kept right on going, coating every interior surface with a congealing skin of frozen moisture. Finally the effect reached Davidson himself: the air inside his helmet abruptly turned into white fog. The tip of his nose burned, then went numb. He could feel his eyelashes grow stiff, heavy with ice. His helmet's faceplate first misted over, then went opaque as the coagulating air coated the high-impact pressure plastic like a shroud.

With the engine gone and the controls useless, Delta pod began to tumble. Without power the tiny craft was nothing more than a tin can with a human filling . . . a human filling about to be flash-frozen like a tin of freezer-burned sardines.

Davidson began to gasp. It felt as if he were trying to fill his lungs with snowdrifts. Reflexively, he cried out for help.

"*Oberon* . . . come in, *Oberon* . . ."

But there was no answer. Only the darkness creeping in from the edges of his eyes, from the edges of his brain. Death by freezing. He'd always heard that was an easy way to go. You just went to sleep . . .

No!

From somewhere he found a final reserve of terror-driven strength. He twisted in his seat, flailed at his helmet, felt his own blows as soft, distant thuds. Fading away . . .

Encased in his deadly icy coffin, Davidson didn't see the monstrous eruption of energy exploding from the heart of the digital cloud like a nuclear blast, this time roaring toward Delta pod as if some secret intelligence were guiding it like a weapon. The ravening discharge reached the tiny craft and swallowed it whole.

Everything that had happened before was like a love tap. Delta pod slammed first one way, then the other, trapped in the force fields like a dust mote in a tornado. Davidson felt gravity jerk him viciously in several directions at once. His helmet tried to twist itself off his head. A crushing weight slammed into his chest. He felt his ribs trying to spring loose. As the last dregs of his consciousness began to fade, he felt a curious lassitude. So easy to just let go, give up, let the darkness carry him down and down in the cold silence of his ruined craft.

Suddenly every piece of equipment in the pod flared back on. The controls beeped, flickered, hummed. The atmosphere system began to whir. Heated air gusted into his eyes, melted the frost on his faceplate, filled his laboring lungs with blessed warmth. His fingers and toes began to tingle.

The control monitor screen crackled with bursts of static, then cleared into sharp relief. The craft's digital time readout was spiraling crazily out of control, running with breathtaking speed backward, forward, then back again. Then it simply shattered.

Davidson stared at the clock and wondered what *that* meant.

He felt his heart rate slowly retreating toward normal. He flexed his stiffened fingers, was relieved to discover that everything still seemed to work. But just as he was allowing himself to hope that maybe he might yet survive this ongoing disaster, he glanced out the pod's window and saw the wheeling stars stretch into elongated needles of light.

The rush of forward acceleration crushed him against the back of his chair once again. Alternating waves of light and darkness rolled across his vision, gradually fading to a complete absence of light. At first he thought something had short-circuited in his battered brain and blinded him. But then a blue halo appeared, vast and glowing, like a gigantic bull's-eye into which he was inexorably tumbling. The blue halo wavered, then faded into a continuous rippling rush of blue and purple, coupled with the gut-wrenching sensation of an endless plunging fall.

This had all been in silence. Now, unexpectedly, he heard a faint whispering hiss that rapidly grew louder. He looked around, trying to discover the source, but had no luck. Yet the sound was familiar—a leak in Delta pod's hull? The sound of the last of his oxygen bleeding out into empty space? Then he realized: it was the sound of the air displaced by his passage through an atmosphere.

The thought stunned him. Only moments before, he'd been in deep space, no planet within light years. And yet somehow there was air around him now, grinding against his hull, slowing him, heating up the exterior of the pod.

A quick glance out the window confirmed it: the tiles of the heat shield on the nose of the pod were white hot, shading into a dull, burning red farther back. Flames leaped and spurted the length of the hull. And now thick, greasy black smoke began to boil from the interior vents, a choking miasma that rasped down his throat and seared his lungs.

Going down too fast, gonna fry like a Cajun catfish, he thought wildly. He groped for the control panel, hoping to fire the retro rockets and slow his reentry—*reentry where, damn it*?—but the panel was so hot it burned the skin on his fingers. He could imagine the delicate mechanisms beneath the panel—now melted into useless slag by heat they were never designed to withstand.

Great, Davidson thought. *Now I'm falling onto a planet whose existence is impossible, locked up in what is basically a burning brick . . .*

And the impossible planet really *was* out there: through the window he could see the vast, curving roundness of it, shading off at the edges into the dark blue of atmosphere. Below him wheeled huge, whirling expanses of deep, forest-colored green, jungle-choked continents surrounded by sapphire-tinted seas, all beneath serried ranks of white, sun-sparked clouds.

The whole mess was rushing up at him as if he'd driven Delta pod over the edge of a thirty-mile-high cliff.

The next several minutes were hectic. Though knowing it was probably futile, Davidson tried everything he could think of to regain some measure of control over the pod. The friction of the atmosphere had slowed him enough that maybe there was a chance. Thank God the heat shield had performed as advertised. It had soaked up enough energy and then dissipated it in harmless flames that the pod's outer surfaces hadn't been destroyed. Aerodynamically, the craft had about the same buoyancy in flight as the average jet plane. But if he could get the engines going, or at least get the thing falling belly-down, he might stand a chance.

Sweat carved pallid trails through the black, smoky grease that coated his face. He worked frantically, one eye on the landscape roaring up from below, and in the final moments of his descent, he thought he just might make it.

Time shattered into a series of instantaneous visual snapshots: breaking through the clouds; the jungle below, amorphous greenery suddenly coming into focus; the flash of water, off to the right somewhere; the trees growing, growing . . .

The pod shrieked in final agony, tortured far beyond its design specifications. Then he could see the tops of the trees, and then, with a bone-cracking jolt, he blasted *through* the jungle canopy and smashed onto a broad expanse of water.

The pod skidded across the water like a skipping stone, throwing up a long, white rooster tail that sparkled in the sunlight. He heard the hull of the vessel creaking and groaning as superheated metal and ceramic hissed into cool, deep water.

Then his forward motion stopped, and the pod began to sink. Automatically he reached for the lever that would blast open the hatch lock. He yanked hard, heard the mechanism activate, but nothing happened. He lunged forward against his restraints, trying to see what had happened. The door had cracked open, but only a little. The outer hinges, obviously melted, had prevented the hatch from fully opening. And now cold, murky water was pouring into the pod. He glanced out the window, saw nothing but water and a few streams of rising bubbles. Delta pod was completely submerged.

He didn't think of himself as a coward, but the thought of drowning in some alien sea, trapped like a rat in the ruined pod, almost sent him around the bend. Panic and terror drove his muscles like pistons, gave him strength he never knew he had as he thrashed about, trying to free himself.

Finally his fingers found the ejection seat release, curled around the red steel handle, yanked it with all the power he had left in him. The cockpit door exploded soundlessly, releasing a boiling torrent of bubbles. The same explosion booted Davidson in the rear so hard he thought his spine had been driven through the base of his skull like a railroad spike.

He blasted through the cloud of bubbles like a torpedo, still strapped into his ejection seat, slashing through the turbid water until finally the pressure slowed him enough to let him move. He clawed frantically at the straps and snaps of his flight suit until he was able to tear the constricting garment away and free himself.

His lungs felt like they were about to explode as he thrashed toward the surface. He was at the very end of his endurance when he finally bobbed like a cork into the life-giving air and sunshine.

Heaving and gasping, he gulped in oxygen as he splashed around, his waterlogged clothing trying to drag him back under. After a while he got himself oriented, looked around, then began to swim awkwardly for the shore. When his feet scraped bottom he tottered to his feet, staggered the rest of the way onto a thin strip of muddy ground, and fell flat on his face in the brooding shadows of ancient, towering trees. Only the faint, slow rise of his chest in the muck showed that he was still alive.

For the time being.

Darkness . . .

The raucous chatter of birds. A blaze of light against his closed eyelids, pink and burning. The smells of mud, decaying vegetation, and a faint whiff of bitter smoke in his nostrils.

His head was pounding. Davidson lay still, feeling as if he'd just gone ten losing rounds with a world-champion heavyweight. Finally he groaned, rolled over, opened his eyes.

He winced as sun glare sent needles into his tender eyeballs. It took several seconds for his vision to clear. He sat up, groaned again as every overstretched muscle, every scrape, every fresh bruise sent out a chorus of agonized protest.

That was a mistake, he thought as he looked around slowly.

He was on the edge of a wide slough, the sunlight bouncing off the water so brightly he had to turn away, temporarily blinded by the glare. Across the narrow, muddy strip the jungle began. From here, it looked impenetrable, a wall of high, green foliage so dark it was almost black. The spaces between the thick, waxy brown trunks were choked with weeds, brambles, and thick-leafed undergrowth. He saw sharp flashes of color in the canopies of the trees, and heard strange-sounding cries; birds, he thought, but no birds he'd ever heard before.

In some ways everything seemed normal enough, but he couldn't shake the sensation that everything was also utterly *strange*, that everything he saw—trees, flowers, birds—was all somehow *different* from anything he knew on Earth. Yet he couldn't quite put his finger on what that difference was.

Maybe, once he got his wits back, figured out what had happened to him . . .

He wobbled to his feet and nearly fell back down when a wave of dizziness swept over him. But he held on, just barely managed to keep his balance, and finally, still swaying slightly, took another look at his surroundings from his new vantage point.

Nothing much had changed, though his vision seemed clearer, and his hearing was definitely sharper. He stared at the ominous wall of greenery, at the flickering shards of color as he listened to the soft flap-*whap* of bird wings, and in the distance, another sound, a woodsy kind of crunching noise, not immediately recognizable.

The scene was, in its own weird way, reassuringly peaceful . . . until he realized what the crunching noise was. Something big, moving through the forest. Moving in his direction.

A blood-chilling scream split through the soft hum and buzz of the other sounds like a cleaver through his skull. He jerked back, startled, and swiveled his head back and forth, trying to locate the source of the terrifying shriek. He couldn't see anything, but that didn't matter. He was a USAF pilot—a trained military man. Old reflexes kicked into gear. First rule about the approach of possible danger: *Get your ass under cover, and do it right now*!

To an amateur, it might have seemed crazy to run *toward* the jungle and the source of the possible threat, but there was no cover on the muddy beach—only in the trees, and if the trees concealed danger, the thick underbrush might also provide a hiding place and safety from that same danger. Davidson didn't consciously think about any of this. He just put his head down and *moved*.

He reached the tree line with a few long, lunging strides and didn't slow at all as he crashed through into the underbrush. The instant shift from the bright sunlight of the beach to the shadowy green dimness of the forest momentarily disoriented him, but he recovered quickly as his eyes adjusted. The adrenaline of panic had supercharged his senses. He still couldn't see much, though every shadowed movement, even the wind through the leaves, raised his anxiety level another notch. His nose didn't tell him anything useful at all. His surroundings smelled like any other old-growth forest choked with rotting mulch and flourish-

ing undergrowth. That left his ears, which had brought
him warning in the first place. He froze for an instant,
straining hard, listening intently. There were no more
screams, but . . .

Yes! It took some effort to sort it out from the background noises of birds and breeze-rustled leaves, but it
was there: in the distance somewhere but growing
closer, desperate, gasping breaths; the soft thud of running feet; the scrape of bodies against branches,
and . . . the chink of metal? That had a familiar feel to
it, but he couldn't quite place what it reminded him of.

Not just one body, either. Lots of bodies.

What the hell . . . ?

The muffled clamor seemed to be loudest off to his
right. That made his decision easy. He crossed his arms
over his head, hoping to protect his eyes, and began to
thrust through the packed shrubbery toward his left.

His waterlogged clothing and boots weighed him
down, made him clumsy as he thrashed along, but at
least it gave him a little protection from the stinging
nettles, ripping thorns, and whiplike branches that
made his mad dash a painful trail of fear and frustration. It was like one of those nightmares where you run
and run, but you just go slower and slower, and whatever it is rushing up behind you gets closer and
closer . . .

There could be no doubt now that he'd blundered
into *something*, though exactly what was a mystery.
Growing closer with every battered stride he took, he
could hear the sounds of frantic flight, soft muttered
gasps of exhaustion, the hammering beat of panicked
flesh against unyielding earth.

The ever-rising tumult was right on his heels when,

without any warning, he clawed his way through a heaving screen of sticker vines, stumbled over a noose of thick brown roots, and lurched wildly into a broad, barren expanse studded with rocks big and sharp enough to snap his legs like toothpicks.

The ruckus at his rear abruptly soared to a crescendo as he scrabbled to turn, to get himself set for whatever was coming after him. The nearly impenetrable screen of sticker vines began to shake, as if something big was trying to fight its way through.

With visions of hideous, man-eating alien beasts dancing in his skull, Davidson frantically looked for something—anything—with which to defend himself, but there was nothing, not even a branch he could use as a club. Only stones. He stooped, grabbed one hefty chunk, and raised it, just as the vines finally parted and a . . .

Man!

. . . smashed through the barrier and skidded to a halt in shock, staring openmouthed at Davidson.

The stranger had long, stringy gray hair and a face tanned nearly brown by the sun, seamed with lines of age so deep and harsh they looked like freshly healed knife scars. Overlaying this was an intricate layer of tattoos, twisting, convoluted patterns that made no sense to Davidson. But this creature who carried a leather sack of odd-looking fruits as he gaped at Davidson, eyes bulging, was human. Definitely a human male, fifty, maybe sixty years old.

And that's impossible, Davidson thought. *So who you gonna believe? The impossible, or your lying eyes*?

Davidson set himself and raised the stone in one hand, ready to club or throw. If this guy was a hallucination, no harm done. But if he wasn't, if he was, maybe, a cannibal looking for something different for lunch, well then, a nice hunk of rock might come in real handy.

For a long, breathless moment the two men stared at each other. Then Davidson caught the barest flicker of movement in his peripheral vision and tried to turn, but too late.

Something struck his wrist a stunning blow. The rock flew from his numbed fingers. He stared at the savage, barbarian woman who faced him, her long blond ringlets as matted and disheveled as any Terran aborigine, her sharp teeth bared in a warning snarl. And if he hadn't been quite so scared witless, he might have also appreciated her fine, muscular legs extending from beneath an enticingly scanty dress that also exposed mounds of nicely tanned breasts.

"Father, they're coming," the woman said.

The native man grunted, pushed forward, shoved Davidson out of his path, and loped quickly out into the stony wasteland. The woman gave Davidson one last warning glare, then wheeled and followed rapidly after the man.

Davidson gaped at the rapidly departing pair, but before he could figure out what—if anything—to do next, more of these strange, primitive humans came pouring out of the forest. Many also carried sacks overflowing with bright-colored fruit, and most of the males bore tattoos similar to those of the first older man. They rushed past Davidson as if he didn't exist, loping after their leader and his daughter with barely a glance in Davidson's direction, as if they had something far more pressing on their minds than a weird-looking human with no facial tattoos and a stunned expression on his face.

Before Davidson could fully catch his breath, let alone his composure, the entire ragged mob had vanished in the distance. He found himself alone again, but his solitude was no relief. It possessed definitely ominous overtones, the main one being . . .

What the hell are they running from?

There had been quite a few of those folks, and some of them had looked pretty tough. Not all the toughies were guys, either. It hadn't looked as if there was a single shrinking violet in the whole crew. Yet they were moving out like the hounds of hell were baying at their heels.

He slowly turned and gazed at the jungle. No hounds baying, hellish or otherwise. But as he leaned slightly forward, squinting at the shadows as if to force them to give up their secrets, he heard a definitely undoglike sound: he'd heard it before, and thought it had sounded vaguely familiar.

Now it came again, louder and clearer: the soft clash of bells, but again, oddly muffled, as if the full tone of the ringing was muted by contact with something else.

As the sounds grew closer and louder, Davidson began to see something moving in the dim green shadows deeper in the jungle. Something big. *Lots* of big somethings. Whipping through the trees as fast as squirrels—and now all the birds had gone stone silent.

A man with an out-of-control imagination might think these dark shadow things coming so fast were ghosts. Davidson doubted that the humans he'd seen were running from ghosts. They looked as if it would take more than a few phantoms to spook them.

But he still had no idea where he was, not even what planet he was on. Did ghosts announce their presence in this place by ringing muffled chimes?

He looked down at himself, at the cuts and scrapes and bruises, at the stinking, ragged, sleeve-ripped, mud-streaked regulation white pants and shirt he'd been wearing under his flight suit, and decided he was in no condition for a street fight with a bunch of alien specters playing some extraterrestrial version of "Jingle Bells."

At least the mob that had just gone past was demonstrably human. He had no idea what was coming toward him from the jungle now. It made his decision fairly easy.

He turned and ran as fast as he could across the rocky barrens until he reached the other side and vanished into the jungle. That woman might have slugged the rock out of his hand, but nobody had actually tried to hurt him. He wasn't sure he could say the same thing about what they were running from. Then it hit him: what *they'd* been running from was now what *he* was running from, too.

For Davidson, the next several moments were a whirling, chaotic jumble. He was at the absolute dregs-end of his strength, yet somehow he found a way to push himself further. Gasping, his chest heaving, he staggered on through the underbrush, too exhausted even to shield his face any longer, simply absorbing the flailing punishment from every passing branch and thorn, as if his skin had been anesthetized.

The forest here was not quite as dense as the one he'd passed through back on the other side of the stony field. In places he would break out into relatively clear patches where he could see a fair expanse toward his front. Once or twice he caught glimpses of the humans he was trailing, a flash of color, even heard high, thin cries of terror echoing in the distance. And now, behind him, the bells were growing louder again, although when he risked an occasional quick look back over his shoulder, he couldn't see anything out of the ordinary, not even the frightening black shadows ghosting through the thick canopy overhead that had scared him so much before.

He turned, redoubled his efforts, and though a red haze was growing at the edge of his vision and his heart was a continuous racing triphammer in his chest, he saw he was gaining on the humans up ahead. He could see several of the laggards clearly. He would have yelled at them to wait for him, but there was no room in his scorched lungs for air to make a cry. There was nothing he could do but keep staggering along and hope he could catch up before whatever was lurking behind caught up with him . . .

He'd reached another one of those relatively open patches where his forward view was almost unimpeded. He could see several of the strange humans, could even see the expressions on their distant faces when huge black shapes suddenly slipped down from the trees above them and fell on them like small dark clouds: clouds lavishly equipped with fangs and claws.

He was still too far distant—and the light under the trees too gloomy—for him to make out exactly what sort of beasts were dropping from above onto the shoulders and backs of the humans, clubbing them and dragging them down.

He could hear the panicked cries, the roars of anger and fear, the pleading and wailing. And he could hear other cries, almost familiar—but reminiscent of what? As he stared at the melee up ahead, he almost had it—but then the notion vanished as a body—a human body—came flying out of the woods on his right side, tumbled across his field of vision like a broken rag doll, and vanished into the thick brush at his left.

What the hell's strong enough to throw a full-grown human around like a kid's toy?

He decided not to wait to find out. In this case discretion, or at least flight, would be the better part of valor. The big question, though, was where to run? Forward seemed like as good an idea as any. A sudden rattling of the nearby shrubbery gave him a good start.

As he pounded along, the tumult grew all around him, shouts and cries of anger, panic, pain, and mixed in with these, a chorus of strange, grunting whines and the nearly continuous jingle of muffled bells. Out of the corners of his eyes he saw weird things: barbarically dressed humans fleeing lumbering, indistinct shapes, bloody wounds gaping; flashes of fur, some dark, some gold, some even red; a hurried glimpse of—armor? Something big wearing a metal breastplate like a Roman centurion?

Could that be? And if so, what the hell *could* it be?

Up ahead the foliage was clearing out, the underbrush thinning, and he was able to pick up speed. With a final burst he approached the forest eaves and saw a sun-drenched horizon beyond long, rolling terrain that culminated in a rise of low, round-topped hills. He spotted the tattooed man he'd first seen, still carrying his bag of fruit, gesturing to his remaining people with his free arm. He seemed to be trying to herd them toward the safety of the hills.

Davidson reached deep down inside himself and found a last surge of strength. He was rapidly closing the gap that would take him out of the jungle entirely when a blood-curdling growl sounded from somewhere above him. He looked up just in time to see a huge black shape hurtle down from the leaf-shrouded upper branches of a nearby tree, to land a few feet in front of him.

A gorilla.

It was a damned gorilla. Davidson skidded to a halt before he ran full tilt into the beast. This gorilla spread his unnaturally long arms wide, opened his mouth in a yawning growl, and showed Davidson a maw full of yellowed fangs.

Which was bad enough. What was worse was that the gorilla wasn't just some overhyped refugee from this planet's equivalent of a zoo. Across his massive barrel chest the animal wore an armored metal breastplate, finely worked with strange shapes and carvings. His head was protected beneath a full metal helmet that looked as big as a cooking pot. The beast also carried a sword in a scabbard at his waist, and wore a suit of dark, massive armor that protected his huge flanks.

Now this snarling, lunatic apparition began to advance, sweeping its grappling-hook arms back and forth like a professional sumo wrestler.

"Jesus!" Davidson blurted.

The ape didn't say anything, just bellowed louder and kept on coming. Davidson scrambled backward, looking for something he could use as a weapon. This monster outweighed him by at least four hundred pounds, and had teeth a lot longer and sharper than his own.

Unfortunately, there were no handy rocks anywhere in sight. Davidson bumped against some shrubbery, then grabbed a branch, held it like a spear, and turned back to face the advancing ape. It wasn't a very impressive spear, though, and so Davidson was amazed when the gorilla immediately stopped—almost as if puzzled—and glared at the makeshift weapon, then at Davidson himself.

Davidson had just enough time to think, *That's one surprised-looking monkey*, before the gorilla's perplexed expression vanished, to be replaced by a mask of utter ferocity. Moving much faster than anything so big had any right to, the gorilla's arms flashed out. He plucked the pathetic spear from Davidson's grip and snapped it like a toothpick.

The next thing Davidson knew, a pair of huge hands latched on to him like grappling hooks and he found himself rising into the air so fast he thought he'd left his stomach behind on the ground. He had a momentary whirling instant when he was looking *down* at the top of the ape's helmet, before he was spun away like a Frisbee.

He crashed back to earth with a bone-twisting, skin-scraping thud that knocked all the air out of him and left him momentarily stunned. When he was able to focus again he looked up, expecting to see the alien King Kong coming at him to finish the job, but the giant animal, evidently having satisfied himself that Davidson was no longer a threat, had turned his attention toward the rest of the fleeing humans.

Davidson huddled on the ground, trying to look as insignificant and harmless as possible, as he watched the rest of the amazing scene unfold. Out of the jungle poured more monkeys, all of them wearing the odd, archaic armor, but they didn't behave like any apes Davidson had ever seen.

They wheeled and moved in sharp battle formations, as smoothly practiced as the best human soldiers Davidson had known in his own training days. The big ape raised one massive arm, obviously a signal of some sort. High-pitched, brassy horns blared as the apes advanced, following their leader's direction.

On the head gorilla's back rode a heavy pack. The ape reached into it and took out a tangle of what looked like ropes and rocks. At first Davidson couldn't figure out what it was. But when the gorilla unsnarled it and began to whirl it around his head as he advanced toward the fleeing humans, Davidson recognized it: a primitive but terribly effective weapon that humans called a bolo, made of three connected ropes with weights on the end to give it the necessary heft.

The ape bounded through the brush, still whirling the ropes over his head, hard on the trail of the nearest stragglers. With a grunt of triumph he loosed the bolo. It whirred through the air toward its prey with a flat, vicious, whizzing sound. The hapless man had no warning. He heard the whine of the ropes at the very last instant and turned his head, enough for Davidson to see the panic in his eyes. Then the bolo snapped around his legs and brought him crashing down.

Almost before the man hit the ground, two more gorillas raced forward with long wooden poles. They fell on the man, clubbed him viciously into submission, then trussed him to the poles with no more dignity or concern than if he were a goat bound for the cook fire.

Davidson gaped, stunned. *Animals don't hunt humans . . .*

But these animals did. As if gorillas with bolos and poles for prey transport weren't bad enough, now a new threat appeared: wheeling out of the jungle in perfect order came the source of all those muffled jingle bells he'd heard. This fresh horror didn't even remotely look like Santa, though. It was a tightly disciplined squadron of gorillas, each one holding the edge of a huge rope net. The jingling sounds came from hundreds of tiny metal bells affixed to the net's strands.

The apes leaped forward, manipulating their net with a precision and grace that couldn't have been more perfect if their separate bodies had been controlled by a single brain. As they moved, they shook the net rhythmically, like human hunters driving scattered game toward a hidden stand of shooters. And that was how the humans reacted: no more than terrified animals, lurching and staggering away from the nets and the bells, succumbing to mindless panic, totally heedless of where they were being herded—or even that they were *being* herded.

Davidson staggered to his feet, sickened and horrified by what he was seeing. He still couldn't quite get his mind around it. These were *monkeys*, damn it! Animals, things you went to the zoo to see, beasts you tossed bananas at. Monkeys you *laughed* at.

Nothing to laugh at here.

His vision was getting hazy around the edges again, too much energy wasted, too many shocks to his system. The human mind can take only so much before it starts to shut itself down. He fought it, bit down hard on his lip, and the bolt of pain pushed the mists back for a moment. The instant of clearheadedness was enough to charge up his instinct for self-preservation and get him running again, but his normal military reflexes were battered into near-uselessness; without realizing it, he ran in exactly the wrong direction. But by the time he noticed his mistake there were gorillas advancing from the rear on either side of him, and in between them, shaking and jingling madly, was a tightly woven net.

But providence—or sheer, dumb luck—saved him once again. Just as the net was about to close over him, he stumbled forward into a shallow ditch. He hugged the ground as the bottom edge of the snare swept harmlessly above him, then continued on. Evidently the apes wouldn't stop to snatch a single human prey, when there were so many left to catch. It gave him a chilling moment of insight into how insignificant these *animals* thought humans were. Not even worth stopping to catch a few strays.

He scrambled out of the center of the melee by following the ditch until he was beyond the worst of it. As soon as he was up and out, he looked for a safer route through the jungle, but just as he started to move out, he found his path blocked by a stocky human running as fast as he could—which wasn't all that fast, because the man was carrying a terrified young girl, maybe five or six years old, in his brawny arms.

The man wasn't paying attention either to Davidson or to the pair of slavering gorillas rapidly coming up on him from the rear. Before Davidson could shout a warning, the gorillas caught up with the man and the girl. One of the apes reached out and plucked the shrieking girl from his grasp as easily as a man picking a daisy. The other smashed him in the back and sent him tumbling. Before the man could right himself, more apes swarmed him, and he disappeared under a scrum of heaving, snarling fur.

Davidson kept moving, but now the whole area was a confused tumult of apes and humans running in every which direction, screaming, roaring, lunging, and darting. To his numb and exhausted mind, there didn't seem to be any way out, at least nothing he could see. The whole area had become a maelstrom of ferocious apes and panicked humans. But it wasn't in him just to give up, not while he was still conscious and breathing.

Then he spotted the pair he'd seen at the very first: the older tattooed man and his fierce blond daughter. From the way they acted, it was plain they were the leaders of this band of ragged humans. Now they were urging a small group of their people through a stand of thin, new-growth saplings, still trying to get out from under the trees, where the apes wouldn't have the natural advantage of being able to attack from overhead.

The old man was wily, Davidson thought, and the woman fierce and brave. Though they were hopelessly outnumbered, they were still fighting. They were taking advantage of the sapling grove, using the tightness of the space between the willowy, graceful trunks as a way to dodge the bigger, heavier gorillas who couldn't slip through as easily. For a moment Davidson thought they might actually be successful. But as soon as the apes saw that their prey was threatening to escape, they came up with a simple way to nullify the human advantage. Roaring in anger, the huge animals simply yanked the saplings out of the earth by their roots, like pulling gigantic weeds.

But the old man wasn't done yet. Even as the apes with the net closed in on him and his charges again, he kept his head about him and watched the approach of the ominously jingling snare carefully. When the apes flung their net, he gave a quick hand signal, and then, with his daughter, dove under the net. Most of the others did likewise, leaving the apes growling in frustration and anger.

But the escape was only momentary. Before the humans could regroup, the same huge gorilla who had nearly caught Davidson streaked into their midst, snarling and clubbing with wild abandon. This ape moved with such speed, such overwhelming power, and such precision that the humans had no chance to escape his onslaught. Within moments the forest was littered with moaning, stunned people, easy pickings for the mop-up crew of apes that now stormed over them. In what seemed like the blink of an eye, only the old man and the woman remained uncaptured, and from what he saw, Davidson doubted that would remain true much longer.

A teenaged male, half-naked and scrawny, darted across Davidson's vision, half a dozen apes in hot pursuit. But with his youthful speed and slithery, slashing moves, the boy managed to keep a few steps in front of the slavering pack, and Davidson found himself inwardly cheering the kid.

Go on, go, keep on going!

But youth and agility weren't going to be enough. Just as Davidson thought the kid would break free and make good his escape, a dark shape swung down from a branch, dangling by hairy, muscular arms. The ape never dropped to the ground. He didn't need to. His bare, long-toed feet, as nimble as any human hands, snagged the boy and swung him screaming high into the air. The boy struggled, beating against the monk's massive thighs with his fist, but Davidson could see it was no use. The kid might as well have been trying to punch his way through a brick wall.

His struggles distracted his captor momentarily, though, long enough for the older man and his daughter to arrive on the scene, running hard toward the little battle. But their quest was hopeless, too. As Davidson watched, two more apes plummeted down from the trees. The first landed feet-first on the man and knocked him to his knees. The second slammed the woman down, rolled her like a bowling ball along the forest floor. The old man scrambled up and flung himself across the woman, trying to protect her. It did no good, just made them a more inviting target when the net settled over them with a harsh clash of bells.

They both struggled against the tough strands of rope, but to no avail. They were trapped like helpless rabbits, as thoroughly taken as the people they'd tried to lead to safety before. The last thing Davidson saw before he turned to run again was the woman, teeth bared, thrashing like some magnificent wild animal as the apes closed in on her.

A wild animal . . .

Davidson knelt behind a rotted-out tree stump, the sounds of the hunt slowly dying away, not so much from distance—he hadn't managed to get very far—but from the fact that the hunted had mostly been

taken, and the hunters were passing out of their raucous frenzy into quieter, less emotional territory.

Davidson crouched, breathing hard, for the first time
trying to *think*, to figure out what had happened to him,
what sort of insane nightmare he'd stumbled into. The
momentary respite lulled him into a dangerous sense
of false security, of having escaped the worst of it. He
even began to think he might escape this mad hunt entirely—though he didn't allow himself to consider
much beyond that. Getting away would be enough for
the moment. He could worry about what he would do
after that later—if he was able to survive that long.

He licked his lips, looked around, began to rise. A
gorilla on horseback exploded out of the woods, almost trampling him as he lunged to get away. The gorilla barely noticed him, busy with controlling the net
he was dragging, and the two humans entangled in it.

Something inside Davidson's brain snapped. He'd
had *enough*! Enough of hiding, of running from *monkeys* . . .

The ape on horseback was almost on top of him
now, still paying more attention to his struggling captives than to his surroundings. Davidson threw himself
at the hairy rider and caught him by surprise. The force
of his launch knocked the gorilla off his perch and sent
him spinning several feet away where he landed hard
and, obviously shaken, didn't get up immediately. His
mount panicked and skittered in the opposite direction,
wall-eyed and snorting. Davidson ran after it, vaulted
onto its back. The two human captives struggled out of
the net, then fled without a word of thanks.

Good idea, Davidson thought, and took off after
them. He didn't see the ape in the trees above him until

he was plucked from horseback and slammed to the ground with lung-crushing force.

The tumble knocked him out for a moment. When he came to, he was flat on his back. A fearsome growl sent chills down his spine as a shadow moved slowly over him, blotting out the sun. He stared up helplessly at the reddened eyes and grinning fangs of the huge gorilla standing over him . . .

3

The first thing he smelled was the stench of terror-sweat choking his nostrils. Davidson let out a soft moan as he sat up, wincing as each movement found a fresh knot of pain somewhere in his battered body. Nausea gripped his belly. His head ached horribly. He wondered if he'd picked up a concussion somewhere in the fight. He felt bad enough . . .

He closed his eyes and sucked air slowly into his lungs, ignoring the too-ripe medley of stenches that accompanied his shallow sips of oxygen.

He was sitting on hard-packed earth with a small group of a dozen or so beaten, thoroughly terrorized prisoners. He didn't recognize any of them, but that didn't matter. The whole scene had a nightmarish aura to it anyway. He came from a time and a place where people who lived like this had utterly disappeared from the Earth, even in its most remote and primitive places. People who wore animal skins and crudely woven cloth, who washed little or not at all, who covered their faces and bodies with myriad tattoos, whose knuckle creases and unshorn fingernails were so caked with ancient dirt it appeared to be an integral part of their flesh and bone—such people were the stuff of videos and e-readers in his time. They no longer existed in what he thought of as the real world.

But he knew his neighbors weren't hallucinations. His own mental figments could not, he was sure, smell as bad as these people did. If he were dreaming them, he would have done a cleaner job. Not to mention the bitter, distinctive scent of the apes he could see moving briskly about the temporary encampment. He pushed himself up on his knees for a better look, and discovered the source of the creaking sound. Several yards from where he sat was a line of bizarre carts covered with barbaric colors and intricate patterns that held no meaning for him.

But on these carts were high cages with metal bars, whose purpose was immediately obvious: as he watched, he saw a crew of apes being directed by the huge black gorilla leader who'd first attacked him. This beast made businesslike gestures as other monkeys grabbed shrinking, shivering, terror-stricken human savages and brutally tossed them into the mobile pens. And though Davidson had come to this place from a world in which the word was not even used any longer, he knew what he was looking at . . . he was looking at slaves.

Human slaves.

Slaves being thrown into cages by animals that, in any proper world, would be living in cages themselves. His throat thickened and he began to shake with rage, but there was nothing he could do except watch.

A small scuffle caught his attention and he saw the apes struggling with the blond woman, who was kicking and scratching and hissing with magnificent ferocity. Her resistance was so inspiring that Davidson found himself cheering inwardly for her, but before he could shout encouragement, the hulking muscles of the gorillas decided the battle and the woman went flying into a cage with the others. He watched as other familiar humans followed: the man who'd carried the little girl, and the teenaged boy, spitting and squirming, after him. Finally the monkeys dragged up the old man, the leader, who was barely able to walk, so badly had he been beaten. His face was bruised, swollen, and patchy with dried blood. The apes paid no attention to his injuries, just heaved him in after the rest.

Davidson didn't think he could get any angrier, but watching how those beasts manhandled that broken old man, he half-rose onto his haunches. He didn't consciously think about it. It was as if something basic to his very existence was commanding him to attack the apes and defend his own kind against them. But his slight movement must have attracted attention, because a huge gorilla appeared behind him, grabbed his wrists, whipped a rope around them, and yanked them tight.

Davidson tried to turn, to confront this new indignity, when he noticed that all the humans around him were bowing their heads, cowering like whipped dogs, refusing to lift their eyes from the ground. Whatever had spooked them so badly was masked by the blazing glare of the sun, and when Davidson tried to look, all he could see was a dark, amorphous shadow slowly approaching his group.

The big gorilla leader suddenly snapped to attention. Davidson didn't consider himself any kind of expert about reading monkey facial expressions, but he would have sworn the black ape looked smugly pleased, dripping with pride about hunting down tattered human prey so efficiently.

Then the light shifted a little, and Davidson finally could see what the big commotion was about. A figure too small to be a gorilla, but a monkey nevertheless, rode toward them on the back of a gigantic black charger. The monkey—a chimpanzee, Davidson decided—was tricked out in a glittering suit of armor that looked as if it were made of solid gold.

At the approach of this splendid figure, everything stopped. The human groans of agony trailed away, and even the apes all turned toward this demigod, following the example of their leader, the black gorilla. Davidson couldn't be sure, but he sensed a nearly religious awe in the way the monkeys regarded the newcomer.

So this one is the real *big cheese, then . . .* he thought, as he stared at the gleaming figure atop the huge horse. He didn't notice that he was the only human watching the approaching monkey, and even if he had, he probably wouldn't have understood what that meant.

The chimp jerked cruelly on the reins of his steed, making it cut and prance as it wheeled toward the knot of humanity where Davidson stood staring at him. The monk's shiny black gaze flashed across the group, passed on, then suddenly swept back as the rider riveted his full attention on Davidson.

For a long instant the two were frozen, their gazes locked as surely as any duel. Then the chimp's eyes widened in outraged surprise. He threw up one long arm, and pointed a stiff, quivering finger at Davidson.

"Attar, this one looked at me!" the chimpanzee general roared, turning to glare at the dark-pelted gorilla commander standing stiffly on the ground.

"He won't do it again!" Attar snarled.

Davidson reacted in reflexive shock. He grabbed Attar's wrists and stared at him in disbelief.

"You talk . . ." he said, amazed at an ape speaking a recognizably human tongue.

The black gorilla commander pulled back angrily. *"Take your stinking hands off me, you damn dirty human!"*

He smashed Davidson's chin with stunning force, sending him spinning away. The gorilla commander looked up at his general.

The Golden General nodded, jerked his horse aside, and rode on.

Seasick . . .

That was Davidson's first thought as he slowly drifted back to consciousness. The rolling, heaving motion he felt, along with the steady, rhythmic creaking that filled his ears, reminded him of his first few times on a large sailboat. He'd spent most of his time draped over the railing, consigning the contents of his belly to the surging waves. He felt the same way now, but the feeling lasted only a few moments before memory came rushing back, and he remembered what the incessant creaking really meant.

His next thought, as he opened his eyes, was that he was getting pretty damned tired of waking up this way. How many times had he been knocked out recently?

Not that there was a hell of a lot he could do about it right this minute . . .

Grunting with effort, he managed to sit up, surprised to find he didn't feel any worse than he had the last time he'd awakened. He didn't feel any better, either, but at least no worse. Maybe, in the larger scheme of things, that was an improvement. He wasn't sure, but he was happy to take whatever he could get.

The stench was, if anything, worse than before. For one thing, there were a lot more people in an even smaller space. The interior of the tiny enclosure was packed with bloody, sweating people; when he sat up, he pushed others aside without noticing. Now he saw them staring at him with empty expressions on their battered features.

None of them looked particularly interested in striking up a nice, friendly chat. Well, that was okay, too. He wasn't feeling very chatty himself.

He craned his neck, the better to see over the unwashed who surrounded him. The cage that held them was as he remembered, a boxy affair that looked crude but also looked more than strong enough to withstand any efforts from the sickly, beaten humans he shared it with.

His cage and cart were one of a caravan of several, moving slowly along a winding road that rose gradually toward a city sprawled across a hilltop in the hazy distance. Squads of heavily armed ape soldiers trudged alongside the wagons, paying no attention to the miserable humans penned like cattle for slaughter inside. But that wasn't what drew Davidson's horrified attention. That was reserved for the beasts of burden putting their work-scarred shoulders to the traces as they slowly dragged the carts along. These dray beasts were young, muscular men, each one wearing blinders that prevented him from looking anywhere but straight ahead.

He'd seen similar contraptions on horses, in history studies of times from mankind's nearly forgotten past. And what had they called those blinkered animals? Beasts of burden.

He winced as, from somewhere at the rear of the slaver train, he heard the sharp crack of a whip, and imagined he could see a cruel flail laying a bloody stripe across straining human flesh.

Up at the head of the column he spotted the black gorilla commander, riding on a horse that looked as if it was used to much better treatment than the pathetic young men dragging the carts. What had that chimp general called the big ape? *Attar?* Yeah, that was it . . .

There was something about the smug arrogance of the overgrown monkey, glittering in his armored breastplate, sneering down from his prancing horse at the misery that surrounded him, that made Davidson long to get close enough with a brick to smash that fang-filled grimace right through the back of the arrogant ape's skull.

He held that thought tight in his heart and let it warm him as the cart train moved closer and closer to the city at the top of the hill. Yet even though he knew what to expect, he was still weirdly shocked when Attar cantered up to the city gates and waved a casual salute at all the apes who swarmed there. Somehow, it hadn't yet quite penetrated Davidson's worldview that this city had been built by monkeys, for monkeys, and not by men. But as his wagon creaked slowly through the gate, and Davidson got his first panoramic glimpse of what lay beyond, it hit him with numbing force: this was a city of apes, and if men had any place in it at all, it was only at the very bottom. Were men slaves here? No. Does a man enslave his dog, his cat, his horse? Not at all. So men weren't slaves here, either. They were something else. Something lower than slaves.

Could humans be subhuman? Or was the proper term here *sub-ape*? But before he could consider the matter further, the sheer spectacle of what he saw overwhelmed him.

The city was sprawling. It rambled across the top of the low hills in a seemingly endless profusion of stone, bright colors, and teeming throngs of apes. The city was an odd blend of new and old: huge piles of ancient gray stone draped with bright tapestries, looming over narrow streets filled with monkeys of every possible size and shape. He saw gorillas, chimpanzees, baboons, even what appeared to be a troop of howler monkeys. In some mad way it looked like any large human city, filled with people bustling along on their daily business, except the citizens were apes, not humans. There seemed to be thousands of them, and none of them paid much, if any attention at all, to the carts loaded with human misery passing through their midst.

He saw several old apes seated around a stone table arguing over some sort of game of chance. These silver-backed graybeards reminded him of old men he'd seen sitting around chessboards set at the edge of sidewalks in big cities, except these apes were smoking what looked like a hookah instead of sipping from cans of beer or jugs of cheap wine.

They passed a stall loaded down with the bright unfamiliar fruit he'd seen the humans carrying through the woods. A group of female apes laughed as they haggled loudly with the vendor, who seemed to be enjoying the argument as much as they were. A couple of the females looked up as the wagon train creaked past, but didn't seem very interested and soon returned to their shopping.

Farther on, a young male tootled merrily on something that looked like an oversized flute, as a group of his friends gathered around him grinning and laughing. The melody vaguely reminded Davidson of something he'd heard before. He groped for it . . . but nothing came. The notion faded.

A young female approached, smiled shyly, and dropped a coin into the hat the young ape had set in front of him. He nodded at her and kept on piping.

Not far beyond the flutist, a chimp moved a knife in flashing strokes over a piece of wood. Davidson squinted; in the bright light it was hard to see what the ape was working on, but eventually it came clear. The chimp was carving a broadly caricatured doll in the shape of a crude human being. Finally they passed an ape juggler, amazingly accomplished, using both his hands and feet to keep a whirl of objects dancing in the air.

Except for the fact that this was all being done by apes, the scenes could have been taking place in any primitive human city. That wasn't what sent a curl of horror creeping up Davidson's spine. Because it wasn't just a city full of apes. Everywhere he looked Davidson also saw humans: pulling, lifting, dragging, carrying, but involved only in the most menial of tasks. And most of the ones he could see wore chains.

In his school days, Davidson had once read a book called *The Invisible Man*. The book had affected him strongly, but nowhere near as powerfully as the reality he now experienced. For as the caravan moved through the city, for all the notice it gathered, it might as well have been invisible, too. The carts were packed full of battered, bleeding, sobbing humans, and almost nobody seemed to notice or care. Was the sight of so much misery an everyday occurrence, not even worth a second glance? What kind of horror had he stumbled into?

But then, finally, somebody did take notice of the line of carts. Up ahead, a small, yelling crowd of youthful gorillas was playing a game that looked like soccer, except in this case, the young apes used both hands and prehensile feet to manipulate the ball. But when the carts approached, several of the gorillas broke off their game, stooped, quickly gathered stones, and began to pelt the cages. Davidson's rage bubbled up all over again as he heard the ugly sound of rock slapping against flesh, and the sharp gasps of agony that followed.

Then a fusillade of missiles rattled through the bars of his own cage, and Davidson hastily put his arms over his head and ducked down. But he looked up again when he heard a feminine voice berating the young gorillas.

"Stop it! You're being cruel!"

Davidson peered over the backs of his fellow prisoners to get a look at this unexpected angel of mercy. She was a female chimp with dark, shoulder-length hair, whose clothing looked both stylish and well-made. And though she was angry, there was an obvious air of the upper class about her. As Davidson watched, she waded right into the group of young apes with no fear or hesitation whatsoever.

"Open your hands!"

The younger thugs shied away from her, but she kept right on after them, a whirlwind of anger as she slapped at their hands, knocking stones every which way. Davidson stared at her in wonder; this was the first ape he'd seen he didn't feel an immediate urge to strangle. Instead he had to stifle an urge to stand up and cheer her on, although after a moment's thought his sense of self-preservation reasserted itself, and he settled for just watching her with a big grin on his face. She was still tearing into them.

"Who told you you could throw stones at humans?"

One of the brats, braver than the rest, faced her: "My father."

She eyed the kid sternly. "Then you're both wrong. And you can tell him I said so."

The young ape looked like he might want to argue further, but the female glared at him and his resistance crumbled. He turned and ran, followed by the rest of his little troupe. Once they'd achieved a safe distance, however, the kids stopped, turned, and faced their nemesis. The leader stuck out his tongue.

"Human lover!"

The chimp woman raised her head and with a single glance quelled this last rebellion. This time the young gorillas ran and didn't look back.

The chimp, Ari, shook her head in disgust, then glanced up as another young female joined her.

"Do you always have to be so intense? I thought we were going shopping," the new arrival said.

Ari nodded absently at her friend, Leeta, but her gaze moved to the carts passing by. Davidson watched her scan the load of human misery groaning past her vantage point. It was hard to believe, but he couldn't dispute what he saw: there were tears welling in the female chimp's eyes. And for one strange instant, he found himself looking directly into her gaze. He felt a spark of—what? He didn't know. And it seemed to shake her, too, because she turned away. Then his own cart creaked past her and she was gone.

Ari began to walk quickly after the carts.

Leeta stared at her in disbelief, then reluctantly followed. "Ari, wait! You're going to get in trouble again."

Davidson didn't see Ari hurrying to catch up with the cages. His initial awe at the strange city of the apes was rapidly fading as the squalor and misery of his fellow captives became too much to ignore. When he tried to shift around, his foot bumped against something soft, and he glanced down to see that he had been kicking a corpse. He looked up in horror, but either nobody had noticed what he'd done, or nobody cared.

Somebody was watching him, however. On the other side of the cage the skinny teenager who had fought the apes so valiantly was staring at him with a level, steady gaze. And though the boy's face was a mask of dried mud and blood, Davidson could sense a bright flame of intelligence burning beneath. Before Davidson could pursue this notion, however, the line of carts abruptly veered to the side of the street. Davidson put his face up next to the bars of his cage and peered out, looking for whatever had caused the detour. It wasn't hard to find. Now passing by them was a line of apes garbed in sober robes, their faces wrapped in scarves, chanting softly.

The measured approach of this stately procession galvanized the big gorilla named Attar. He pulled away from his position at the head of the column and approached the monks with great reverence. The line of holy men came to a halt and the leader faced the big ape soldier. He raised his hands and offered the gorilla his divine blessing, as Attar bowed his head, a beatified expression on his craggy features. Even Davidson was impressed by the deep sense of spirituality he felt emanating from the gorilla. It shook him more than he wanted to admit, that something which looked so much like an animal could also seem so human.

He turned away from the scene and approached one of his fellow captives, a man hunkered down with his face in his hands.

"Where am I?" Davidson whispered urgently.

The man raised his face from his hands, gave Davidson a terrified glance, then jerked away from him as if he had some deadly contagious disease.

Davidson stared at the man in disbelief, then tried again, this time with an old woman huddled against the opposite wall of the cage.

"What is this place?"

The woman stared at him dumbly, obviously too terrified even to reply. Davidson wanted to shake her, but knew that would make matters only worse. But his frustration at his own ignorance was almost impossible for him to control, and before he could stop himself, he blurted, *"Somebody's got to tell me where I am!"*

The old woman only shrank away from him, but the raw urgency in his voice did finally attract the attention of someone willing to speak to him. At the front of the cage, the old man whom Davidson had first seen leading these people in the forest roused himself and pushed toward him. As he approached he looked around to make sure nobody was watching, and then said, *"Head down! Mouth shut!* You'll get us all killed!"

Davidson wanted to protest, at least ask a few questions, but then he saw the blond barbarian woman hovering behind the old man's shoulder glaring at him, and decided to let it drop. He was in enough trouble here. No sense in making needless enemies.

Then the gorilla, Attar, returned to his position at the head of the column, let out a guttural shout, and the carts creaked into motion again. Davidson sank down and huddled with his chest against his knees, feeling as hopeless and depressed as he ever had in his life.

The quadrangle was a wide dirt square enclosed with high sturdy walls. In the center of the quadrangle stood a single orangutan, a squat little figure with orange fur. With a measured beat he slapped an ugly little flexible club called a sap against the palm of his hand as he watched Attar lead the first carts of the column through the open gates into his courtyard.

The chimp's name was Limbo. He stared without expression as the rest of the train straggled in and ground to a halt in a rough line before him. Only once all motion had ceased did he finally stop tapping his nasty-looking weapon against his hand and stride toward the carts. He moved up and down the line, peering into the cages, his sharp, cruel gaze evaluating their contents as emotionlessly as an accountant adding up a column of figures. Davidson felt the chimp's attention pass over him almost like a cool whispering lash. He shivered and crouched lower. It was the first time in his life another living being had looked at him in that cold, dispassionate manner, as if he were nothing more than a side of meat for the carving.

So this, he thought, *is what the steer feels like as it passes under the eye of the butcher on its way into the slaughterhouse . . .*

Limbo finished his inspection and ambled over to one of Attar's soldiers. As he approached he sighed heavily.

"Are you trying to put me out of business? These are the skankiest, scabbiest, scuzziest humans I've ever seen."

"You don't want them?"

Limbo sighed in mock resignation. "I'll take the whole lot. I'll have to make it up in volume."

As he spoke, several new apes approached from the far reaches of the courtyard, evidently menials or employees of some kind.

Limbo noticed them and waved one arm casually toward the cages.

"Get them out, get them cleaned!"

Evidently this was nothing new. The handlers, all huge gorillas, their faces shrouded in germ prevention masks, swarmed over the carts in a tidal wave of fur. They moved with the speed and ease of long practice, as they ripped open cage doors and waded into the clots of cowering humanity. They worked without passion, dragging the humans out and down to the dirt of the quadrangle, then sorting out men, women, and children into separate groups.

Only this last seemed to finally rouse the numbed humans from the stupor that had gripped them in the cages. Men fought and howled as they tried to keep their families together. Women screamed as their husbands were dragged away, and children cried in panic as they were torn from their mothers' arms.

As Davidson struggled with one gorilla, he saw another drag the old man and the blond woman away from each other. The woman fought even more viciously than before, but with the same futile results.

The old man stretched out his shaky arms as she was jerked away. "Daena, don't be afraid!" he called to her.

"I'll find you . . ." she cried back to him.

Limbo strolled up as this pathetic scene was playing out, and eyed the pair sardonically.

"Very touching," he said. "Really. I can't see for the tears in my eyes."

Then, with a brutal savagery that belied the calm tone of his words, he reached out, twined his fingers in Daena's hair, dragged her to a nearby pen already filling up with other women, and threw her inside. She landed in a twisted heap and glared up at him.

The old man, Karubi, struggled against his own handlers, trying to reach her, but they yanked him backward with equal brutality toward a different cage and threw him bodily inside, nearly breaking his arm in the process. Karubi shrieked as the pain hit him, tottered a couple of steps, and then fell writhing to the ground.

Worst of all were the children, because they were the most helpless. Davidson could barely watch as the ape slave masters dragged them from their families and shoved them into their own pens. But he forced himself to look, because in the back of his mind he was promising himself revenge for those kids, somehow, someday.

Davidson found himself in a male pen with the man he'd seen carrying the little girl in the forest. He thought he'd heard somebody call the man Gunnar. More apes came right behind dragging the boy, Birn, whose fighting spirit was still not even slightly quenched. Davidson watched as one of the gorillas tried to get a better grip on the boy's head, and the kid sank his teeth deep into the soft meat of the ape's palm. The ape let out a roar, grabbed Birn by his scrawny shoulders, and shook him like a dishrag. Davidson could almost hear the boy's teeth rattling in his skull. After a few seconds of this, Birn was limp enough for the gorilla to throw him into the pen, where he landed on the hard-packed earth with a soft thud.

The head chimp wandered over in time to see the outcome, which he watched with an uncannily human expression of amusement on his grinning face. Davidson had never felt his own hatred as strongly as this. It frightened him and at the same time lifted him up, gave him a reason to keep on fighting.

Limbo glanced at Davidson, then at the handlers. "How many times do I have to tell you? When you handle humans, wear your gloves."

"Are you softening, Limbo?"

Davidson saw the chimp whirl to see the big boss himself, the Golden General on horseback called Thade, bearing down on him. In that one short instant Limbo transformed himself from a preening, sneering slave master to a cowering toady. He seemed to physically shrink as he stared up at the imposing figure looming over him.

"You used to hack off a limb," the general observed.

"Yes, General. But he's worth more intact."

The general tilted his head back and stared haughtily down his nose at the slaver, then proceeded to ignore him as beneath notice.

Commander Attar, who had followed the general over, now approached the men's pen and gave Davidson a fast once-over. He obviously didn't seem to like what he saw. He glanced at Limbo.

"Don't turn your back on this one. He's feisty."

Davidson didn't know how he felt about this unwanted attention, but he noticed out of the corner of his eye that Karubi, battered and nursing his twisted arms, had suddenly looked over and fixed him with an intent stare.

What's that all about? Davidson wondered.

Limbo was chattering nervously at the two soldiers. "These ones raiding the orchards, sir? I know an old country remedy that never fails. Gut one and string the carcass up . . ."

General Thade gave the chimpanzee a look of disdain. "The human rights faction is already nipping at my heels."

Limbo obviously saw an opportunity to kiss some gorilla butt. He almost stumbled over his own tongue before he managed to say, "*Do-gooders!* Who needs them? I'm all for free speech . . . as long as they keep their mouths shut."

Evidently General Thade approved of the sentiment, because he left off staring at the obsequious chimp and urged his mount toward a pen filled with weeping, ter-rified children. He rode right up to the fence and looked over, appearing for all the world like a mildly interested window shopper.

"I promised my niece a pet for her birthday."

Limbo, his merchant's nose twitching hard on the scent of a possible profit, hopped right over and said fawningly, "Excellent. The little ones make wonderful pets. But make sure you get rid of them by puberty. If there's one thing you don't want in your house, it's a human teenager."

A small female ape accompanied by her protective mother approached the pens. General Thade looked down from his horse and nodded in approval. The little girl walked up to the fence of the children's pen, glanced shyly up at her uncle, and when he nodded again, she began to examine the children on the other side with all the excitement any kid would show given free run of a pet store.

Finally her attention settled on one of the "pets." She raised her hand and pointed at the little girl Davidson had seen Gunnar carrying through the woods earlier.

"Excellent choice," Limbo said with greasy approval.

General Thade glanced at Commander Attar. The huge gorilla immediately entered the children's pen, extricated the weeping girl, and patting her head like a puppy, carried her back to the waiting ape girl. Care-fully he settled the child into the ape's arms while her mother looked on with an expression Davidson thought was noncommittal at best.

Probably wondering if she'll be the one who winds up having to housebreak the kid, Davidson thought. He was astonished at the depth of the bitterness he felt.

The innocent evil of the female ape child frustrated him enormously. There was no way she could understand the horror of what she was doing, but the horror was being done anyway.

Then, as mother and child walked away with their new pet, they did something that nearly blasted Davidson's sanity right out of his brain. As the girl ape coddled the wailing child, the mother reached into a bag, took out a collar and leash, and fitted the little girl with them.

Speechless, Davidson looked at the pen holding the adult women, expecting to see the girl's mother in hysterics. But the woman was simply standing quietly, staring dully at the ground, her eyes as empty of expression as polished granite marbles.

Behind her, though, the blond woman, Daena, who was standing in equally stiff silence, held rage enough for both of them. Davidson could see the inner fire boiling in her eyes, and knew that while *he* might have problems doing it, this savage woman could slaughter the little ape girl without a second thought. The thought made him shiver, and yet he knew that he would not be the one to hold Daena back if she got her chance to wreak vengeance. These were monsters who treated human children as nothing more than cuddly animals to be petted, and loved . . . and leashed.

General Thade watched his sister and niece depart with the newest member of their little family. After they had vanished beyond the gates of Limbo's compound, he wheeled his horse, took a final survey of the slave pens, then headed for the gate himself. Limbo evidently couldn't resist one final chance to ingratiate himself and scurried after the general, fawning words dripping from his rubbery lips.

"They say if you piss along the fence line it will keep the humans away from the fields."

General Thade aimed a disdainful growl back over the flank of his steed that stopped the chimp in his tracks.

"Close enough. You stink of humans."

Limbo skidded to a stop. Thade gave him one last haughty glare, then spurred his mount hard and galloped on out of the gate. Limbo watched him go, a mournful expression on his features. After a moment he lifted his right arm and sniffed. Davidson might have thought Limbo's discomfort was funny, if he hadn't wanted, with every last ounce of strength in his lacerated soul, to throttle the sleazy little ape slaver to death.

Ari and Leeta were hiding just inside Limbo's gates as Attar went thundering after General Thade out of the compound. Leeta peered gingerly around the edge of the gate, then recoiled at the sight beyond. She turned to Ari, unable to hide her growing nervousness.

"No way I'm going in there. It's disgusting."

Ari barely noticed that Leeta was speaking to her. Her attention was riveted on the horrific scenes inside the compound.

"What's disgusting is the way we treat humans," she said. "It demeans us as well as them."

She moved closer to the entrance, obviously intending to go inside. Leeta plucked at Ari's hand, tugged her to stop.

"Ari, we should go home."

Ari gave her an annoyed glance, then pulled her hand away.

"Then go home," she snapped.

Out in the quadrangle, the bored gorilla handlers were continuing with the processing of their new human captives. Limbo watched the ugly procedure with a jaundiced but discerning eye.

Inside his pen, Davidson kept moving around the fence, uncertain and trying to figure out what might come next. Limbo seemed to be the obvious one to watch, since he was the ape in charge. Once the dusting procedure was finished, the chimp glanced over at a large fire that had been set in a stone pit near the pens.

"Get them marked! I've got orders to fill."

As soon as he gave the command, two of the gorillas reached into the flames and pulled out red-hot branding irons. Davidson watched, horrified, as other apes approached the pens, carrying long wooden poles with wire loops affixed to their ends. The apes used these implements to reach into the pens and snare their helpless captives.

The initial target was the women's pen. Evidently Daena's fearlessness had attracted attention, because she was the first one they snagged. They dropped the wire loop over her head, then yanked it cruelly tight around her neck, and dragged her out of the pen to a wooden post set up near the fire pit.

The old man, Karubi, spitting with rage, flung himself at the bars of the pen and shook them violently.

"No!"

His despairing shriek caught Limbo's notice, and the chimp reacted immediately, twisting his mobile, rubbery features into a laughing mask of scorn. He raised his hands in mock terror, and this time got a big round of laughter from his employees. But he tired of this dumb show soon enough, and headed for the stake where Daena struggled with her captors.

As he approached, the gorilla holding her stripped the top of her dress down, exposing her shoulder blades. One of the apes with a branding iron stepped up and pressed the scorching metal deep into her flesh, leaving behind a smoking wound in a shape that reminded Davidson of something, though right then he couldn't think of what it was.

If the apes were expecting their victim to provide them with a new source of humor, they were sadly mistaken. Daena flinched, but not one sound passed her lips as she glared at them defiantly, with eyes that smoldered just as hotly as the brand that had burned into her skin. Disappointed, the apes dragged her roughly away and tossed her back into the pen.

The apes continued with their grisly duties until finally Davidson's turn came around. It took two of them, but in the end they had no problems dragging him to the post. They pinioned his arms as the gorilla with the branding iron approached. The monkey was quick, but Davidson was quicker. He twisted in the grip of the two apes who held him and kicked the white-hot torture instrument out of the third ape's hands.

Limbo exploded with fury. He stalked over, snarling at his hapless underlings.

"Do I have to do everything myself?" he asked as he reached for the branding iron. As he did so, a ruckus erupted at his gates as Ari came storming in, then raced right up to him, her eyes flashing. She grabbed the branding iron from him before he could react and threw it aside.

"Oh no," he groaned. "By Semos, not you again."

"I cannot stand idly by while humans are being mistreated, tortured . . ." she flared at him.

Dumbstruck, Davidson stared at Ari. Karubi and the others also rushed to the bars of their pens, amazed at the sight of ape threatening ape. In the distance, Leeta peeked around the edge of the gates, saw what was going on, and quickly darted back.

Ari rushed to the women's pen. Fending off the angry gorilla handlers one-handed, she fumbled with the lock on the women's pen and finally thrust the gate open. But before the women could escape, one of the handlers dodged around Ari and snarled ferociously at the frightened humans. The women retreated back inside the pen as Limbo charged at Ari.

"The only reason I put up with your nonsense is because of your father," he growled.

Ari raised her head, nostrils flaring. "If you want me to stop, give up your bloody business!"

Limbo shook his head. "Hey, I do the job nobody else wants. I don't see any of you bleeding hearts spending all day with these dangerous, dirty, dumb beasts."

"They're not dumb! They can be taught to live with us . . . and I'm going to prove it!"

Limbo sneered at her. "You forget who you're talking to. I work with the dirty creatures."

Ari glanced at the women huddled at the back of the pen. "They're smart. And I'm going to prove it," she said stoutly.

Davidson had been watching all this with one eye, but with the other he'd also been noticing how lax the handlers had become, their attention entirely caught up in the strange confrontation between the female chimp and their own master. Nor did he miss how the iron grip of the two who held him had slackened almost into nonexistence.

Now or never, he thought suddenly, and lunged forward, grabbed a chain lying in the dirt, whipped it around the leg of the nearest handler, flipped him, then grabbed his spear before he could react.

Before Limbo had any notion of what was happening, Davidson was holding Ari, the point of his spear aimed directly at her neck.

Limbo stared at them, but didn't seem much ruffled. He nodded to Ari and said, "There's your *proof*."

Davidson, trying to look in all directions at once, saw that some of the gorilla handlers had already slipped in at his rear and cut off his retreat through the gates. More were easing in from the sides as he edged Ari along.

He had nothing against this ape woman—she seemed well-meaning enough—but right at the moment, Davidson decided that his own hide was more important. He kept on going. As he progressed, Ari's head turned, and their gazes accidentally met. They locked for an instant, as Ari felt the shock run through her nerves. No human she'd ever seen or heard of would dare to look directly at her like that. She didn't know how it made her feel.

"Please . . . help me," Davidson whispered.

Limbo watched this all sadly. He ignored Davidson entirely, seeming almost unaware that he was present, or that it was his own handler's spear that was threatening the ape woman. He spoke to Ari. "Now I'll have to put him down."

He didn't seem especially saddened by the prospect.

4

In the female pen, Daena was watching everything through squinted eyes, a hard and thoughtful expression on her features. The door to the pen was still open. Suddenly Daena took a deep breath, put her head down, and ran for all she was worth out of the pen and toward the gate of the compound.

She startled the slow-moving gorillas, who were far too large to get up to speed as quickly as she had. Arms pumping, legs flying, a triumphant grimace on her face, she almost made it.

Then Limbo, bounding across the compound like a berserk jumping jack, streaked in from the side and delivered a tremendous clout to the side of Daena's head, knocking her sprawling. She landed, limp as a flounder, and didn't move.

Limbo returned to Ari and Davidson, so furious he was practically spitting.

"Look what you started. I'm getting a headache."

Davidson looked first to his right, then to his left. Then he tightened his grip on Ari and pressed the spear more firmly against her neck. He looked at Limbo, trying to appear as determined and deadly as he possibly could. He didn't know if he could murder this strange ape woman in cold blood, but his life might depend on convincing Limbo that was exactly what he would do if he had to.

"Get back," he told the chimp.

Limbo raised both his hands, palms out, and ducked his head as if Davidson's threats terrified him.

"Oh, please don't hurt her."

Limbo's sudden transformation from ferocious slaver warrior capable of knocking out Daena with a single blow to whining, fearful supplicant didn't fool Davidson for a moment. He knew there must be some nasty bit of trickery at work here, but he thought that as long as he kept the spear at the throat of his hostage, remained aware of the other gorillas, and kept a sharp eye on Limbo's shifty, dangerous hands, he might be able to back out of here in one piece. He was right about Limbo's hands, at least. They never moved.

But he'd forgotten something he'd seen on his way into the city. The pack of gorilla kids playing their version of ape soccer, using their prehensile toes as easily as a man might use the fingers of his hand . . . as easily as Limbo's right foot whipped up and plucked the spear from Davidson's grasp.

In the same fluid motion, Limbo walloped Davidson in the side of his head. To Davidson it felt as if the chimp had hit him with a pillowcase full of horseshoes. He staggered, then sank to his knees, his eyes full of stars, and missed the sight of Limbo doing a full backward somersault, still holding the spear. The chimp landed next to Ari. He glanced at her, looked back at Davidson, then shrugged and nodded at his gorillas.

"Who needs this aggravation?" He hefted the spear meaningfully, glanced at Davidson, then ordered his handlers, "Hold him."

Ari flung herself between the chimp and Davidson.

"Sell him to me!"

Limbo raised one hand, halting the gorillas who were moving toward Davidson. He stared at Ari as if she had suddenly turned into a butterfly before his eyes.

"Are you crazy? He's wild."

Beyond Davidson, Daena was beginning to stir. Limbo pointed at her. "They're *both* wild."

Ari straightened her shoulders. "Then I'll buy them both."

Limbo opened his mouth, and snapped it shut. A strange little war fought itself across his face. He obviously thought Ari had lost her mind. On the other hand, there was definitely a huge profit to be made here. Common sense and wariness fought with greed. With Limbo, such a battle would not take long to decide.

Slowly, he said, "That would be expensive, very expensive." He scratched his chin, as if reluctantly considering.

"I'm sure we could reach a deal," Ari said contemptuously.

Limbo thought about it, and finally nodded.

Ari glanced at Daena, now her property, who had staggered to her feet, her senses slowly returning. Daena glared back at Ari, nothing but hatred visible in her fiery gaze. Ari sighed.

"Deliver them to my house," she said.

Limbo didn't quite clap his hands in glee. However, he did grin nastily at Davidson.

"I'll have to mark him first."

With that, he snatched the still red-hot branding iron and thrust its curiously shaped tip against Davidson's shoulder.

And that was what Davidson would most remember about his first meeting with Limbo, the chimpanzee slave trader: the stench of his own seared flesh burning in his nostrils.

Dusk drifted like velvet over the city of the apes as the monkey metropolis drowsed beneath the rising moons. As the feverish activity of the day died away, shadows continued to flit through the streets. Here and there metal chinked softly, as apes in full armor moved out on patrol.

In the better neighborhoods, lights gleamed from behind high walls that protected the residents from the hurly-burly of the street. At one such house the gardens were strung with red lanterns that cast warm, glowing shadows against huge tapestries that flapped softly in the night breeze.

The peaceful scene was abruptly shattered by the sound of loud voices.

"Father, please. I'll pay with my own money." Ari's voice came floating from the kitchen's open window.

Ari followed her father, Sandar, around the kitchen. He had a harried expression on his face. Sandar stopped in the middle of the room and looked around.

"Your *own money* is going to make a pauper of me. Where are they?" he said sternly.

The several occupants of the room stared back at

him. Krull, a huge, aging silverbacked gorilla going rapidly gray, pointed at the other side of the room, where Davidson and Daena knelt on the floor.

The two humans, with their matted, disheveled hair and torn clothing, made a sharp contrast to the second pair of humans who knelt beside them. Tival was a middle-aged black man, Bon a tiny Chinese woman. Both were painfully neat, and wore clean, floor-length robes. They kept their heads down and refused to meet their master's gaze.

Krull turned, growled at them. "Rise when your master enters."

Slowly, Davidson came to his feet and turned to face the old chimp. But Daena continued to scowl at the floor and refused to move. With a startling speed that belied his advanced age, Krull yanked her to her feet.

For his part, Sandar ignored his two servants as he stared at the new arrivals. After a moment he groaned softly.

"Semos help me, wild humans in my house."

Ari winced at Daena's attitude, but directed her father's attention toward Davidson, who was at least standing properly in a respectful posture.

"This one seems different."

Sandar stared at Davidson. After a moment his eyebrows rose dismissively.

"How different could he be? You can't tell one from the other."

Davidson caught Ari's gaze, but she refused to look at him.

Before she could say anything else, a sudden babble of voices drifted through the door from the stairway up to the main rooms.

Sandar looked even more agitated. He turned nervously toward the stairs. "My guests are here. Keep the savage ones out of sight. *Especially* from General Thade."

He pushed past his daughter and headed for the door. Just before he vanished, he looked back at her. "And you'd better be nice to him!" he added fiercely.

Ari whirled to follow. "Father!" she cried.

But he was gone.

Sandar and Ari's dining patio glowed pleasantly beneath the red lanterns, as candlelight sent shadows dancing in the abundant trees and flowers. A long, wooden table garlanded with flowers and groaning beneath mounds of beautiful fruit occupied the center of the patio. Several apes stood around the table, engaging in a lazy stream of small talk.

At the patio entry, Sandar bustled up and exchanged greeting touches with an older orangutan compatriot and fellow senator, Nado, and Nado's latest wife, Nova, a beautiful chimp far too young for the aging politician.

"Good evening, Senator Nado." Sandar squeezed Nova's fingers lightly. "You look lovely tonight."

Nova simpered. "I'm having a bad hair day." She sighed and coquettishly stroked the abundant fur on her face.

Nado gazed on her fondly, then glanced at Sandar and rolled his eyes. "Yet she spends a fortune grooming herself."

Sandar offered his friend a knowing grin of male complicity.

Beyond the table Ari stood with Leeta, chatting softly, wearing a beautifully embroidered robe. But it wasn't just the robe that gave her such an air of elegance. She possessed a natural grace that was only accentuated by her garb. This was in contrast to Leeta, who was dressed similarly, but loaded down with garishly oversized jewelry. In her case, the expensive baubles gave her something of the look of a Christmas tree.

Leeta watched Sandar escorting Senator Nado and his wife into the room. She shook her head.

"Thade is powerful and aggressive. What else could you want in a male?"

Ari sighed. They'd been over this before. "Someone I can respect . . . and who respects me."

Leeta leaned closer. "Don't play so hard to get. Say yes to him, and you'll be invited to every exclusive party in the city." The prospect obviously seemed agreeable to her.

"How many parties can you go to?" Ari asked, wondering what Leeta would say.

"How many are there?" Leeta replied.

Krull suddenly appeared, ringing a small dinner bell. Sandar opened his arms wide and swept everybody toward the table.

"Please, everyone, sit."

Tival and Bon were standing just inside the kitchen, at the foot of the stairs leading up to the dining patio, each carrying a tray, when the sound of Krull's bell came tinkling down to them. Immediately they lifted their trays and began to climb up to the dinner party.

No sooner had they gone than Davidson jumped to his feet and hurried to one of the shuttered windows. He grabbed the heavy shutters and shook them hard, but they wouldn't budge at all.

Daena was watching him stoically when he turned and saw her.

"How the hell did these monkeys get this way?" he asked.

He'd lost her. She stared at him, dumbfounded.

"What other way would they be?" she asked.

Davidson snorted. "They'd be begging me for a treat."

This confused Daena even further. She shook her head slightly, as if something had gotten stuck in her ear. Finally she spoke.

"What tribe do you come from?"

Davidson's jaw tightened. "It's called the United States Air Force. And I'm going back to it."

The stairs leading down from the dining patio abruptly creaked as somebody heavy approached. A moment later Krull entered the kitchen. He regarded his two unwelcome new charges with disapproval.

"Finish your work. And no talking."

He glared at them a moment, but then a crescendo of noise from the stairwell reminded him of his primary duties. Several trays of food were arranged on the top of a preparation table. He picked one up, turned, and hurried out.

Davidson waited until the big gorilla was gone, then picked up a tray, went to the door, and peeked up the stairway.

By the time Krull returned to the dining patio, Sandar had everybody seated around the long table. Ari and Leeta were placed across from each other. Senator Nado and his new wife were next to Leeta. The space next to Ari remained empty.

As Krull moved up to the table and began to serve,

he overheard Nado say, "We just returned from our country house in the rain forest."

Sandar replied politely, "And how was it?"

Nova leaned toward the two older men, her eyes sparkling. *"Boring!"*

Sandar and Nado exchanged glances over her head.

"I find it relaxing," Nado protested. "Being away from the frantic pace of the city."

It was obvious Nova disagreed. "I wanted to go out. But there was no place to go. Nothing but trees and rocks." She glanced at her husband accusingly. "All *you* did was nap."

Krull worked his way around the table, offering each guest something from the platter.

"Exactly," Nado replied. "A bit of time away from politics is what is needed for a weary soul like me."

Nado reached up to Krull's tray, took a bite, nodded his thanks. Sandar examined Krull's tray carefully before selecting a particularly appetizing piece of fruit.

Ari leaned closer to Leeta and whispered, "Look at the old fool. He left his wife and children for her. Now he can't keep up."

Leeta had her own priorities. "But he's worth a fortune," she protested.

Nado touched Sandar's hand, a gentle, friendly gesture. "We used to lose ourselves for days in the forest when we were young. Now I can barely climb a tree."

Sandar chewed, swallowed, and nodded agreement. "It's trite, but true. Youth is wasted on the young. Now that I have so much to do . . . I'm exhausted. Still, some nights I dream of hurtling through the branches . . ." He sighed heavily. "How did I get so old so fast?"

A voice from the shadows of the garden answered him. "Living with your daughter would age any ape quickly."

Startled, everybody turned just in time to see General Thade, trailed by the hulking Attar, enter the dining patio. As Thade stalked toward the table, Ari jabbed her friend in the ribs and hissed, "Quick! Switch seats!"

Leeta shook her head. "No, he's here to see *you*."

Thade waited for Krull to pull out his chair, but the old gorilla didn't move. Attar saw this, and moved quickly to take the back of the chair next to Ari and pull it out for his commander. Thade grunted at him and sat down without much grace. Attar sat down next to him.

And though Sandar's daughter did not seem as pleased as she might have been with the new arrivals, her father was a picture of hospitality.

"You are too long a stranger in our house," Sandar said.

Thade nodded brusquely. "My apologies, Senator. I stopped to see my father."

"How is my old friend doing?"

General Thade shook his head and sighed.

"I'm afraid he's slipping. I wish I could spend more time with him. But duty keeps me away. These are troubled times. Humans infest the provinces."

Ari wasn't about to let that pass. Her eyes flashed as she replied, "Because our cities encroach on their habitat."

Thade spoke with both condescension and distaste. "They breed quickly, while we grow soft with our affluence. Even now they outnumber us ten to one."

Nova broke in. "Why can't the government simply sterilize them all?"

Nado answered her. "The cost would be prohibitive. Although our scientists do tell me the humans carry terrible diseases."

"How would we know?" Ari said scathingly. "The army burns the bodies before they can be examined." She glanced at Sandar. "Father!" she pleaded for support.

Now Thade also turned to give the senator a questioning look. Sandar dithered from one to the other, obviously not enjoying being caught between them. He flushed. His discomfort made him stumble a bit before he finally managed to say, with precarious delicacy, "At times . . . perhaps . . . the senate feels the army has been a tad . . . extreme."

Thade's eyes turned to stone. "Extremism in defense of apes is no vice."

Senator Nado had been following all this, apparently with mixed feelings. Absently, he raised a piece of fruit to his mouth, but before he could bite into it, a guttural growl froze them all.

Attar, the gorilla commander, had a beatific expression on his face as he closed his eyes and began to pray.

"We give thanks to you, Semos, for the fruit of this land. Bless us, Holy Father, who created all apes in His image. Hasten the day when you will return, and bring peace to your children. Amen," he declaimed in deep, sonorous, reverential tones.

When he finished, Attar sat in silence, without opening his eyes. He seemed to be waiting for something. General Thade cast an inclusive glare around the table, and was quickly rewarded with an emphatic chorus of *"Amen!"* from the rest of the guests.

Attar looked up and saw Krull staring at him. He seemed to wince, and looked away from the old ape's eyes.

Ari stared down at the table, deep in thought. She'd been trumped with religion, and could not continue the argument without appearing to be sacrilegious. She was conscious of Thade surreptitiously glancing at her from the next chair, but she didn't look up. It was going to be a long evening.

In the foyer at the top of the stairs from the kitchen, Davidson, wearing a hastily supplied brown robe that matched Tival's, stood holding a tray as he listened with one ear to the buzz of conversation from the patio. However, he had no intention of joining the dinner party.

There has to be a way out of this place, he thought. *All I have to do is find it.*

But his search was interrupted by one of Thade's bodyguards lounging in a corner. The big soldier saw him standing there, grunted, and shoved him through the entry onto the patio. Davidson stumbled, caught his balance, and quickly covered himself by carrying his tray toward the table and beginning to serve.

Thade looked up and saw Davidson. Evidently he remembered their initial confrontation, because his lips curled in a half snarl, exposing a fair amount of yellow fang.

"What is this beast doing in your house?" he asked angrily.

Ari exchanged a worried look with her father, but

when she realized Sandar was too befuddled to reply, she quickly said, "He'll be trained as a domestic."

That didn't please General Thade at all.

"Your ideas threaten our prosperity. The human problem will not be solved by throwing money at it. The government tried once, and all we got was a welfare state that nearly bankrupted us."

His voice rose as he spoke. It was obviously a subject to which he'd given a great deal of thought.

As had Attar, who piped up from Thade's other side.

"And changed the face of the city," the big gorilla added.

Now even Ari's friend abandoned her. Leeta leaned forward and joined the conversation for the first time.

"I think the city has about as much diversity as I can handle," she said firmly. Ari shot her a betrayed glare, which Leeta ignored.

Still trying to hold her anger in check, Ari held up one edge of the beautifully embroidered scarf that draped her shoulders. She turned to show the lovely handwork to everyone at the table.

"This garment was made by one of my humans."

As she spoke, she glanced up at Bon, and smiled at the Chinese serving woman. Bon gave a little jump and averted her eyes nervously.

Ari turned back to the table, her voice now intense with deep conviction.

She said, "Can you deny the skill? Isn't it obvious they are capable of a real culture?"

Thade eyed the scarf with distaste, obviously unimpressed.

"Everything in 'human culture' takes place below the waist," he growled.

This sally brought a roar of laughter from all the guests, Sandar most loudly of all. After a moment, Nado, still chuckling, turned to his host's daughter.

"Next you'll be telling us that these beasts have a soul."

Out of the corner of her eye, Ari could see the new wild human male, who had been holding a spear at her throat just a short time before, watching her intently. There was something about him. He was different from any human she'd ever known before. Nor was she certain of her own feelings regarding him. One thing for sure: his steady, burning gaze wasn't helping her peace of mind any.

She looked quickly away and took a moment to gather herself. Finally she answered Nado's question.

"Of course they do."

Attar had finally roused himself from his religious contemplation. It was quite obvious that Ari's words offended him deeply, because there was a disgusted scowl of anger on his face as he replied, "The senator's daughter flirts with blasphemy."

This dark, threatening pronouncement brought the entire conversation to a screeching halt. Thade turned and looked at Attar. The moment of silence stretched. Suddenly Thade leaped from his chair, whirled, and grabbed Davidson by his shoulders so powerfully that he knocked Davidson's tray to the floor. He slammed Davidson backward against the table, pushed forward right into the human's face, pried his clenched jaws open, and stared deep into his gullet, as if searching for something there.

"Tell me," he grated. "Is there a soul inside you?"

Then, disgusted, he threw Davidson aside.

Davidson felt his own rage ignite all over again. He was shaking as he knelt and began to scrape up the spilled food. As he scrabbled in the mess, his fingers closed on one of the small, pronglike instruments the apes used as a fork. Covering his action with his body, he slipped the utensil into his robe.

He'd just finished doing this when Thade made a disgusted sound deep in his throat and pushed Davidson away as if he'd touched something filthy. He held up his hands. "Quick," he said, "a towel."

Almost everybody laughed at this sally, but Ari, her face stiff with anger, pulled her beautiful shawl tightly around her shoulders and pushed her chair back.

"You're all cruel and petty. And I've lost my appetite!"

She stood, ignoring the sudden air of embarrassment that seemed to settle over the gathering.

What's the use? she thought. *I'll never make them understand.*

She turned and stormed away from the table.

Everybody at the table was either too polite or made too uncomfortable by the scene that had just played out to watch her departure. Only Davidson, still scraping garbage off the floor, watched her go, his forehead creased in thought.

Finally Sandar glanced at Thade, and gestured for him to go after her.

Ari's bedroom was large, but cozily furnished. Shelves and tables were filled with hundreds of handmade human artifacts: bright scarves and hangings, colorful woven baskets, intricately painted pottery, carved figurines all jostled for space in the inviting room. Next to her bed, which was covered with a spread that had obviously been loomed by human hands, was an icon of Semos that portrayed His divine self, surrounded by a golden penumbra, descending from the clouds.

Beyond the bed, a door opened onto a balcony that overlooked the gardens. The sweet evening scents of ripe fruit and new blossoms wafted in through the opening.

As Ari stooped to light a candle set in a beautifully worked piece of human-crafted glass, the back of her neck suddenly prickled. She froze for an instant, and then her sensitive nostrils told her who had silently entered her room.

"I have no patience for these society dinners," Thade rumbled. "I only came to see you."

"Then you've wasted your time," she cut him off.

She finished what she was doing as Thade crept up softly behind her. He began to run his fingers through her pelt, the rhythmic motions somewhere between grooming and a lover's caresses. Against her will, she felt herself beginning to respond, and hated herself for it. Hated her weakness. Suddenly he gripped her hard, held her tight.

"My feelings haven't changed," he rasped huskily. "You know how much I care for you."

Repulsed, as much at herself as at him, she pushed him away.

"You only care about my father's influence . . . and your own ambition."

He flashed his fangs at her.

"I know about the trouble you caused today. I could have you arrested."

She faced him. "What I did was *right*. And I'd do it again."

The general's big hands reached slowly for her neck. She gave a slight start when his fingers gently lifted the scarf from around her shoulders. When she turned, Thade was running the rich cloth lightly through his hands.

She spun away, moved to the edge of her bed, and sat down. She folded her hands in her lap, and began to examine the pattern of the bedspread, as if it were the most interesting thing in the room.

His fingers suddenly closed on the scarf, crushing it. It was obvious that whatever he thought his mission here had been, he now understood it was done. He spun on his heel and stalked toward the door, then suddenly paused. From where she sat, it looked to her as if his shoulders might be shaking. His voice was so soft and choked with emotion she had to strain to make out his words.

"You feel so much for the humans. Yet you can't feel anything for me."

A moment later he was gone, leaving her to stare out into the empty night for a long time.

The street outside Senator Sandar's house looked almost empty, except for Attar standing beneath the shadows of several huge trees as he held the reins of both his and Thade's horses. He looked up, his ears twitching and his gaze intent, then stiffened as General Thade, still holding Ari's scarf, came storming out of the house.

The general's rage was plain for anybody to see as he stomped up, snatched the reins from Attar's hand, and turned to mount his charger. Before he could leap into the saddle, Attar made a quick move, touched his elbow, and stopped him.

"A moment, sir."

Thade was so lost in his anger that Attar wasn't sure the general even saw him, but at least he stopped. He looked down at the bright scarf he was still holding, as if surprised to find it in his hand.

Attar spoke gently but firmly. "It's important."

General Thade took a deep, shuddering breath, and seemed to visibly pull himself up out of whatever fog he was in. He stared at Attar blankly.

"What is it?"

Attar made a sharp hand gesture. There was a soft rustle, and then two ape soldiers stepped out of the deeper shadows beneath the trees, and marched toward them. The troopers looked nervous, even a bit frightened, but determined nevertheless. They approached the general and the commander and came to a rigid halt.

"My men insist on speaking to you. They won't tell me what it's about."

General Thade eyed the soldiers, then raised his eyebrows in question. After a moment one of the soldiers began to speak.

Night spread vast, black wings over the city of the apes. The poorer sections were already dark. Now the lanterns and candles began to flicker and die in the good neighborhoods, as the parties and dinners came to an end, and the aristocracy, in small, chatting groups, made their way back to their beds.

And in various hovels, kennels, pens, and cages

throughout the city, human slaves curled tighter against their straw mattresses and bundled rags, moaning softly as nightmares chased them through the land of sleep.

In the kitchen of Senator Sandar's villa, the old gorilla majordomo, Krull, slammed shut the door on the cage that housed his master's slaves. Krull's bones ached, his feet hurt, and after the exhausting tension of the dinner party that evening, he was feeling more tired than usual. He rattled the lock on the cage door to make sure it was secure, then turned and trudged away, thinking no more of locking up Tival and Bon and the two new wilding slaves than a human would have thought about putting a dog in its crate for the night.

As soon as the door slammed shut, Bon immediately curled up on her blanket on the floor. But Davidson waited by the cage door until he heard Krull's heavy tread vanishing up the stairs. When he was certain the old gorilla was gone for good, he reached into his shirt and carefully withdrew the small pronged fork he'd salvaged from the mess at the dinner party and hidden in his robe. Squinting in the dim light, he crouched down and hunched over the lock mechanism. He had to reach through the gate in order to work on the front of the lock, but he managed. At first it was slow going, especially as sweat bloomed on his forehead and dripped down into his eyes. Behind him, the black slave, Tival, sank down on his own sleeping mat and closed his eyes, ostentatiously ignoring what Davidson was doing.

But not Daena. With her fierce barbarian eyes wide open, soaking up what little light there was, she edged closer, watching Davidson work. He was aware of her presence but didn't allow it to distract him, though her earthy, musky scent was strong in his nose.

Senator Sandar evidently didn't spend much time worrying about his house slaves escaping, because after only a few minutes of work, Davidson gave a final twist to the fork, and heard a sharp click from the lock's innards. He breathed a sigh of relief and jerked the bolt out of its socket. A moment later he pushed the cage door wide and stepped out into the freedom of the kitchen.

Daena silently followed him out. When he looked back into the cage, he could see that the other two slaves had not moved. However, both of them had their eyes open and were watching him. Bon, in particular, looked scared to death. Davidson couldn't understand it. Wasn't he offering them a chance at freedom? Could they be so degraded by their captivity that they were unable to even *try* to escape?

Bon's eyes gleamed at him out of the darkness as she spoke. "There's a curfew for humans."

Davidson stared at her in amazement. Evidently his worst speculations about the two slaves were true. Then Tival shifted slightly on his own mattress.

"If you're found on the street at night . . . they kill you on sight."

Feeling sickened, even shamed for his own humanity by their fear, Davidson moved closer to the cage. He peered down at them as they cowered on their mats.

"If you stay here . . . you're already dead."

Bon stared at him and shivered. But Tival, after a long moment of thought, suddenly nodded as if making up his mind about something. He grunted as he got his feet under him; then he rose and walked out of the cage, an uncertain but determined expression on his dark features. Bon watched him go, then curled herself more tightly and retreated farther back into the cage. Her thin voice drifted out like the cry of a ghost.

"Our mistress has been so kind to us."

Daena moved back to the cage and looked in the door at the little servant. "She's your enemy," she told her.

But Bon was unable to overcome her long, deep conditioning. She uttered a soft whimper and retreated even farther, watching Daena as if she were afraid the barbarian woman might leap on her and eat her.

Davidson was paying no attention to this. He was too busy opening doors, rummaging through drawers, checking boxes and shelves, looking for anything he might find that would make a better weapon than the tiny fork he'd used to open the cage's lock. Finally he struck pay dirt when he found a long, dangerous-looking knife.

Tucking the knife away, he turned back to Daena. "Can you find your way back to the place where we were captured?"

She stared at him, a look of consideration in her eyes, as if she were weighing his own resolve against hers. Evidently he satisfied her inner questions, because finally she nodded slowly.

He was beginning to feel the urgent beat of time pressing in on him. Anybody—Krull, some of Thade's soldiers, for all he knew, even Thade himself—could come walking in on them at any moment. And then what was he supposed to do? Fight them off with his kitchen knife? He grabbed Daena by the arm and began to urge her toward the stairway door. She came reluctantly, and after a moment, pulled away from him.

He turned, his eyebrows rising in question.

"Not without my father," she said.

It all seemed so simple to him. You pick a lock, you break out of your cage, you find a weapon, and you get the hell out. What was so hard about that? And why was everybody making it so difficult?

He shook his head. "Too dangerous. We have to go right now."

Daena stepped back, her chin coming up stubbornly, her eyes flashing. Davidson recognized the signs, and if he hadn't needed her so badly, he would have just left her there. But he did need her, and so he had no choice but to convince her.

"You don't have a clue who I am. Or where I'm from. And you wouldn't understand if I told you. But I can help you."

She showed him her teeth. It didn't really look much like a smile.

"Find your own way back," she said flatly.

Davidson groaned inwardly, but did his best to keep his expression unmoved. It wouldn't do him any good to show her the slightest sign of weakness. But he also couldn't help the spark of admiration that began to burn inside him.

Damn, she was *tough*.

The moons danced above the dark green forest like great, glowing cue balls across perfect felt. The hard, clear brightness they cast through the trees was not quite daylight, but it would do.

The smell of the bog at the edge of the jungle filled Thade's nostrils, and he booted his horse into a trot. Behind him, the two soldiers struggled to keep up.

When they came out from beneath the trees, they found themselves on a narrow, rocky, mud-packed beach.

Thade urged his steed to the water's edge, looked around, then looked back at the two soldiers. The first soldier waved vaguely.

"Here! This is where I saw it."

Thade nodded as he dismounted. "Go on."

The second soldier moved forward. "Something fell from the sky."

"With wings of fire," the first chimed in.

"There was a terrible thunder and the ground itself shook! I thought we'd all be killed," the second ape added.

Thade led the way along the edge of the boggy water, leaving the two soldiers to scurry after, trying to keep up.

"Are you sure you didn't dream this?"

The two apes glanced at each other nervously. Finally the first ape spoke.

"It was no dream, sir. Look!"

They'd progressed some distance down the beach now, with the jungle at their backs. The soldier who had spoken looked at the trees, found what he was seeking, and pointed.

Thade turned to look, and saw a line of charred and broken trees standing like skeletons in the moonlight. It was as if a great, burning knife had been thrust straight into the heart of the forest.

Thade stared at the track of shattered trees, then turned and looked out over the still, moonlit waters, thinking furiously. Whatever it was, it must have been huge!

After a long moment, Thade grunted and turned to look thoughtfully at the two soldiers, who were watching him with obvious apprehension.

"Who else did you tell?" he asked, in as calm a tone as he could muster.

Neither one of the soldiers wanted to be the first to speak, but finally the first one said, "No one, sir. We knew we had to come right to you."

Slowly, Thade smiled. Those who knew him well might have been unnerved by the sight of his fangs, but these troopers didn't know him at all. If they had, they would have understood what it meant.

"You did exactly the right thing," he said soothingly, as he rested his hands on their shoulders.

5

The blossoms filled the bowl, mounds of them, a bowl full of beauty. Suddenly a long-fingered hand streaked with red-tinged fur hovered above the bowl, holding a stone pestle. Slowly, the hand lowered the pestle into the bowl and began to crush the flowers. The clean, heady scent rose into the air and hung in fragrant clouds around Limbo, who regarded himself in a tall mirror as he worked.

When he'd reduced the flowers to mushy paste, Limbo stopped and looked himself over in the mirror again. He raised his head, wrinkled his nostrils, and sniffed. He couldn't smell anything out of the ordinary, but he had somehow offended General Thade's sensitive nose, and that meant that measures must be taken.

He sighed, looked down at the bowl of mashed flowers, then scooped up a handful and began to smear the stuff beneath his arms and across his chest.

It didn't stick very well. Bits and chunks fell off, but

some did remain in the appropriate places. And he had to admit that he certainly did smell . . . different. He grabbed another handful and kept on smearing, as he thought some more about Thade.

Limbo had no illusions that the smell of crushed rainbow bud and morning blue would make the general like him any better. The general would never actually like him, no matter what he did. Just like the rest of the quality apes. They all looked down on him, even despised him, because of what he was. A slave trader. It was his occupation, not the flavor of his armpits, that stuck in their oh-so-delicate nostrils.

Sometimes it made him angry. Who were they to look down on him because he was the one who supplied them with what they needed? If not for him, who would cook and serve their food, pull their carts, clean out their manure pits? They wanted all the benefits of human slaves, without having to face up to where those beasts came from, and how they were obtained.

In a way, if only to himself, he had to admit to a certain amount of grudging respect for Ari, Senator Sandar's crazy daughter. She might be dead wrong about the nature of the humans, but at least she didn't shrink from the truth of them. She *knew* the source of the well-groomed, well-behaved beasts who kept her father's house. And she hated him for all of it, because she *did* know.

Well, in the end, he wasn't sure he didn't prefer her honest, knowledgeable hate to the reflexive condescension of somebody like Thade. Although he had to admit that Thade, at least, also knew where humans came from. It was Thade, in fact, who supplied him with many of his slaves. Which was why he was standing in front of a mirror in the middle of the night, smearing smashed posies on his armpits.

Life was funny like that, sometimes.

Outside in the quadrangle, in the ramshackle male slave pen, the old man, Karubi, lay on the ground, his head resting against Gunnar's shoulder. Gunnar's chest rose and fell as he snored softly, but Karubi was wide awake. The pain in his mangled arm made sleep impossible.

Across the way, he could see that the boy, Birn, was also awake, peering restlessly through an opening in the slats of the pen wall at the tiny sliver of night sky visible beyond.

Karubi watched the boy, pitying him for the loss of his freedom at such a young age, and at the same time envying him his youth and strength.

Suddenly Birn leaped to his feet. He stood, head cocked, almost quivering with the intensity of his listening.

A chill snaked up Karubi's spine. Then he heard it, too. A faint scraping sound coming from above, as if somebody were creeping across the roof of the pen. As the noises grew more distinct, others began to stir, and Karubi waved for everybody to be quiet.

Outside, a pair of Limbo's hulking gorilla guards ambled slowly along the line of pens, beneath a night sky that sparkled with a million stars. One of the gorillas abruptly came to a halt. He turned and carefully scanned along the top of the roof line above the cages.

After a moment, he turned to his partner and asked, "You smell that?"

The second gorilla cast a cursory glance at the top of

the pens, then sighed in exasperation. "Don't start now. We're off duty. And I'm starving."

The first gorilla listened a moment more, not quite satisfied, but then he shrugged, and the two guards trudged slowly away.

Up above, along the part of the roof where the first gorilla had looked, a shadow moved. Down below, in the male pen, a new sound, heavier and louder than the first, shivered in the silent air. Another shadow rippled past, casting a stroboscopic glimmer across the ragged openings in the slats. Karubi lurched to his feet against the back wall, groped around with his good arm, and found a wooden plank that would serve as a weapon. He hoisted it and made ready for an attack as he strained his eyes toward the darkness beyond the walls and ceilings.

Daena's face appeared in one of the openings. Karubi gasped and lowered his club. For a moment he stared at this apparition in stunned disbelief, until Daena extended her hand toward him. Then he rushed forward, took her fingers in his own, and kissed them.

As tears of gratitude at the sight of his daughter leaked slowly from Karubi's eyes, he heard something rattling at the gate to the pen. He dropped his daughter's hand as a rope slithered through an opening in the door. He hurried over, took the end of the rope, and fed it back outside . . .

. . . where Davidson quickly lashed both sides of the rope loop to a wooden stake. He tested the knots, then began to turn the stake, quickly tightening the pressure of the loop on the wooden slats of the pen. Tighter . . . tighter . . . the slats snapped with a sharp firecracker sound that froze them all.

Davidson didn't move for several heart-thumping seconds, listening so hard he began to hear a buzzing in his ears. But no shouts of alarm, no hurrying thud of running feet, no clash of spears or swords or clubs.

No gorillas.

Slowly he let his breath out. They were still okay.

Daena and Tival slipped around him, went to the gate of the pen, and carefully pulled it open. Birn came bounding out first, his eyes glittering with excitement. Then Gunnar appeared, hard and watchful, his fists clenched. Karubi was last, barely able to shuffle along, clutching at his twisted arm.

As soon as Daena saw her father, she hurried to him. "You're hurt!"

Carefully, so as not to do any further damage to himself, Karubi folded his daughter in a heartfelt embrace. Daena clung to him until finally he disengaged himself and pushed her gently back.

"How did you get away?" he asked her softly.

She paused, then slowly turned and looked at Davidson. Karubi followed the direction of her gaze, then carefully looked Davidson up and down, as if inspecting a cut of beef he was thinking about buying. But slowly his suspicious expression softened, as if almost against his will, he liked what he was seeing.

"Who are you?" he asked.

Davidson shrugged. "Just somebody trying to get the hell out of here."

Gunnar, his muscular body still taut with tension, was eyeing Tival, Senator Sandar's black houseman, with an expression of surprise and dislike on his blunt features.

Davidson saw him looking, and cocked a questioning eyebrow in his direction.

Gunnar's lips twisted. "This is one of their house humans. He thinks he's better than us." He gave Tival a poke. "He thinks he's part ape."

Davidson stared at him. He'd just about had enough. First he'd given the two slaves at Senator Sandar's house a shot at freedom, and one of them had been too frightened to even give it a try. Now he'd risked his own neck to come back here and break people he didn't even know out of their cages, and some of them had started to give him a load of grief as well.

He shot a glance at Daena. "You promised to show me the way back."

Karubi listened to this exchange with bright-eyed interest, then shot a questioning look at his daughter. She glanced at Davidson, then at her father.

"We'll go together," Karubi said decisively.

Davidson stepped out onto the roof of a building near the slaver compound, followed by Karubi, then Daena, and the rest trailing after. Everybody stayed low, but moved quickly, painfully aware of how they were silhouetted against the bright, moonlit sky. All any ape had to do was glance up at the stars, and it would be all over. Davidson, for one, didn't look forward to another meeting with Attar or General Thade, and he doubted any of the other humans were much interested in finding out what Limbo might do to punish a bunch of recaptured slaves.

As they crept along, nobody noticed that on a rooftop lower than them, but directly in their path, four youthful male apes were passing around a jug as they indulged in a time-honored tradition of all teenaged boys: the monkey equivalent of a late-night kegger.

One of the ape kids sloppily placed a finger over his numbed lips and blurted out, "Shhh. I hear something."

His friends stared at him in goggle-eyed shock. One of them, more paranoid than the rest, shot drunkenly to his feet.

"I think it's my mom! Hide it!"

A third grabbed the jug and went lurching toward the edge of the roof, looking for a hiding place. His eyes bulged and he reared back in stunned surprise as he found himself face-to-face with Davidson. The young male might have been drunk, but he recovered quickly and lunged for the man, who stepped nimbly out of his way.

Overbalanced, his brain fuddled with alcohol, the ape tumbled over with a crash that alerted his friends. Davidson saw what was happening, whirled, and sent his foot smashing through an attic door that opened onto the roof. It slammed open and he plunged through, with the others piling after him as he raced down a narrow stairwell. Behind them, the teenaged apes roared in outrage, bellowing alarm after alarm.

The panicked humans scrambled pell-mell down the stairs, fanning out in wild disorder as they reached the bottom. Davidson veered off from the pack, took a hard right, and crashed through a door into a bedroom.

Nova, Senator Nado's popsy, sat up in bed, her eyes bulging as she tried to cover herself. Next to her, Nado snored, so deeply asleep even this racket couldn't waken him.

Davidson barely looked at them, only to note that

Nova was too frightened to be a threat, as he kicked through another door and burst into another bedroom.

Here an old ape was taking off a wig, revealing a bald head. As she placed it onto an ape bust, Davidson came through, overturned the bust, never slowing for an instant.

He dove through a window, landed rolling on a balcony, leaped over the edge of the railing, smashed through another window, and kept on going.

The interior of the ape apartment house was a spreading mass of chaos as frantic humans collided with an ever-growing circle of terrified apes. In one room, unconscious of the rising din outside, a little ape girl put her new pet human to bed in the human girl's small, cramped cage. The ape girl was just mouthing a goodnight kiss at the trembling human child when Davidson and Karubi burst into the bedroom, followed by Daena.

The two men barely noticed the drama with the little ape and the little girl, but Daena did. She'd been there when General Thade had snatched the human child from the children's holding pen and given her like a pretty toy to his niece.

Daena's rage was a coal burning in her chest, but she managed to be almost gentle as she shoved the little ape girl aside, reached into the cage, and lifted the human child out into her own arms. As she turned to follow her father and Davidson, the little ape girl opened her mouth wide, revealing a row of sharp, tiny white canines, and let out a thin, childish howl of anger. Daena ignored her, which was a good thing. If she had to touch her again, she could probably not have kept herself from snapping the ape's neck like a rat bone.

* * *

Not far away, Limbo, with a glum expression on his face, was carefully scraping half-dried patches of mashed flower blossoms off his once-clean pelt when a chorus of outraged gorilla roars suddenly began to thunder beyond his window. He turned to stare, his jaw dropping open, as the din grew louder.

Great Semos, he thought, *now what?*

He moved toward the window . . .

A few streets from where Limbo stood, staring worriedly out his window, Attar was at the head of a troop of apes thundering down the street, heading for the apartment house where most of the reports of wild human atrocities were coming from. What few citizens were still on the streets scattered before the onslaught of grim-jawed, snarling gorillas and chimpanzees. Within seconds the troop swept past and vanished around the far corner, leaving behind a stretch of deserted pavement still echoing with the roar of their passage.

High above, a pair of human legs extended out over the gutter, then dropped. Davidson hung there for a moment, then let go and landed on the street in a springy crouch that absorbed the impact of his fall. Daena appeared at the edge of the roof, looking down at him as she extended the little girl she carried. Davidson looked up at her and nodded, setting himself. Daena took a breath and released the girl. She dropped like a stone, straight into Davidson's waiting arms. He sighed with relief, and smiled into her wide, blue eyes.

Daena hit the pavement a moment later, quickly followed by Gunnar, then Birn, and finally Tival. They stood in a tight group, looking up at Karubi, who dangled precariously by one arm, trying to catch a grip with his other arm. He almost made it, but missed by a finger's-length, and lost his hold entirely. He fell awkwardly and landed hard in a crumpled, groaning heap.

Daena hurried to him, knelt, cradled him in her arms. He looked up at her, his breath coming hard, sweat blooming on his brow.

"Leave me . . ." he gasped.

She shook her head. "No."

Karubi licked his dry, cracked lips. "I'm tired." He paused, rasping air into his lungs. Looking up into her eyes, he saw the tears gathering there. "And just too old. And old men get scared," he whispered.

Davidson was standing over them, listening. When Karubi finished, Davidson caught the old man's eye and said, "You might be old and tired. But you're *done* being scared."

Karubi glanced at his daughter, then back at Davidson. Their eyes locked. Something invisible but terribly important passed between them. Slowly, Karubi lifted his good arm.

Davidson took his hand, and together with Daena, helped the old warrior to his feet. Daena slipped his arm across her strong shoulders, helping him to stand. She looked at Davidson, an odd expression on her face. Davidson nodded at Karubi.

From across the street, Gunnar's deep voice shattered the moonlit silence.

"Apes!"

Davidson wheeled, jerking the kitchen knife out of his shirt, as two dim forms materialized from the shadows. A huge gorilla and the smaller shape of a chimpanzee. Davidson tensed, getting ready to attack, sensing Daena and Karubi at his back also preparing to fight. Off to the side, Gunnar was also moving toward the new arrivals.

We can take them, Davidson thought. *Maybe . . .*

The two apes reached a lighted patch of the street, and Davidson was finally able to make out their features.

The gorilla was Krull, Senator Sandar's majordomo. The chimpanzee was Ari, the senator's daughter.

Davidson threw up one hand, stopping Gunnar. But he still held the knife in his hand, and Krull saw it. The big ape moved with a speed amazing for his age. His mighty fingers closed over Davidson's hand, twisted, and suddenly Davidson found himself unarmed.

Ari began to speak as this was happening. Her tone was upset, her words rapid and filled with both anger and worry.

"You're lucky I found you before *they* did! Come back with me to the house. I can reason with them."

Karubi came limping up, along with Daena, whose face had turned fierce and cold. She glared at Ari.

"I know how apes *reason*," she told the female chimp scornfully.

Ari's lips tightened. Behind her, another figure appeared, shuffling up to stand behind her in a hunched, fearful posture. It was Bon, the small Chinese woman who was Ari's servant. Bon saw Tival staring at her and quickly lowered her head, whether in shame or fear, Davidson couldn't tell. And it didn't matter anyway. Bon had made her choice. Let her live with it.

He pressed toward Ari and spoke urgently.

"Is there another way out of the city?"

Ari started to reply, caught herself, glanced at Krull, then looked back at Davidson. Davidson could see it in her eyes. She knew something, but was trying to hide it. Krull knew it, too. He eased closer to her, glared at Davidson, and growled, "Do not get involved with these humans."

Davidson ignored him, moved even closer to Ari, invading her space. He could see it unnerved her. That was good. Somehow he had to convince her, and her uncertainty could only help.

He spoke forcefully.

"Why did you save me? Why'd you take the chance?"

His question upset her even more, not to mention that Krull's lips were now pulled back, exposing a mouthful of huge fangs. Davidson thought it wouldn't take much more to send the big gorilla over the edge, but he couldn't worry about that now, either.

Ari dithered helplessly a moment, then said slowly, "I . . . don't know. You are very unusual."

Davidson grinned mirthlessly. "Like you can't even imagine. Come with me, and I'll show you something that will turn your whole world upside down."

Daena had been listening to this conversation with growing agitation. Now her anger boiled over.

She glared at Davidson and barked, "So this ape will understand you but I can't?"

Why me? Davidson thought, but he couldn't spare time for Daena and her jealousies—if that's what they were. He could see that Ari was thinking furiously, and began to hope that maybe he'd gotten through to her. He hoped so. The street around them was still empty, but he could hear the blood-chilling howls as the ape patrols tearing up the city grew closer and closer.

Finally, obviously fighting her own inner battle

every step of the way, Ari reached some kind of decision, and spoke again.

"When I was little I found a way to sneak outside the city walls. Where no one could find me. I can lead you there."

Krull's frustration and concern had reached a fever pitch. He looked into his mistress's eyes and pleaded with her: "If you are caught even your father won't be able to protect you."

But Ari had reached her decision.

"You know what the soldiers will do to them."

Davidson could tell that Krull obviously didn't care whether the soldiers ground up every human on the street for monkey chow, but Ari was his mistress. The big gorilla fell back on his last, and to his own mind best, argument. "Your father did not order it."

Ari winced. It was obvious Krull's words carried weight with her, but not enough. She raised her chin, adamant. "He didn't forbid it, either."

The old gorilla was helpless. He had spent his life in her father's service, and he respected him, but he loved his daughter.

He turned and stared at the ragtag band of humans as if nothing would make him happier than if all of them vanished in a sudden puff of smoke. But they obviously weren't going to do that. He sighed as he spotted the little girl Daena had rescued from Thade's niece, who was now clutching Daena's hand as if it were her last lifeline.

"This human child cannot survive the journey."

Ari glanced at the human girl, then looked over her shoulder at Bon.

"My servant woman will hide her in my house."

Ari reached for the little girl's hand, but Daena pulled her back. No matter how necessary it might be, she just couldn't bring herself to release a human child into the care of an ape.

For a moment, Davidson feared there might be a new confrontation, as Daena glared at Ari, and Krull glared at Daena. But then Karubi walked up to his daughter, reached down, took the little girl's hand, and gently tugged her away. He took the child to Ari, nodded, and stepped back.

Bon turned and raced off into the shadows. Ari and Davidson exchanged a long look. A moment later, Ari was racing down the street, with Davidson and the rest of the humans trailing after.

The street was long and narrow, cloaked in shadows, and echoing softly with a thud of running human feet. Darkened clifflike houses loomed on either side.

Karubi lurched along as best he could, his crushed arm dangling, pain etched across his sweating features. His eyes darted back and forth, watching everything. He was an old man. He had not survived to become an old man by being stupid, or by being unaware of his surroundings. To him, with his wilderness-trained senses on high alert, the city was like a vast living, breathing thing. Light and shadow, sounds and smells. The very air carried messages to him.

There was a sort of collective howling all around him, as if the city itself had been roused to the hunt. He knew that wasn't far wrong. There had to be literally hundreds of ape soldiers searching out and tearing apart every possible human hiding place; it was inevitable that, if they couldn't get beyond the city walls soon, they would be captured again.

He glanced at the chimp female, Ari, running at the front with Davidson. The humans had put their lives in the hands of these two strangers because Karubi had shown that he trusted them. But what if he was wrong? He was old; he'd made mistakes before. And so much depended on his being right this time . . .

Up ahead, Davidson and Ari, in the lead, pounded around the corner into a new street as empty as the last. To Davidson, it was like racing through some vast, vacant mausoleum, with the sound of distant ghosts howling in their ears.

He knew that there was almost no margin for error remaining. This was a city built by apes for apes, and it was filled with apes. A pack of wild humans running through the streets could not hope to go unnoticed for long. It was a miracle they hadn't been spotted by one of the roving bands of troops already.

And just as that depressing thought skittered through his mind, several large, dark shapes wheeled around the far corner and began to thunder down the road toward them.

The humans scattered. Krull grabbed Ari and pulled her into a shadowed doorway, with Davidson diving in right after. But they were too late.

It was Attar at the head of that troop of soldiers, and he recognized Ari's willowy silhouette as easily as he would know the palm of his own hand. The sight of an aristocratic ape woman, the daughter of a senator, consorting with a pack of blasphemous beasts, maybe even helping them, sent a bolt of white-hot rage blasting through his brain. He let out an earth-shaking roar and charged forward, the rest of his squad an avalanche of enraged apes behind him.

Krull took one look at the nightmare rushing down on them, and knew the worst had happened.

"They've seen us!"

Daena and Karubi slipped into the doorway just in time to hear Krull's despairing cry. The warrior woman supported her father as he took in the sight of the approaching apes. His expression was odd, half smile, half resignation, and over all, determination. He laid a light hand on his daughter's shoulder.

"Hurry," he whispered.

Somehow, with only that single word, she understood what he intended. Her voice was choked with emotion—pride, fear, anger, resignation—as she answered him.

"*No*, Father . . ."

His eyes glowed as he brushed her cheek with his fingertips. "Don't worry," he whispered. "I'll be right beside you. Just like always."

With that, he twisted out of her grasp, slick as an eel, and darted out into the street, one lone man charging toward a whole squadron of heavily armed, angry apes, as the sound of his daughter's final cry rang in his ears . . .

"*Father!*"

He smiled to himself as he rushed forward. He was doomed, he knew it, but he'd never expected to live forever. And if by throwing his own body on the warrior's altar he might save his daughter and his fellow humans, well, then, that was a sacrifice worth making. Besides, he'd never wanted to go out as a sick old man.

Far better to leave the world as he'd always walked it, as a man and a fighter, strong and brave, a weapon in his hand with which to slay his enemies.

On that thought, he swerved sharply toward the side of the street. His hands were empty, but his eyes were still sharp, and he'd spotted a great wooden poleax left standing beside some ape's door. If he had to take on a squad of armored gorillas and chimps, he'd much rather do it from a distance, with a good, stout bow and a quiver full of arrows. But he didn't have the luxury of that, and the poleax, though old, felt strong and deadly in his rejuvenated grasp.

And so it was with a light heart that he stepped out into the street again to face Attar's wild stampede. He aimed the point of the poleax at the closest gorilla, spread his legs, braced himself to absorb the shock of collision, and waited.

What came was not entirely what he expected, but not much of a surprise, either. He'd already seen this Attar ape in action. He knew him, knew how he felt about humans, and so when the huge, armored gorilla didn't simply cut him down, but instead jerked aside at the very last instant, Karubi only turned to keep him in the sights of his poleax.

Trampling me to death probably isn't personal *enough for him,* Karubi thought. *And that's just fine with me. Maybe I can surprise him a little, before he figures out he's got a little more on his plate than just squashing a cockroach . . .*

Attar's red-rimmed gaze was watchful as he spread his arms and began to shuffle in a circle around Karubi, who kept on turning to face him.

Karubi was dimly aware of the rest of the apes

pulling up, gathering around to watch their commander and his sport with the wild human.

Good, he thought in the back of his mind. *More time
for the others to get away . . .*

But the contemptuous way Attar was refusing to
take out his sword and *fight* him, as if his blade were
too good for soiling on human flesh, finally goaded
Karubi beyond endurance. He lunged toward the gorilla, jabbing ferociously at his throat with the sharp
end of his poleax.

Attar was a highly trained warrior, his reflexes
keyed to a fever pitch, as strong as any five men. His
right arm flashed out and slapped the tip of the poleax
aside as if it were no more bothersome or threatening
than a buzzing gnat.

Karubi felt the parry as a tremendous blow that
nearly ripped the weapon from his grasp. The power of
it spun him halfway around, exposing his undefended
blind side to the ape's ferocious attack. The next thing
the old human fighter knew, down was up, up was
down, and he was flying through the air, his poleax
spinning from his numbed fingers like a child's toy top.

He crashed back to the pavement with stunning
force, felt something snap near his spine, and then
everything went fuzzy and distant. When the world
came back, it was with a ringing of bells in his ears,
and a splash of white stars across his vision. Finally the
fireworks faded away, and he looked up to see Attar
looming over him, looking down. Vaguely, Karubi
could see the rest of the ape soldiers gathered in a circle surrounding them, and he felt again that flash of triumph at helping his people to escape.

A curious calm settled over him. He felt no fear as

he looked up at the grinning ape, only a spreading lassitude, and a sensation of peace.

Attar, evidently, had been expecting a different reaction. His forehead wrinkled. He tilted his head to one side, then the other, suddenly uncertain. Finally he spoke.

"Why do you not tremble before me?"

Karubi felt no fear at all. Instead, a sudden rush of freedom filled him and lifted his spirit, the freedom that comes to a man when his life moves beyond everything that has come before, moves beyond even himself, and rests at last in something greater. Death may wait in that place, but fear is forever banished.

The strange human, Davidson, had been right, Karubi realized.

His cracked, bruised lips spread in a slow smile, and when he spoke, his voice was clear and strong.

"I'm done being scared," he said.

Only four words, but their impact on Attar was clearly visible. His head jerked back, his forehead wrinkled, and his eyes suddenly grew wide, as if he were seeing this human prostrate before him for the first time.

All thinking beings recognize bravery beyond self, for it is the quality that transcends the beast, and lifts the heart toward the stars. Nothing is more prized by a warrior, and as a warrior, Attar recognized it now, even though he was seeing it in the most unexpected of places.

Karubi, whom he'd thought a beast, stunned him. He raised his arms, lowered them. His ferocious leer became uncertain, faded, vanished. He'd set out to squash a bug, exterminate an animal, but what faced him now, even though vanquished, was as brave and pure and bright as any ape he'd ever faced. This battered, matted, tattooed *man* smiling up at him so serenely was *as good as any ape*!

Something deep inside Attar's simian soul creaked, cracked, and was transformed forever. And as he locked his gaze with Karubi's own, he realized that things would never be the same again . . .

A thunder of iron-shod hooves crashed across the pavement. A foaming, rearing stallion shattered the circle of mesmerized troopers, as General Thade arrived in all his fury.

The chimp leaped from his steed, his armor flashing white-gold in the moonlight. Attar staggered back from his general as Thade flashed past, a sword gleaming like a flame in his hand.

The rising moons cast shadows on the walls, and in those shadows danced a picture. A sword, rising, falling, rising again.

A terrible cry shattered the night.

In other shadows, rapidly growing distant, the humans ran for their lives. They heard Karubi's final shout. Daena turned, blood in her eyes, for she knew the source, and the cause. But Krull was there, blocking her passage like a wall, her furious blows falling on his chest with no more effect than a gentle rain. Finally the huge old gorilla took her in an iron grip and handed her over to Davidson, and after a long moment, she grew quiet.

But it wasn't Davidson who calmed her. It was the death cry itself. As she listened to it again in the silence of her memory, she realized there had been no fear in it, no hopelessness, not even any pain.

It was her father's farewell message to her, and now she understood. Not a wail of despair, but a cry of triumph.

Thade ignored the odd look Attar gave him as he led the troops away from where Karubi's body lay bleeding on the stones. He had no time for odd glances, or anything else that distracted him from his duty as a general. In the back of his mind, something whispered to him that he'd perhaps missed something important, but he paid no heed to whispers, either.

He turned to his commander. "Where are the other humans?"

They'd reached the end of the street again. Attar looked around, then pointed. "This way. They can't have gone far."

He made a terse hand gesture, and the apes fanned out, searching across the silent buildings, the shrouded trees, the empty doors.

Attar stepped out into the intersection, raised his head, sniffed at the night. He sniffed again, then looked around, puzzled.

Nothing. Nothing at all.

He looked at Thade. "They've disappeared."

A little growl of exasperation rumbled in the general's throat. "Ring the city!" he roared. "Block every gate!" He paused, considering, then continued, a deadly certainty filling his voice. "When you find them, kill them all. But keep the troublemaker alive. I must talk to him before he dies."

Attar hesitated. Despite what had just happened with Karubi, he had no real objection to the general's orders. Whether the humans were cockroaches or kings, they still had to die. But there was another problem, a problem that wouldn't improve Thade's mood at all. Nonetheless, it had to be said. Attar might be many things, but one thing he never shirked, not even for a general, was his duty. He took a deep breath and said, "Sir . . . ?"

General Thade looked at him.

"The senator's daughter is with them."

Thade's eyes widened. Suddenly he looked like a man who'd just been kicked in the belly. He opened his mouth, closed it. "They took her?" he asked slowly.

Attar shook his head. "She is helping them. I saw her myself."

Thade stared at him, emotions warring across his face. Attar felt a wash of sympathy for his chief. He knew of the relationship the female and his general had once enjoyed, and he knew why that relationship had frayed into near nonexistence. But what a quandary for General Thade! The woman he had loved now consorting with a pack of wild animals, committing public blasphemy *literally* in the streets for all the world to see. Watching the ape's agony made Attar sick to his stomach, but what could he do? Only be a soldier, and tell his commander the truth as he knew it. What Thade did with that knowledge was up to him. But Attar silently thanked Semos it wasn't his problem, or his decision to make.

At last Thade began to stutter out a reply. "She had no choice," he said. "She was terrified." His voice grew stronger, more certain. Attar wasn't sure if Thade was trying to convince him, or convince himself. If it was the latter, it seemed to be working, because Thade gave a small nod and said, almost pompously, "I will report the matter to the senate myself!"

While Attar tried to imagine *that* scene, a knowing smile began to spread across Thade's saturnine features. "They'll beat their chests and ask for my help."

Attar stared at Thade, struck with awe. Yes, it might just work. The sad tale of a senator's daughter—one of their own!—captured and brutalized by a nest of filthy humans. It could happen to any of them! Only if they gave Thade what he wanted, what he needed, would he be able to protect them.

Now Attar truly understood why Thade was a great general, and he was only a commander.

The idea was diabolical. It was heartless.

It would work.

The two apes nodded at each other in perfect understanding.

"They are weak without you, sir," Attar said. *And now they will be terrified as well . . .*

Thade nodded brusquely. He didn't care what they were. He *knew* what they were. He cared only what they could give him.

"Has she taken the old silverback with her?"

Attar sighed. He regretted the answer he must give. He'd known Krull for many years, beginning from the time he'd been a green trainee in the army under Krull's tutelage. He knew how badly the decision he'd had to make, the choice between the senator and the senator's daughter, must have torn him. And he thought he knew why Krull had made the decision he had. That blasted female! Her father loved her. Krull loved her. Even *Thade* loved her. But whom did *she* love?

Wild beasts. Animals. The worst, most sinful filth imaginable.

Poor Krull. But he had to answer, had to tell the truth. "Yes, sir."

Thade stared at him. They'd been together a long time, too. The general had a pretty good idea what Attar was thinking. "I trust this will not be a problem for you?" he said searchingly.

Attar stared right back at him, his gaze raw but steady. "No, sir. As of now, he is a criminal."

Thade nodded, satisfied, and turned away. But Attar thought of Karubi, and Ari, and Krull—and even Thade—and his expression remained troubled for some time after.

From the crest of the low hill downward, time and wind and water had wrinkled the frozen flow of lava like an old woman's gray cheeks. The ancient fires were long dead, but the once molten tide remained, still and silent beneath the lowering moons and the glittering stars.

At the bottom, looking nearly as old as the rocks on which it rested, was a springhouse built around a cistern. The mortar between the stones had long crumbled away, but their massive weight was sufficient to hold them in place. The springhouse had been built into the side of the hill, and that it remained at all was a reminder of a time when apes had lived here, and drawn out buckets of water by hand to water their fields and fill their bellies.

The disintegrating structure looked as deserted and abandoned as the mountains of the moons, but somebody had taken the trouble to prevent accidents. Covering the front entry, sealing the opening, was a dauntingly heavy wooden door, as thick as two apes' fists. The vagrant breezes had carried a thick coating of lava dust down from the hills to coat the planks, dust that had lain undisturbed for years, maybe decades.

Now, something struck the door a mighty blow from *inside* the springhouse, and the dust jumped and hung in the air before it. Somewhere a bird, disturbed by the alien sound, squawked and flapped away. Small crawling things scurried for shelter.

The muffled sound of voices. Another thumping blow. But only the resulting puff of stony powder flying from the wood showed there'd been any movement at all.

A long moment of silence as the dust settled back. Then, suddenly, a guttural, growling roar, followed by a tremendous thud, and the thick wooden planks exploded outward as if a bomb had been set off behind them.

Krull came powering out, mighty fists clenched, shedding broken planks off his massive shoulders like jackstraws.

He pushed out into the moonlight, then waited patiently as the humans, their chests heaving as they gasped for air, stumbled out after him.

Amid all the hacking and wheezing as the humans struggled to catch their breath, Ari was the last to step out into the open. Krull quickly walked over to her, as she turned to stare back at the sleeping ape city in the blue-black distance.

The old gorilla saw the direction of her gaze, and knew what she was thinking. He put a gentle hand on her shoulder and said, "We can still return."

She didn't take her eyes off the now-faraway place that had held all the years of her life, but she did shake her head, slowly, sadly. "No," she whispered. "We can't."

6

It took a little while for the ragtag band of fugitives to settle down and realize that, for the moment, at least, they had escaped their pursuers. But, gradually, it sank in that they'd reached a place of safety.

The air was cold and clear. Small animal night sounds issued from the darkness beneath the eaves of the forest that extended almost up to the base of the looming lava cliff.

The sky overhead gleamed silently down, as all of them, in their own way, absorbed the changes they'd undergone in the previous several hours. Some had more to absorb than others.

Daena stood in silence a little bit off from the others, her palpable grief at the murder of her father surrounding her like an invisible barrier. Her head was bowed. Streaks of tears glimmered in tracks across her dusty cheeks.

Ari saw this and, thinking of how she would feel if

her own father met such a horrible end, moved hesitantly toward the barbarian woman. As she approached, Daena looked up and saw her.

"Your father was a brave man," Ari said gently.

Daena's eyes opened wide, focused on Ari, flashing
with rage. The ape woman hesitated again, because she
could see that, even though she'd been trying only to
offer solace, the human woman was clearly too upset
to take it in the spirit Ari intended.

But even Ari didn't expect what happened next.

Daena made a soft, choking sound deep in her
throat, curled her fingers into sharp-nailed claws, and
launched herself like a thunderbolt right at Ari's face!

Ari thought of herself as civilized, but the fact remained that a chimpanzee's reflexes were about fifty
percent faster than a human's, and their natural
strength varied between two and five times as much as
a normal human. Daena never had a chance. Ari's long
arm flicked out, and her open palm slammed into the
side of Daena's skull. The blow sent Daena flying side-
ways, limp as a rag doll, until she crumpled onto the
ground in a huddled heap.

Krull and the humans rushed to separate the two females, although the old gorilla was much less worried
about Daena than he was about shielding Ari from any
vengeful harm as he stepped between his mistress and
the rest of the party and let out a warning roar.

Davidson got his hands around Daena's shoulders
and helped her to her feet. She shook her head, still a
little woozy, and grated through clenched teeth,
"Let . . . me . . . go!"

He thought he knew what she had in mind, and
since the last thing he needed at that moment was a

full-tilt brawl between the two main females in the party, he tried to keep a restraining grip on her. He might as well have tried to hold back a panther. She jerked, jerked again, and was free. He reached for her, but she was running now, hard, leaping strides, and before he could say or do anything to stop her, she'd reached the edge of the forest and was gone.

Davidson watched her vanish with a sinking feeling.

Now *how am I going to find my way back?* he wondered.

Daena ran like a deer before the wind, twisting and dodging through the thick shrubbery, thorns and stickers tearing at her clothes, her skin. She welcomed the sheer physical exertion, and the pain also, because she was able to lose herself in it, and forget, for a few moments at least, the terrible weight of the grief that threatened to crush her.

Karubi, she thought as she ran. *Father!*

The words raced through her mind, finally blending together in a continuous shriek of loss, as other pictures, like a riffled deck of those cards the apes used in their games, flashed up and vanished as quickly as they'd come: sitting on Karubi's knee as a little girl, his strong arm around her shoulders as he showed her brightly colored birds flashing through the treetops and told her their names. Walking with him along the edge of a bright stretch of water, the day summery and hot, as she struggled to cope with the changes her body was making as it slipped from childhood to womanhood. How gentle he'd been, how much he'd tried to understand, even though she could tell he was uncomfortable.

And how strong and brave he'd been!

"We are *men*, he'd told her a hundred times, his voice quivering with emotion. "Not slaves or beasts! The apes listen to their filthy god, Semos, who whispers these lies in their ears and their souls, but they are *lies*! Never forget, my darling daughter, the truth: they may be stronger and faster than we are, but that doesn't make them better. Only different. But we both look up at the stars at night, and dream . . ."

Now he was gone. His death cry still echoed in her ears and in her heart. She knew she'd still be hearing it on her own dying day, and that was good. Because it would always be there to remind her what it meant to be human.

She knew he'd feared the apes. What rational man wouldn't? But he'd struggled against his oppressors all his life, and in the end, he'd conquered his own fear even in the face of death. He'd gone out as what he said he was, a man, fighting until the very end.

And he'd saved them. That was a precious gift. In dying, he'd given her and the rest of them their lives, at least for a little while longer. That was a grave responsibility, and a great challenge to live up to. She couldn't—*wouldn't*—throw that chance away, not for some sleazy, tricky ape woman, and not for a stranger who looked human but who, she sensed, was something else, something strange and frightening, beneath the familiar shape of bones and skin.

Gradually she'd been slowing, as the sharp edge of rage and grief and hate was dulled by the effort of her flight. Now she could hear them pounding along behind her, growing closer. The stranger, Davidson, was closest, gaining steadily. She could tell it was him. He had almost no woodcraft, and lumbered through the woods like a great cow—or a gorilla.

The chimp was close, too. The female. She knew chimps. She knew that if Ari wanted to catch her, she might very well be able to do it. But the female was holding back, keeping pace with her huge gorilla servant.

What did she want? Why was she here?

It made no sense. The ape was the daughter of a senator, a rich, powerful ape leader, and all she'd known, from the day of her birth, had been comfort, wealth, maybe even power. Why would she risk that, risk losing everything, to help beasts that everyone in her ape world told her to despise?

It had to be a trick, she thought, and yet a part of her wondered. The ape woman was *here*, after all, running through the trees just as she was. And she'd rescued them at least twice, first from Limbo's slave pens, and then on the street, leading them to a way out of the city.

Daena's thoughts were so confused, so all-absorbing, that when she began to hear a harsh, guttural rasping, it took her a moment to realize it was her own breathing. And now there was a stitch of pain growing in her side.

Better slow down, let them catch up. Davidson—*what an odd name for a man!*—thought she'd promised to take him to where he wanted to go. She hadn't, not in her own mind, but she decided she would anyway. He was different from any human she'd ever seen. And she sensed a strength, a determination in him, that perhaps matched even her own. He must have secrets. And if his secrets could help her own people, then she would learn them.

She owed Karubi that much. And infinitely more.
If Davidson could help her pay, then so be it!

Davidson was galloping along, running on almost
nothing but willpower. Back on the *Oberon*, he'd
thought he was in pretty good shape, but an hour on a
stair stepper was about as tough as a peaceful nap,
compared to what he'd been doing the last couple of
days—not to mention what everybody else, mostly
apes, had been doing to him.

It wasn't as if he had any choice, though. He was a
stranger here, and the tangled, trackless paths of these
forests were nothing like the neat, manicured national
parks he'd hiked through and camped in as a kid. Without
Daena to show him the way back to where he'd crashed,
his chances of ever finding the pod were somewhere between slim and none, and from what he could see, old
slim had been out to lunch for quite some time now.

And he *had* to find the pod. Without it, he was as
helpless as a baby. Oh, sure, he was a lot more techno-
logically advanced than the barbarians who passed for
human here, and even, from what he could see, well
ahead of the apes, too. That general, Thade, thought he
was pretty handy with a sword. Wonder what he'd
think of finding himself on the business end of a fully
automatic, laser-sighted assault rifle?

He let the thought of that percolate warmly in his
brain for a while, because it was a lot more cheerful a
thought than the reality that he *didn't* have an assault
rifle handy. He didn't even have a flashlight or a book
of matches. All he had was himself, his boots, and a
ripped-up set of regulation United States Air Force
pilot's underclothing. Too bad he'd had to shed the

pilot's suit. There'd been a few minor things in the pockets that might have come in handy. But not so handy it was worth drowning over them . . .

Damn it, that woman must be half rabbit! Was she *ever* going to slow down?

When she'd first gone charging off into the jungle, from his point of view, she hadn't gone alone. She'd taken his last, best hope of ever getting himself out of this bizarre mess right along with her, and the knowledge of that had lent wings to his feet.

Now those wings felt more like concrete boots, and his lungs burned as if somebody had poured boiling sulfuric acid down his throat.

Just when he'd about decided he couldn't go on any longer, he saw her up ahead, just a flash of blond against the darker green of the jungle. But a moment later, another flash, and then a glimpse of smooth, golden, high-kicking legs.

Maybe she was slowing down at last. The thought gave him a bit of second wind, and he lunged on ahead. Yes, she was definitely slowing! And she knew he was behind her, because now she cast a quick glance over her shoulder.

She didn't exactly smile, but she no longer looked as if she wanted to murder everything within a ten-mile radius. Now if she'd just decide to stop, take a break, let everybody catch up and catch their breath . . .

Maybe he'd be able to get out of this after all!

Something began to rustle the bushes right behind him. The rustling continued, keeping up with him as he heaved himself along. He risked a fast look, and saw the kid, Birn, running easily, barely breathing hard, and grinning at him. He had that look in his eyes again, like Davidson was about the most fascinating thing he'd ever seen in his life.

Hero worship, Davidson thought sourly, though he didn't feel much like a hero, and for the life of him couldn't figure out why a teenaged boy with a smudgy face would even begin to think of him that way.

Stupid, annoying little problems. He didn't really dislike the boy—didn't think much about him one way or the other, as far as it went, but who had time for kid stuff like that?

Then Ari blew by him like he was standing still. Davidson looked up just in time to see her looking back at him. She appeared to be expending no more effort than he would on a peaceful morning stroll. Damned monkeys! It wasn't fair, how much stronger they were than humans, and it didn't help any that she was female, to boot. All the females around here, human and ape alike, seemed to be able to run him into the ground.

He gave up. If Daena really intended to leave him in the dust, then it was going to happen, and there wasn't anything more to do about it. Besides, it was either stop now because he chose to, or stop because he fell down.

He stumbled to a halt, bent over, put his hands on his knees, and spent what felt like a long time getting reacquainted with his lungs, his heart rate, and his ever-growing collection of bruises, scrapes, and lacerations. After a while, he grew aware that everybody else had stopped, too. Maybe he *wasn't* the only wuss in the neighborhood.

Ari came loping back, barely breathing hard. As she rejoined the group, Tival vanished into the trees and returned a short time later with freshly picked fruit and some water. He immediately took this to Ari and offered it to her.

Even Daena had decided to stop imitating marathon woman. He saw her standing near the edge of the group, arms folded, glaring at something. Something that, for once, didn't seem to be him.

Gunnar sidled over to where Ari was, glaring at the sight of the human servant tending to his mistress.

"Look how they pamper her," Gunnar growled.

Ari glanced up, looked over at them, then turned back to Tival, shook her head, and waved him away.

"I'm fine," she said.

Daena gave her a jaundiced look. "Apes are always fine, as long as you have humans to serve you."

Ari lifted her head, her lips tightening, as Davidson watched and came to the conclusion that the two females were never going to get along. It could become a problem, but right now there were more pressing things to worry about.

He'd pretty much recovered his breath, and despite his growing collection of aches and bruises, he thought he was good for a few more miles. He moved through the group and checked their back trail as well as he could in the night gloom. Which wasn't very well. Something was itching at him, a nagging little scratchy feeling on the back of his neck, as if somebody he couldn't see was watching him.

He had nothing concrete to go on, but any soldier learns to trust his instincts in the field, especially when danger might be present. He thought their current situation certainly qualified as dangerous.

He herded everybody back together and said brusquely, "Let's keep moving."

It took a cruel amount of willpower to ignore the looks of exhaustion he got from folks like Tival, but Birn gave him a puppylike look of worship that said he was willing to follow Davidson for another hundred miles if necessary, and Daena showed him a flashing glimpse of teeth that he took to mean she'd be happy to run him right into the ground. Ari's and Krull's capabilities he already knew about.

Eventually he got them all moving again, with Daena reluctantly in the lead. As Davidson started to follow, Krull grabbed his arm. The old gorilla might be going gray, and his mighty back a little stooped, but there was nothing weak about his grip.

He leaned close and growled, "If this is some human trick, I will kill you."

Davidson thought, but didn't say, that he'd pretty much already figured that out. He merely nodded and headed after the others, and after a final moment of hesitation, Krull followed.

As they left, something stirred in the shadows. For just one instant, a pair of yellow eyes gleamed in the light of the fading moons. The eyes looked feral, vicious.

Hungry.

After Davidson and the rest of the party were gone, the eyes began to slip out of the shadows and into the trees, following them.

Dawn finally came as both suns peeped above the horizon at about the same time, sending a tangle of cross-hatched shadows weaving through the woods. Davidson thought that the two moons had been bad enough. But the sight of two suns, each a slightly different color from the other, made this whole world seem like some bizarre fantasy.

Davidson was running easily, pounding along the muddy beach that edged a broad expanse of deep, still water, where ripples and tiny waves glittered softly in the light of the rising suns. He didn't quite recognize his surroundings yet, but everything looked familiar: the dark, looming jungle on his left, and the steely glitter of water on his right.

After everything that happened—the beatings he'd suffered, the injuries, and then a night spent running through a nearly impenetrable jungle, he knew he should be ready to drop. But he felt fine, even exalted, racing along on the mixed fuel of adrenaline and hope.

He'd taken the lead now. Behind him, the rest stumbled along in a wavering gaggle of exhausted humans and apes. Finally he found what he'd been looking for all along, and he screeched to a halt. He turned, looked back, and saw the others also slowing and stopping, their jaws dropping in expressions of mingled surprise and awe.

Here the forest looked as if it had been split by a giant's flaming sword. The leafy green canopy had been seared away. All that remained was a line of mighty tree trunks charred into twisted matchsticks, leading directly toward the water.

Davidson found himself staring, too. He remembered the wild ride in, when he thought his death might come first by ice, then by fire. Now, looking at the vast, black scar, he was privately amazed that he'd survived at all. He gestured at the devastation as the others came straggling up.

"This is where I flew in . . ."

The humans simply stared, their confusion at the massive devastation plain on their faces. Davidson could also see an uneasy fear growing among them as well. Ari and Krull, more sophisticated, looked mostly puzzled, as if trying to figure out what could have caused such a thing.

Finally, Ari stepped forward. She pointed accusingly. "You *caused* this?"

Davidson shrugged. "My retro burners . . ."

Then he saw the look on Ari's face and realized what he had said. She knew as much about retro burners causing forest fires as he knew about a world with two moons and two suns where apes were in charge.

It was hard to keep from laughing in her face, especially with his own excitement bubbling up inside him like an unquenchable fountain. He saw the kid, Birn, staring at him wide-eyed. Davidson knew the boy was picking up on his own burgeoning hopes.

Gunnar, looking even more dour and gloomy than usual, stomped up to Daena, his uneasiness more than obvious.

"The soldiers will be hounding us. We can still make it to the mountains."

It was plain he held this mysteriously scorched jungle and Davidson's pipe dreams in equally low regard. Daena barely heard what he said. She walked over to the nearest tree and put her fingers on its scorched hide, a look of wonder on her face.

"I don't understand. You fell from the sky?" she said.

Davidson grinned at her, then nodded. "With my ass on fire," he replied.

Krull looked no happier than Gunnar, and he obvi-

Mark Wahlberg stars as Captain Leo Davidson, a pilot on the USAF *Oberon* in the year 2029.

Swept into a powerful electromagnetic storm, Davidson's ship crashlands on a mysterious planet where apes rule and humans are slaves.

Davidson fights his way out of his submerged ship with nothing but the clothes on his back.

Fleeing humans are brutally hunted down by a band of ape soldiers.

Dragged in wheeled cages, the captured humans enter the shocking city of the apes.

Stunned, Davidson sees human slaves everywhere.

The slave trader Limbo (*left*, Paul Giamatti) with General Thade (*right*, Tim Roth), ruthless leader of the ape army.

After they leave the city walls, Ari's servant gorilla, Krull (Cary-Hiroyuki Tagawa), reminds Davidson that apes are still superior to humans.

Estella Warren stars as Daena, a beautiful and fierce leader of the captured humans and Davidson's reluctant ally.

Helena Bonham Carter stars as Ari, an altruistic ape committed to helping the humans.

Davidson makes radio contact with his ship—now he must reach the signal source within 36 hours.

Enormous and terrifying ape effigies guard the path to Calima, holy city of the apes.

Michael Clarke Duncan stars as Attar, a ferocious but devout gorilla captain who embodies much that is best about the ape's culture.

Davidson and the other humans leave the apes' camp in flames as they escape across the river.

Thade and Attar lead the ape army to battle.

Inspired by Davidson, the humans gather at Calima for a final stand against their ape enemies.

ously was extremely skeptical of Davidson's unenlightening account of his arrival. His glance in Ari's direction made his feelings extremely plain.

Ari caught his look and said reassuringly, "I'm sure he'll explain everything."

Krull grunted scornfully. "How can you explain what can't exist?"

Davidson had had just about enough of listening to a lot of guff from a bunch of jumped-up monkeys. Krull definitely qualified. He caught the hulking gorilla's eyes and said, "I'll tell you what can't exist. You. Talking monkeys." He swept his arm in a wide gesture. "This whole place."

Krull leaped over a couple of the others at Davidson, tackled him, held him down as he growled, "Apes. Monkeys are lower on the evolutionary ladder. Just above humans."

After a long moment, Krull released Davidson, who stood, peered at the scorched black line slashed through the jungle, then turned and tried to estimate where the pod, traveling along that line, would enter the water. Farther out, the water showed the dark blue of great depth, but in closer to the shore, the bottom was shallow and boggy.

Still trying to figure it, he stepped out into the shallows. Ari started after him, but Krull touched her shoulder, stopping her. Davidson noticed and said, "What's wrong?"

Ari stared at the water. "Apes cannot swim," she said. "We will drown in deep water."

Daena came up behind her, and said malevolently, "That's why we pray for rain every day."

For a moment, Davidson thought he was about to

have another brawl between the two females, but then Daena backed off. Uttering an inward sigh of relief, he turned and began to splash along the shore, and a moment later, Ari followed.

Both suns were now burning brightly above the horizon, casting a blinding glare across the water. Davidson shielded his eyes and squinted, trying to find what had caught his gaze earlier.

It took him a few moments, but then he saw it: several yards out, the remnants of a rainbow-colored oil slick still floated on the water. He pointed at it.

"There's where I went in!"

Before anyone could do much more than stare in the direction he was pointing, he made a running dive into the bog and vanished beneath the water.

After that, everybody waited for what seemed like a long time. Nobody had much to say. None of them, neither ape nor human, had any idea what Davidson had been raving about. What were retro burners?

Birn went right to the edge of the bog and stood silently, staring at the spot where Davidson had vanished.

Ari seemed as if she were the most nervous of them all. Finally she muttered to herself, "How long can a human hold his breath beneath the water?"

Birn glanced at Daena, the question plain in his eyes: was Davidson in trouble?

Daena made no reply, but suddenly ran out into the water several feet and then dived. Ari watched the woman vanish in a flurry of powerful kicks, and marveled at Daena's grace. She might be three times as strong as the human, but she couldn't match her in the water.

Daena pulled herself along beneath the surface with powerful strokes, though the going was difficult. The bog plants that showed their tips above the surface of the water were like small trees below, and there were wavering forests of weeds as well. Finally she fought her way past an especially dense thicket and broke into an underwater clearing.

She almost gasped, which would definitely have been a mistake several feet down, but she caught herself in time. Still, for a woman who had lived her entire life in a society where the horse was considered high-tech transportation, the sight of Davidson's wrecked pod was easily the most amazing thing she'd ever seen.

She'd come out of the weeds almost on top of the pod; a couple of short, powerful strokes put her right next to it, close enough to slide her hand across the scorched metal skin of the ship. She ran her fingers in wonder along the surface, trying to puzzle out the bizarre pictures that were painted there: USAF, which made no sense at all, except it looked sort of like the stick-men paintings her people sometimes found in ancient caves; and another form, which reminded her vaguely of something with which she was quite familiar.

Suddenly a cloud of bubbles erupted from the alien vessel, followed by Davidson, who was cradling a metallic box in his arms as if it were the most precious thing on earth. He saw her, smiled, jerked his head toward the surface, and began to kick in that direction. She followed, but before they'd gotten more than a few feet, a pair of frightening shapes drifted up from the murk and blocked their path. She recoiled, then realized that the two waterlogged ape corpses weren't any threat; something had hacked them almost into pieces.

Neither she nor Davidson had any idea who the apes were, or how they'd gotten there, but General Thade would have recognized the two soldiers he'd slaughtered not a hundred yards up the beach . . .

Davidson tugged her away from the grisly sight, and a moment later they broke through to the surface and began to splash back toward shore. As they sloshed through the shallows and up to the stagnant little beach, Davidson saw Krull staring at him. He grinned.

"You guys don't go near the water?"

Krull bared his teeth, but turned away as Davidson carefully sat his box down on the ground. As with almost everything from the *Oberon* that was part of the official stores, the box had the ship's logo embossed on its lid.

Davidson stared at the box a moment, then shook his head and turned to the others.

"How come there're two monkeys down there?"

Now everybody stared at him, and a few began to mutter. Krull pushed forward, angry. "Someone else knows about you," he said.

Davidson shrugged him off. Now that he had what he wanted, he didn't have to care about monkeys, no matter whether they were alive or dead. He knelt, worked at the catches on the lid of the box, opened it, and began to rummage through the contents inside. After a few moments he found what he was looking for, and stood up holding what looked like a small laptop computer.

None of the natives, whether ape or human, knew what to make of this, and Davidson was in no mood to enlighten them. He walked off a few paces, scanning the woods, the sky, and the water, checking for lines of sight and optimum transmission windows. Once he found a likely spot, he set up the transmitter, initiated its maintenance routines, and waited for it to warm up, mentally crossing his fingers until he saw a couple of digital lights flicker.

Thank God, he thought, *the water didn't damage anything* . . .

As he worked, Birn gingerly approached the box, squatted, and peered inside. After a moment his curiosity got the better of him, and he began to pull things out. The first item he discovered was a compass. He held that up to the light, shook it, watched the needle whirl and then steady. He handed it to Daena, reached in for more, and in quick succession came up with a flare, a packet of field rations, a thermal blanket, a high tensile strength rope, and finally a medical kit.

All of this garnered quite a bit of interest, since most of it was several hundred years advanced over the current state of their own civilizations. As the bits and pieces went from hand to hand, accompanied by grunts and puzzled expressions, it became obvious that while nobody knew what to make of these things, the fact that Davidson had them and seemed to know what they were for went a long way toward backing up his wild claims.

Gunnar ended up holding the package of field rations, examining the sleek plastic cover with a mixture of curiosity and distaste. This wasn't surprising, since his world was at least a century away from developing a plastics industry.

He peered at the markings on the cover but, not being able to decipher them (Meals: Ready to Eat— Baked Chicken, Gravy, Generic Vegetable, Rice,

Dessert . . .) he soon lost interest and turned to the package itself. He poked it, twisted it, and finally got the notion of trying to tear the tough plastic sack open. It was harder than he expected, but with a powerful jerk he finally succeeded in ripping the bag apart and spilling some squarish brown lumps of desiccated air force–issue chicken onto the ground.

Why would they wrap up little chunks of shit in such a fancy bag? he wondered to himself. *They must be very strange people . . .*

He'd jumped suddenly, as he heard a sound that had never before been heard in his world: the distinctive electronic squawk of a digitized vocal transmission coming through a high-gain filtered speaker.

Ari's eyes widened. "What is it?" she asked.

Davidson glanced up, amused. "It's called a messenger. It keeps an open frequency with my ship so I can talk to them."

Ari's eyes widened. She stared at the little instrument as if it might suddenly sprout wings and start chasing her.

"It can talk?"

Davidson nodded. "With radio waves."

From the looks everybody gave Davidson, as well as the messenger, it was plain that the term *radio waves* hadn't done much to clear up the general confusion. Davidson sighed. "Invisible energy that floats all around us," he added.

Evidently the notion of energy hadn't yet gained much traction in either ape or human society, either.

"This is sorcery," Krull growled, eyeing the little electronic box menacingly.

Davidson waved one hand soothingly. "Not sorcery, science. I just have to monkey with it a little."

I wonder if they caught that one?

Ari and Krull glanced at each other. Maybe they did, Davidson thought.

A high-pitched, piercing tone, the electronic equivalent of a four-alarm scream, spiked through the air. It caught everyone by surprise, even Davidson, who had been hoping to hear it. Everybody jumped like startled jackrabbits. The two monkeys covered their ears. Davidson jumped, too, but for different reasons.

"Contact!" he shouted, pumping his fist in triumph.

Behind him, Birn crept forward and peered carefully over his shoulder, snatching a peek at the mysterious alien machine. What he saw on the screen, though it didn't make any sense to him, was a single brightly colored line sweeping back and forth. As the line reached different parts of the screen, two tiny pinpoints of light would blaze up and then disappear. When Birn looked up into Davidson's face, he saw that it was shining as brightly as the lights.

"Jesus," Davidson gasped. *"They're already here!"* With one trembling finger, he traced the short distance between the two flickering lights.

Ari moved closer, her mouth open in amazement. Daena also approached, her face a study in contrasts. She glanced at Ari, then at Davidson, and said, "You'd better warn them about the apes."

Davidson stared at her in disbelief, and then snorted out loud. "Better warn the apes about *them. We're* in control now. We're the eight-hundred-pound gorilla!"

Ari's mouth slowly closed, and her eyes slowly

widened. She stared hard at Davidson, as if she'd never seen him before.

"It's time you told us the truth," she said. *"Who are you?"*

Davidson stared back at her, then stiffened, threw his shoulders back, and straightened to his full height.

"I'm Captain Leo Davidson, of the United States *Oberon*. I come from a galaxy called the Milky Way. A planet in our star system called Earth."

The look in Birn's eyes had passed from the everyday hero worship he'd shown previously to something that was very near awe. "Is it far?" he breathed softly.

Davidson gestured at the sky. "Past any star you can see at night."

Birn blinked. He was a smart kid, and he tried to get his mind around it, somehow take it all in and have it make sense. It was obvious that he couldn't, but it was equally obvious that he wouldn't stop trying.

From her expression, Ari was as conflicted as the boy, but written deep in her shining eyes, plain enough for anybody to see, was a simple truth: Leo Davidson, whoever and whatever he was, had captured her imagination, and maybe her dreams as well.

Poor Tival, still confused, blundered timidly forward and said, "Your apes permit you to fly?"

"Our apes live in zoos," Davidson said scornfully. "They do what *we* tell *them*."

On that note, Davidson picked up the messenger and snapped it closed.

"I'd call this hostile territory. So I've got exactly thirty-six hours to rendezvous with them." He paused, a dreamy look passing across his features. "And then my ass is out of this nightmare."

Gunnar shoved past Tival, distraught and surly. "What happens to us? Where do we go?"

Gunnar's question was on everybody's mind. But nobody knew the answer, not Davidson, not Ari, nobody . . .

A dark, red-streaked shape dropped from the trees and landed on Gunnar, wrapping him up as tight as a furry straitjacket.

"*You're* going nowhere," Limbo growled into Gunnar's ear." He looked up, saw Ari staring at him in horror. *"This one still belongs to me!"* he snarled at her.

Gunnar was a hard, strong man, and he looked almost twice as big as the chimp slave master. On top of that, panic, fear, and the adrenaline of rage fueled his panicked struggles. No normal man could have held him, but Limbo handled him as easily as a helpless baby.

He let Gunnar struggle for a few moments, then hauled off and delivered a stunning slap to the side of Gunnar's skull that took all the juice out of him, left him staggering on legs as weak as dishrags. Limbo paid no more attention to the rest of the group than if he'd been standing in the center of his own compound as he pulled out a pair of leg irons and snapped them around Gunnar's ankles, effectively immobilizing him.

Ari moved toward him, raising one hand. "This is an outrage. *Stop!*"

Limbo barely spared her a glance, but he *did* show her his fangs.

"*You*, I've had enough of!"

Birn was the first to break the shock of paralysis. He took off for the jungle like a scalded jackrabbit, dodging and weaving, but as he entered the forest proper, something from the trees reached down, grabbed him, and yanked him off the ground. His legs were still pumping frantically as he rose into the air, the apes hidden in the thick green canopy now becoming visible.

Two more gorillas exploded from the underbrush and charged the rest of the party as, with frightened cries, all the humans scattered.

Davidson sat quietly next to the box he'd retrieved from the sunken pod, watching the chaos. Although only a handful, it seemed as if Limbo's apes were everywhere, chasing the humans, catching them, slamming them to the ground. The air echoed with screams and shouts of anger and pain, and the satisfied growls and grunts of Limbo's gorilla slave handlers as they captured another of their escaped cargo.

Limbo was wrestling with Birn, trying to shackle him, but the kid was slippery as an eel and thrashing frantically, so that all Limbo's superior strength wasn't doing him much good.

"Hold *still*!" Limbo panted. "I'm not going to hurt you. I wouldn't hurt my own property." The tone of his voice said he couldn't think of any greater stupidity than that, inadvertently breaking the goods and costing himself money.

But just as he spoke, Birn managed to wriggle one arm free and deliver a sharp punch right in the center of Limbo's face. The chimp's reaction was immediate and unthinking. He growled and backhanded the boy right across the chops, leaving behind a red, rapidly swelling bruise.

"For you," he muttered, "I'll make an exception."

Davidson, still calmly watching this, saw Limbo draw back to strike the helpless kid again. He reached into the box, rummaged a moment, and withdrew his hand, which was now holding a compact gray hand weapon. Davidson put his finger on the trigger, then made a small adjustment to a control dial on the butt of the weapon.

Birn twisted away from Limbo's second blow, but it was a dumb reflex; the boy was too stunned to evade the monkey much longer—and Limbo knew it. He grinned as he drew back, this time with his fingers bunched in a fist—

A sound like a thunderbolt, but sharper, flatter, split the air. A thick tree branch right above Limbo's head exploded, showering him with splinters.

Everybody froze. Slowly, Limbo looked up to see what had fallen on him, and saw the shattered remains of the branch. He lowered his head and looked over at Davidson, his eyes bulging out of his skull.

Davidson smiled faintly, nodded, and showed him the weapon.

"You saw what it did to the tree," he said softly.

As Limbo continued to stare in goggle-eyed confusion at the innocuous-looking thing Davidson held so casually, and the immense destruction that had been wreaked right above his head, apparently by the same weapon, the rest of his crew were not so slow to react.

He'd trained them well. They were as loyal to him as he was honest to the rest of the world. They dropped their struggling human captives and vanished into the jungle even more quickly than they'd come out of it. Limbo's sharp ears could easily hear the rapidly fading rustle of their precipitate retreat. He knew what it meant.

He would have liked to join his employees, but that infuriating, mysterious human was still staring at him with a quizzical, taunting expression, as if he'd like nothing better than to have the slaver make a run for it—and maybe test his weapon again, see how big a hole it would put in a running chimp . . .

Limbo very carefully raised his head and smiled at Davidson, being careful not to show his impressive canines. He reached down, snagged Birn, and solicitously helped the boy to his feet. Brushed him off a little, and said to him, "No harm done. You're not hurt. You're young . . ."

He turned to Davidson. "These kids bounce right back," he said hopefully.

Davidson raised his chin slightly, and his weapon a bit more than that. Now it was pointing right at the center of Limbo's chest.

In the same tone of voice he might use to command a disobedient dog, Davidson said, "Play dead."

Limbo had never had a dog for a pet, but he understood the tone well enough. He'd used it on his own humans before. A sickly grin played across his features as he slowly sank to his knees and raised his arms high over his head.

Daena came storming over, fire in her eyes as she glared at Davidson. She wasn't exactly sure what had just happened, but she could see who held the upper hand. She could also see the white, broken remains of the tree limb over Limbo's head.

"Kill him!" she cried, pointing her finger at the chimp slaver, just in case Davidson had any doubts whom she was talking about.

Gunnar came stumbling up, partly restrained by his shackles, and snarled at the kneeling monkey: "Slave trader!"

He slammed his foot hard into Limbo's back, then

drew back to deliver another blow. But before he could do so, Ari pushed in between him and the slaver, shielding the cowering ape from Gunnar's wrath.

"If you kill him," she said heatedly, "you'll only lower yourself to his level."

Limbo looked up at her earnestly. "*Exactly . . .*" he said eagerly. He glanced at Gunnar, then at Daena, and finally at Davidson. "She's extremely smart. You know I've heard her talking . . . about apes and humans . . ."

He paused, frantically trying to remember what sort of blasphemous, moronic drivel he'd heard the crazy senator's daughter spouting on the many occasions she'd tried to make his life miserable. He could recall the misery okay, just not whatever monkey dung she'd been yelling at the time. He felt a sinking feeling at the unfairness of it all. How could he have known that his life might one day depend on having paid attention to a lunatic?

He stuttered a bit, then thought he recalled a few phrases. Had it been she yelling them, or some other moron? He guessed he'd find out soon.

"Separate but *equal*," he went on. "Uh, to *each his own!*" He blinked. "Right? Whatever it is, I agree with it *completely!*"

This totally insincere speech was received in dead silence.

Limbo blinked again. Not exactly what he'd hoped for—maybe his ability to lie was slipping a bit under pressure—but at least the two wild humans weren't trying to kick him anymore, and that ugly stranger with the thunderstick in his hand, who was eyeing him the way Limbo might regard a tasty cake with a worm on top, hadn't blown a large hole in him.

Yet.

And still . . . how dumb *were* these humans? In Limbo's experience, pretty dumb. But was this stranger, this Davidson, as dumb as the rest of them? He'd tricked him once. Maybe . . .

He put on his best smile, the one he used on human children when he was trying to soothe them for the branding iron, rose shakily to his feet, and keeping his hands high, slowly approached the human male.

"Can't we all just get along?" Limbo pleaded, counting the inches of his approach. Maybe it *would* work. The fool was letting him get close enough, anyway.

Gathering himself, never taking his eyes off the weapon Davidson held, Limbo flexed the muscles of his right leg, envisioning the lightning-fast move he'd use to snatch the thing away with his foot.

But he'd barely twitched when the human moved his hand, and a smoking hole about half the size of a chimp's grave suddenly appeared not more than a hand's-breadth from Limbo's right big toe.

"Find a new trick," Davidson told him.

7

"Take them off," Davidson said, pointing at the shackles around Gunnar's ankles.

Limbo could hardly tear his horrified gaze away from the smoldering pit that had nearly swallowed his right leg, but Davidson's words galvanized him from his terrified paralysis. He might have had questions about Davidson before, but no longer. Whoever the man was, and wherever he had come from, he was the most dangerous being Limbo had ever seen. And there was nothing like the fear of his own imminent death to concentrate an ape's mind wonderfully.

Limbo leaped to comply. It was but the work of a moment to free Gunnar, who backed quickly away, glaring at the slave master as if he'd like nothing better than to continue his little exercise on the chimp's ribs with his boot heels. Limbo began to sense that these humans *really* didn't like him at all. And if that was the case, discretion was definitely the better part of valor.

He began to edge slowly toward the forest, still smiling hard, trying to look as harmless as he possibly could.

"Well, I'm probably just in the way now. So I'll get going . . ."

Daena speared him with an accusing finger. "He'll lead them to us," she warned Davidson.

Davidson gave Limbo an appraising glance. "Then we'll make him our guest," he said.

He scooped up Gunnar's shackles and tossed them to Birn, who snatched them from the air with a wide grin. The boy turned to the slaver and snapped the manacles around his wrists. Limbo submitted with a resigned expression. He was a practical ape. He might be chained up now by his former slaves, but at least he wasn't a smoking hole in the ground.

His natural sneakiness hadn't totally vanished, though. He looked pleadingly at Birn and said, "Ouch! These things hurt!"

Birn only grinned at him, as if to say they probably weren't hurting *enough* . . .

Suddenly the trees above Davidson's head rustled as a massive arm covered with thick gray hair snaked down, and fingers like steel cables clamped around Davidson's gun hand. Davidson leaped backward, rubbing his wrist, as the rest of Krull tumbled out of the greenery, did a backflip, and came to his feet before him. Krull raised the gun he now held and examined it curiously.

"What the hell are you doing?" Davidson demanded furiously.

Krull gestured with the weapon. "You can turn this on me. I can't allow it."

Davidson started to speak, but before he could say anything, Ari's huge servant turned, raised his brawny arm, and smashed the gun down with pulverizing force on a rock. It took him two or three tries before he managed to reduce the high-tech weapon to useless rubble.

Davidson stared at Krull with a stunned expression on his face, unable to believe what had just happened. Then Ari wheeled on him and said, "Who would invent such a horrible device?"

Davidson screamed at her: *"That device was going to keep me alive!"*

Ari sniffed. "We're better off without it."

Right, Davidson thought. *You apes are bigger, stronger, and faster than we are. Of course you're better off. In the Old West, the cowboys who carried them didn't call them the Equalizer for nothing.*

Daena pushed toward the angry female chimp. "There's no *we* here," she said.

Ari misunderstood. "Why must you be so difficult?" she asked sadly.

Daena snarled at her. "Why don't I act more like a slave?"

Ari backed off, shaking her head. "That's not what I meant."

But Daena bored right in, and Ari really didn't intend to back off *that* much, so once again the two females began to wrangle. Davidson watched Krull take a final look at the crumpled wreckage in his hand, then shrug and toss the useless shards away.

Davidson could cheerfully have murdered him, but that wouldn't solve anything now, either. But he needed some outlet for his frustration, or he was afraid his skull would explode.

He whipped around on the two females whose dispute was growing louder and more heated by the instant.

"Shut up!" he roared. He looked around. "That goes for all species . . ."

Reluctantly, Ari and Daena stepped away from each other, both looking wronged.

Finally Daena muttered, "You can't trust them."

Davidson stared at her, utterly disgusted. With Ari, with her, with *everything*.

"You know who I trust?" he said at last.

Daena gave her head a tiny shake. No.

"Myself," Davidson snapped.

He picked up the messenger, flipped it shut, and stomped away.

The city of the apes was like an anthill that had been brutally kicked over. Ape soldiers of every description swarmed everywhere: some in pairs, some in squads, and even a full detachment or two. Young ape males peered down from the roofs of buildings or dangled from windows, excited by all the activity. The females stayed mostly off the streets, while their males stayed close to home and kept watch. The rumors of the wild humans' escape, even some darkly muttered tales of atrocities committed, had galvanized the city and terrorized the residents into a fever pitch.

Senator Sandar, looking years older than he had only a few days before, walked down one of the main streets with a grim-faced General Thade. Sandar was obviously distraught, his face etched with lines of worry as he knit his long fingers together in his distress.

"If I ever thought that those humans were capable of

kidnapping my daughter . . ." Sandar's voice cracked with grief, and he fell silent.

Thade's glowering features were frozen in what seemed to be a permanent snarl. He glanced at the senator and said, "Don't blame yourself, Senator. Your family above all tried to be compassionate to the humans." He paused, looking around at the chaos in the city. "And look how they repaid you."

Sandar's shoulders jerked. Next to Thade's arrogant presence, he looked suddenly frail and weak, almost fragile. He turned to the general, his hands raised in a desperate plea. "Can you find my daughter?" he begged.

Thade gave him a considering look, and then said, "If you untie my hands."

The senator had evidently been expecting some soothing bromide for a reply, and now he raised his eyebrows, startled at the implications of what he'd just heard.

"What do you want?" Sandar quavered.

Thade stopped abruptly. He turned to Sandar, a bold, almost obsessive light gleaming in his eyes.

"Declare martial law. Give me the absolute power to rid our planet of humans once and for all!"

Sandar's interlocked fingers now looked like a small nest of nervous worms. He hesitated before replying. He understood far too well what a terrible thing it was that General Thade was asking of him.

But Thade felt the senator's indecision, and pounced into the breach as he would on any weakness.

"Now is not the time to be timid and indecisive." He moved closer, violating the senator's personal space, pressing his advantage.

"I am the only one who can bring your daughter back to you . . . alive."

Thade's presence was nearly overwhelming as he waited adamantly for a reply. Sandar backed away a bit, unable to look into the other ape's eyes. Instead he looked at his city, and saw the panic caused by just a few wild humans. Even that he might have dealt with, except for one thing: those animals had his daughter. In the end, he valued her more than anything else, even justice. Even compassion.

But still, at the very end, he couldn't bring himself to speak their doom out loud. Instead, he looked into General Thade's eyes and nodded, once.

With that, overwhelmed by what he had just done, Senator Sandar turned and scurried away, and so he did not see the slow, horrible smile of triumph that came over General Thade's face as he watched him go.

Thade was still staring at Sandar's retreating back, a dreamy, terrible expression of anticipation on his face, when Attar approached him at a brisk march. Thade nodded at the gorilla.

"They're not within the city walls," Attar reported. He sounded disappointed, but not surprised.

Thade grunted. "We underestimate this human," he said, remembering the beast that had sprawled before him while he searched its gullet for a soul.

At the time, he hadn't thought he'd seen anything there but the mute dumbness normal to such animals. But maybe he'd missed something . . .

He made up his mind. "I will hunt him down myself!"

Attar started to salute, but Thade was already turning away, his foot seeking the stirrup of his horse. He threw himself up into the saddle just as another rider approached at a gallop and reined up beside him.

The newcomer was an old ape wearing dark robes and a worried expression. Thade had known him well since his childhood; he had served as his father's manservant all of Thade's life.

The old ape leaned out of his saddle toward Thade and spoke in low, hurried tones: "Your father has sent me to find you. You must come quickly."

Thade involuntarily clutched at his reins, then let them drop, his expression shaken. This could be no surprise. His father had been failing for some time. Once, he'd been the strongest of them all, but even the great ones eventually succumbed to the ceaseless rubbing and wrecking of time.

Why now? Thade roared silently to himself. *Couldn't he have waited? Damn the Semos-cursed luck!* But then, horrified at his own disrespectful thoughts, Thade pushed them away. Of course he would go. He wasn't some bestial human, to leave his father dying alone in the street, like that barbarian woman had done . . .

He gathered himself, turned to Attar, nodded him closer. "Alert the outposts. Make sure the human does not pass."

Attar half-saluted. "I understand, sir," he replied.

The general stared searchingly at his underling, as if wondering how much he could say to him. He began slowly: "Except for my father, you're the one I depend on most. We're not just soldiers, we're friends." He paused, then continued: "I'm depending on you . . ."

Attar nodded, deeply touched by his general's confidence. He was a tough fighting ape to his very bones, but he'd been with Thade for a long time, and he understood at least some of what drove his commander. He had no qualms about Thade's intentions toward the wild human male he'd seen at Senator Sandar's dinner. After all, Attar was a devout believer, and Semos had placed apes above all other beings. Killing or capturing wild beasts who threatened apes was neither sinful nor criminal, merely duty. And Attar was an ape who knew his duty.

The room was as dark as the bottom of a mine shaft, and nearly as stuffy. The chamber smelled of sweat, and age, and sickness. The windows were heavily shrouded, as if for a tomb. A single candle flickered uncertainly on the stand next to a simple wooden bed. The thick silence was broken only by the low rasp of heavy, labored breathing.

On the bed lay an ancient ape, whose thinning, faded gray fur gave him the appearance of a ghost. He looked as if he might vanish entirely at any moment, so wasted and desiccated had he become.

Thade approached the ape on the bed with a mixture of grief and pity for one who had once been strong, but was now only a short step from his grave. It was painful for Thade to even look at his father, at what his father had become, but he owed him this final duty, and he would carry it out. He *always* carried out his duty.

The old ape didn't know he was there. Thade came to the bed wrapped in his own silent pain, leaned over, and gently smoothed the old ape's lank, lifeless hair away from his raddled features.

"Father . . ." he whispered.

Slowly, the old ape opened his eyes. Once so sharp and clear, now they were scarred with the pale, milky clusters of cataracts. He recognized his son more by smell, sound, and touch, than by the power of his nearly ruined sight. But he did know, and he smiled.

"I don't have much time." His smile widened slightly. He was amused at stating such an obvious thing. "Tell me about this human who troubles you."

Thade didn't really want to talk about humans. Even the one who worried him seemed a small matter in this room. He made a short gesture, waving the subject away.

"He'll be captured soon. And little trouble."

His father lifted his head from his pillow, trying to see him better.

"You're not telling me everything." His eyes widened a bit. "You believe he's not born of this world."

Thade gave an involuntary twitch of surprise. How had his father known? He'd been this bad for weeks now, with nobody but his old servants and his son talking to him.

"Has he come alone?" his father said.

Thade nodded. "Yes."

His father sighed. "More will come looking for him."

Thade stared at him. "How can you possibly know?"

His father stirred restlessly on the bed. He was considering how best to say what he had to say. The words were difficult, but finally he found them.

"I have something to tell you before I die. Something my father told me, and his father told him. Back across our bloodline to Semos."

He began strongly enough, but his voice faded as he went on, and Thade leaned closer until his ear was only a hand's-breadth away from his father's lips.

"In the time before time," his father said slowly, "we were the slaves and the humans were our masters."

Reflexively, Thade jerked back, his mind boiling with the unbelievable implications of that revelation.

"Impossible," he roared.

Slowly, the old ape stretched out one skeletal hand, like some dire phantom warning of doom. He pointed a shaking finger at a sealed urn on a table across the room. From the earliest time that Thade could remember, the urn had been there. His father had never said anything much about it, but everyone understood it was not to be meddled with. Thade had always assumed that the jar played some role in his father's private religious observances. That had never been confirmed, but now he wondered if he hadn't been right all along.

"Break it," his father said flatly.

A curious, half-expectant fear electrified Thade's muscles as he hurried across the room, lifted the urn from the table, and smashed it on the floor.

His father watched intently as Thade sank to his knees, pushed aside the shattered bits of ceramic, and slowly lifted a corroded metal object into the candlelight.

Thade stared at this thing, utterly confused. He couldn't imagine why his father considered it so important. It was nothing more than an oddly shaped hunk of rusty metal. Not even big enough to use as a club.

He didn't know what to call it, because even the concept of a gun had never entered his mind. He looked at his father, the question plain on his face.

"What you are holding in your hand is called a gun. It is proof of their power. Their power of invention. Their power of technology. Against which our strength means nothing."

With wonder, and not a little touch of fear, Thade turned the deadly thing back and forth in his hands as he stared at it. Its name was meaningless to him. Nor could he understand his father's obvious awe and terror of the harmless-looking artifact.

His father's voice grew stronger, as if to impart by the sheer force of sound the truth he was trying to speak.

"It has the force of a thousand spears," the old man warned.

But his efforts, and his determination, were agitating him greatly, and causing him pain. He grimaced as he tried to gather himself, fighting against the urge to fall back in exhaustion as the world swam away from him. With nearly super-ape effort, he pulled himself back together, and continued.

"I warn you, their ingenuity goes hand-in-hand with their cruelty. No creature is as devious or violent. Find this human quickly. Do not let him reach Calima."

Now even more confused, Thade stared at his father in disbelief.

"The ancient ruins? There's nothing there but some old cave paintings."

But his father shook his head. "Calima holds the secret of our true beginning." The effort had cost him too much. He let out a low, guttural groan of pain.

Thade hurried to him. He still didn't really understand what this great secret was supposed to be, or how the strange wild male was connected to it, but he knew what his father wanted to hear.

"I will stop him, Father."

But Thade's father barely heard him. He'd exhausted what little of his strength remained, and now he fell back against his pillow. He spoke his last words in a nearly inaudible whisper.

"This human has already infected the others with his ideas," he gasped. Death rattled deep in his throat. "Damn them all to hell . . ."

His hands went limp. His eyes rolled back in his head. Thade looked down on him, feeling his own eyes well with tears. Gently, he touched his fingertips to his father's eyelids, and closed his eyes for the last time. Then he straightened, turned to the bedside table, blew out the candle there, and plunged the room into darkness.

Somehow it seemed fitting.

After the enervating heat of the junglelike lowlands, and the swamps and bogs that clutched at their every step with soft, muddy sucking sounds, Davidson and the rest of the party—the humans more so than the gorillas—found the transition to the foothills of the mountains a welcome relief. But they'd been running for a long time, without much food or rest, and everybody, even mighty Krull, was exhausted. More dispiriting, after the initial relief of not having to fight for every foot through impenetrable underbrush or across treacherous quagmires, was the discovery that the mountains, even the foothills, were hostile to both humans and apes, and placed their own unique obstacles in their path.

It grew cooler the higher they went, but there was little or no cover from the burning suns. Tender, exposed skin, used to the soft, green-tinged light of the forest, baked and burned beneath the harsh, pitiless light that scoured the stones on which they climbed.

Worse was the way their journey kept traveling across steeper and steeper ground until, for all intents and purposes, they were climbing instead of hiking. The apes were better at this than the humans, because they had four appendages capable of grasping the treacherous stones. However, nature had designed the apes' skills for trees; Krull especially had trouble hauling his massive weight up dizzying escarpments, where his hand- or foothold might give way at any moment.

The chimps, with their small size and extreme strength relative to that size, had it easiest, though Limbo, the slave master, had some trouble with his shackles, and spent most of his time complaining bitterly. The humans tended to straggle along, scratching and clawing their way up the rocks, though Birn, smaller than the others and with the agility and endurance of youth, did better than everybody but Ari and Limbo.

It was getting on toward the high heat of noonday, with no place to hide from the heat that turned the sky into a white furnace, when Davidson, sweat burning in his reddened eyes, called a halt on a narrow stretch of relatively level ground.

As everybody sat or squatted, glad for a moment of respite in which to catch their breath and rest their aching muscles, Krull and Tival hurried to their mistress and offered her a cup of water from the sack Krull carried on his back.

Ari took the water with a nod of thanks, but didn't drink. Instead, she bounded over to Davidson and handed the cup to him, a look of—*of what?* Davidson wondered. *Something more than friendship, and that is just plain weird . . .* in her eyes.

That look unsettled him. If Ari had been a human woman, he would have understood it, known how to deal with it. But she was an ape, and to him, no matter how smart or literate or compassionate, that meant she was an *animal*. And humans just didn't *have* that kind of relationship with beasts . . .

Reluctantly, he accepted the cup from her, took a single sip, then handed it back. Ari looked disappointed, as if she'd expected something more, but Davidson couldn't imagine what that might be.

Surely she doesn't expect me to . . . ?

But his mind couldn't quite wrap itself around that notion, either. To *what?*

Then he saw Daena silently glowering at him and Ari a few paces distant. Ari saw her, too, and carried the water to her. Daena looked down at the female chimp as if she were offering something filthy, pushed the cup aside, and quickly stomped away.

Great, Davidson thought. *Maybe I should just let them kill each other.*

He knew why Daena hated the apes. Hell, who wouldn't? She'd just seen her father die horribly on the cold pavement of the ape city, murdered by brutal ape soldiers. But her attitude toward Ari seemed to go even beyond the usual, and the suspicion was growing on Davidson that it was all tied up with him, somehow. But even thinking about it gave him a headache and made his stomach twist queasily. Women!

Not that Daena was acting like a woman in love or anything. Mostly she looked at him as if she'd enjoy smacking him upside the skull almost as much as she'd enjoy doing the same to the apes. If he thought he'd have to spend any length of time trapped with the two females, he would probably have to do something about them. But once they found the place where the signal was coming from, he'd be out of here, big-time. No sense in making mountains out of what were, for him, only molehills. He could put up with it for a while, though thank God a *while* was all that was required.

When they finally got moving again, Ari seemed to gravitate naturally to Davidson's side. Their little break had put some spring back into his stride, though not nearly as much as Ari's.

She seemed excited, bursting with energy, and chattered nonstop as they climbed.

"I have so many questions I want to ask," she said.

Davidson glanced down at her and shrugged. "Get in line," he replied.

Ari ignored the implicit rebuff as if he hadn't spoken. "What are these zoos you speak of? This word is unfamiliar."

Right, Davidson thought. *In your world, you call them slave pens . . .*

And maybe it was the memory of his brief, painful experience in those pens that flavored the venom in his answer to her.

"Zoos are where you'll find our last few apes," he said.

Krull was, as usual, right behind Ari, and when he heard what Davidson said, he uttered an involuntary growl. Ari blinked.

Krull pushed closer and glared at Davidson—*everybody glares at me*, Davidson thought—as if to make sure he'd heard what he thought he had.

"What happened to the rest of them?" the gorilla rumbled ominously.

Davidson sighed. "Gone. After we cut down their forests. The ones that survived we locked in cages for our amusement . . . or use in scientific experiments."

So put that banana in your bowl and swallow it . . .

Ari recoiled, her shocked anger making her stiff with revulsion. "How *horrible!*"

Davidson glanced at her. No sense in starting another brawl. After all, she hadn't tried to harm him. Not intentionally, at least.

"We do worse to our own kind," he told her.

It took a moment for that to sink in, and when it did, Davidson could see it confused and upset her even further.

"I don't understand," she said slowly. "You seem to possess such great intelligence . . ." Her voice trailed off.

Davidson could understand. It puzzled him sometimes, too.

"Yeah, we're pretty smart. And the smarter we get, the more dangerous our world becomes.

Odd. He'd never thought about it quite that way before. Nothing like a little travel to open a man's eyes.

But Ari seemed almost willfully determined to put the best possible spin on anything he might say.

"You're sensitive. I knew it. It is an uncommon quality in a male."

Davidson thought about Thade and Attar, and even the treacherous, coldhearted Limbo. Not to mention the gorilla breathing heavily over his right shoulder. Or even his former commander, the captain of the *Oberon,* that pig-headed, stubborn man. Hell, with evidence like that, there might even be something to what she was saying.

Krull didn't think so. He just couldn't quite get it. A world like the one Davidson described was so foreign, so *alien,* that it remained a few steps around the corner of his understanding.

"Why don't your apes object to the way you treat them?" he asked harshly.

If you only knew, Davidson thought. "Our apes can't talk," he replied.

Ari didn't really get it, either. "Maybe they choose not to, given the way you treat them," she said earnestly.

Limbo had pulled up next to them, clanking his shackles like Marley's ghost. He'd overheard the last part of the conversation, and not only did he not get the notion of a world where apes weren't in charge, he obviously didn't give a damn whether he got it or not. He snorted, his disbelief in Davidson's fantasy obvious.

"Apes in cages," he muttered sardonically. *"Right . . ."*

Daena certainly could imagine such a thing, even if she didn't yet quite believe it could be possible.

"Sounds like paradise to me," she chimed in.

Birn, as usual grinning silently, was close by, watching Davidson with that worshipful gleam in his eye. Davidson noticed, and smiled at the kid. What the hell. Birn's hero fixation might be a little embarrassing, but at least the boy didn't spend half his time trying to make a man miserable.

Surprised at the unexpected response, Birn blushed, ducked his head, then scooted quickly on ahead of the rest of the party, as if any acknowledgment from Davidson was more than he could cope with in public.

The terrain, dangerously steep and rocky for quite some time, now turned downright treacherous as they reached an area that was, for all intents and purposes, a nearly vertical cliff wall.

Davidson raised one hand to halt the rest of them, and watched to see how Birn would do with the sudden obstacle.

The kid scrambled up almost as well as a monkey, but even he found the going hard. Bits and pieces of rubble tumbled in his wake as he worked his way higher. The boy seemed fearless, but Davidson found himself holding his breath even so.

Then Birn reached an upward sloping ledge, one whose lip he couldn't see beyond until he actually reached it. He was climbing blind, working his way up by feel and luck, when he reached the rocking lip, thrust one hand over it, and grabbed hold of something furry.

Surprised, he pulled himself up enough to look over the ledge and then up, to find that he was holding on to the foot of the biggest gorilla he'd ever seen, massive arms spread wide, leering down on him with a mouth full of fangs that seemed as long as swords. He let go as if he'd latched on to a red-hot branding iron, threw his arms wide, and began to tumble helter-skelter back down the precipitous rise, bouncing from rock to rock.

By the time he rolled to the bottom, his terror at the sight of the gorilla, and the pounding he'd taken on the way down, had pretty much scrambled his brains. He struggled reflexively at the arms that wrapped around him, stopping his fall, until he realized it was Davidson.

Davidson glanced back up the cliff, then down at the boy, and shook his head. "They're not real," he told him.

And indeed, when Birn's vision cleared and he looked for himself, he could see it was true. All along the top of the crest stood dozens of the things, twelve, fifteen feet high, like gigantic ape scarecrows.

Their bodies were made of bundles of weathered sticks bound together, impossibly long arms extended up and out from massive shoulders. Draped over these skeletal forms were furs and rotted swaths of cloth that drifted menacingly in the mountain winds. The chests and bellies were sheathed in rusty armor, and on the skull-like heads sat corroded helms from which rose fearsome crests. Flimsy and monumental at the same time, they were kept in constant movement by the wind, simulating life.

Still, once you saw what they were, they weren't so scary. Not in themselves. Why they'd been put there, what they meant, that was a different story.

Daena joined them, also looking up at the line of effigies, a thoughtful, worried expression on her face.

"The apes put them where they don't want us to go," she told Davidson. "Crossing means certain death."

Davidson thought about how much work it must have been to haul all the materials up here, then put those things together and get them planted.

"What's so important on the other side of this hill?" he asked.

Krull knew the answer. In doom-laden tones he said, "It leads to the ancient ruins at Calima."

Which told Davidson exactly nothing. "Calima?" he asked slowly.

Ari knew some answers, too. She said, "Our holy writings say creation began at Calima. Where the Almighty breathed life into Semos, the First Ape, in the time before time . . ."

Krull nodded. "And where it is said Semos will return to us one day."

Sounds like he not only believes in the prospect, he'd welcome it, Davidson thought. *And who am I to judge? We've got religions like that on Earth, too . . .*

"Of course," Ari went on, "most educated apes consider such religious notions as fairy tales, metaphors we use to explain our origins. I doubt there ever really was a Semos."

Somehow, standing beneath that line of ape effigies twitching ominously in the breeze, she sounded both pragmatic and worried at the same time.

Daena was staring at the ape scarecrows as well. "His *friends* aren't fairy tales. They're real."

Davidson could see where *that* conversation could lead, and decided to break it up before it could go any further. He pushed on ahead, retracing Birn's path up the stone wall, until he reached the top, and then, with only a curious glance, passed the invisible line of death that the effigies demarcated.

Krull gave Limbo a rough shove to get him going. The chimp glanced at Davidson, then glared at Krull in exasperation.

"Doesn't he *ever* stop?"

Krull didn't care whether he did or not. He just gave Limbo another push, and off they went.

The rest of the party came after, making their way

up as best they could, until all of them stood just in front of the row of apes, afraid to cross the deadly line.

Birn was watching Davidson as he trudged slowly onward, beyond the fake apes. He licked his lips, took a breath. Suddenly closed his eyes and bounded forward. As soon as he was past, he opened his eyes again, found Davidson, and loped up to a position near him.

Daena wasn't about to have her own courage outdone by a green boy. She followed almost immediately, and behind her, the rest of the group finally conquered their fears to follow as well.

The crest was only a few hundred yards on beyond the line of apes. Davidson reached it first, along with Birn. He crouched down before he actually topped it, lest he be silhouetted against the dusky, fading evening sky, easy pickings for any ape who happened to be wandering around with a bow and some arrows out there.

Gingerly, he moved forward until he could peek over, with no more than his head exposed. He could feel Birn moving up beside him, and motioned the boy to stay back.

He found himself looking down on a narrow valley nestled between two huge peaks, and the river that had cut the valley from the stone in the first place. The floor of the valley was an inviting meadow, green as emeralds in the clear mountain light.

It would have been a pleasant place, a good spot to lay up for some much-needed rest, except for the cluster of colorful tents arrayed along the edge of the river.

By Davidson's earthly standards, the tents looked strange. Dusky rose-red, patterned with blue, they reminded him of miniature circus tents, with high peaks and spear-pointed tent poles. But there was nothing circuslike about the massive, armored apes who tended to their armored warhorses, or ate, or sharpened their weapons, or all the other things soldiers do while in camp. Nor was there anything cheerful about the gorillas, their eyes alert, their weapons ready, who patrolled the pass leading down into the valley.

As the rest of the party came up, Davidson made sure everybody stayed hidden down in the rocks. Those apes looked like they weren't in a very good mood, and Davidson doubted that his own people, after days of running, hiding, and climbing, were in any shape to do much about it if the monkeys decided to stage another human hunt. Which was probably exactly why they were camping there in the first place.

Not for the first time, Davidson inwardly cursed Ari's old servant, Krull, for smashing the gun that could have given him the advantage over even an entire camp full of apes. It was all well and good to piously rant about terrible weapons the way Ari had, but whether a high-powered explosive bullet or a low-tech bronze spear went through your chest, you were just as dead either way. And the apes had a lot more spears than he did.

On the other hand, at least Krull had had a reason Davidson understood. He knew the gun was a threat to him personally, and possibly to his mistress as well, so he'd just taken what he'd considered the logical precaution. Understandable, if infuriating. And not much worth getting all upset over at this late date.

Davidson scratched his chin thoughtfully as he peered over the rocks at the camp below. The apes had penned up their horses in a natural stone corral between their camp and his own position.

Hmm. Maybe some possibilities with that . . .

Daena slithered in next to him, carefully looked down, and then hissed, "*Monsters!*"

Davidson turned, stared at her.

"What are you talking about?"

"I've heard the apes feed them human flesh," Gunnar added.

And even Tival had his own fantastic two cents of myth to toss in the conversational pot.

"I've heard they're possessed by the spirits of great ape generals," he said.

Davidson regarded them all with weary disbelief. They might be his people, they might be human, but they were as primitive as, well, as apes. Maybe even more so. He sighed.

"They're just horses. They'll do whatever you tell them to do."

He hoped they would, at least. It had been some time since he'd had anything to do with horseflesh, but from what he remembered, horses sometimes had a mind of their own.

Gunnar was his usual dour, pessimistic self. "We should try to cross the river another way." He looked around, shrugged. "Over the mountains."

Davidson shook his head emphatically, the vision of the messenger's screen in his thoughts, and those two flashing red dots.

"I've got no time for that. We'll go through them."

He turned and headed back down the hill, not bothering to see if they followed. He knew they would. Where else did they have to go?

Ari and Krull exchanged worried glances as they scrambled down after him, but Limbo still wasn't having any.

"Where should we bury your remains?" he hooted softly after Davidson, then chuckled nastily to himself.

8

A brisk and bitter wind blew up from the far end of the valley's constricted throat, gusting upstream to the ape encampment, ruffling the banners, whipping the sides of the tents with sharp, cracking sounds.

In the way of soldiers through all time and all places, the apes were hunkered in against the unforgiving weather, glad to be dry, fed, and warm around a crackling campfire.

In the same way, once their basic necessities were taken care of, they faced the same problem of all garrison troops ordered to spend an indeterminate amount of time performing an indeterminate mission: they got bored.

But boredom was better than the alternative, at least from a soldier's point of view, and the military—at least the grunts on the ground—had a time-tested solution for that, as well.

One of the apes around the fire threw down a large

playing card from his hand. The deck was well-used, but the pictures of apes in ancient clothing painted on the card faces were still visible.

"Semos smiles on me. I win again!" the lucky ape bragged, to the consternation of his mates.

Crowing with triumph, he stretched out his long arms to gather in the pot of winnings. But one of his fellows, a surly-looking brute with an evil temper, grabbed one arm and stopped him.

"You win too often," this one growled. "What have you hidden up your sleeve?"

The would-be card shark bristled right back. For a moment it looked as if things might come to blows, or worse, but the first gambler, after a quick look around the circle of his opponents, decided that he might get the worst of such a confrontation.

He relaxed a little, and extended his arms toward his accuser. The second ape pulled back first one sleeve, revealing only a thick, hairy wrist. He got the same results with the other.

The first ape, his face wreathed in the triumphant grin of the wrongfully accused, reached again for the pot, but once again, before he could rake in his spoils, the second ape stopped him.

"All of them," he growled, jerking his fearsome visage at the first ape's feet.

The gambler stiffened, but he didn't have much choice as his tormentor peeled back the cuff of his right pant leg.

Nothing again.

The inquisitor reached for the second leg, and the gambler twitched. The second ape grinned an evil grin.

He reached beneath that side, groped a moment, and then his grin grew even wider and nastier.

He pulled up the pant leg to show the first ape's left foot, and the card still grasped firmly in the long, prehensile toes.

"Cheater!" the second ape yelled.

He backhanded the would-be flimflam artist with a clout that knocked him sprawling. That was all it took. Everybody else piled onto the hapless ape as well, kicking, gouging, punching, kicking.

It might have gone very badly for the first ape, except that his tormentors were interrupted in their carnage by the sound of a commanding growl from above.

Heads turned, tilted up, and then eyes bulged.

Commander Attar, astride a gigantic charger, was not ten feet away, glaring down on them as if they were the sorriest excuse for soldiers he'd ever seen.

For their part, the troopers stared up at him as if they'd just been surprised by their worst nightmares. Which wasn't far off the mark. Some of them knew who he was. For those who didn't, the badges of rank gleaming on his armored shoulders told them all they needed to know. More, in fact: every one of them recognized the iron air of command he carried, muffled though it might have been by the hard-riding dust that coated him like a thin gray layer of smoke.

He spurred his mount closer to the abashed brawlers, leaped down, shattered the card game, and barked, *"Who is in charge here?"*

Everybody glanced at one another. Nobody was in any hurry to answer the question. After all, this high-and-mighty commander wouldn't stay here forever.

But their captain would, and he had a long memory for the slights of enlisted apes.

In any event, they were saved further deliberations by the arrival of the captain himself, hurriedly stumbling from his tent as he struggled to button his uniform.

"I am, sir," he stuttered as he got his disarray more or less under control and managed to sketch a half-hearted salute.

The look Attar gave him was even more ferociously disgusted than the one he'd used on the hapless troops. After all, Attar was no piddling milksop, like some senators he could think of. He'd served all his life, had even once, long before, been one of just such men. If they didn't fall to brawling every once in a while, especially on remote duty like this, he'd be surprised, and wonder if they'd become soft.

But that was no excuse for this fumbling, bumbling fool of an officer now trembling before him. The men were one thing. But the people in charge were supposed to set an example.

"They didn't tell me you were coming . . ." the local commander added sheepishly.

Really? Attar thought sourly. *And if they had, I guess I would have found your camp all shipshape and starched, instead of the mess in front of me now.*

For a moment, he thought that maybe he really should spend more time out in the field, inspecting the troops, if this was any example of what was going on. But he shelved the notion for another time. He had bigger rats—or, to be precise, humans—to fry today.

Although it couldn't do any harm to make this lump sweat off some of that fat he could see jiggling beneath his pelt . . .

"This camp is a disgrace!" he roared.

The local man flinched as if Attar had whipped him across the face. Already, visions of losing his command—maybe even jail!—were dancing in his skull. Attar's reputation was not a cheerful one. He had no doubt the famous ape would ruin him without a second thought, and he was terrified.

He stared dumbly up at Attar, waiting for the ax to fall, but after a long, scornful examination of the errant underling's person, Attar snorted and climbed down from his horse.

He tossed the reins to a waiting trooper and stomped toward his cowed underling. "Some humans have escaped," he growled.

Faced with an opportunity to redeem himself, the captain visibly pulled himself together, straightened, and said with as much conviction as he could muster, "If they come this way, we'll *crush* them!"

Attar figured that was probably right, at least if it were only humans this buffoon had to deal with, but there were delicate side issues that must be considered, too. Attar hated delicate side issues, but nonetheless, these had to be handled properly, which meant handled in such a way that this idiot couldn't possibly screw them up. After all, General Thade might be angry at Ari now, but there had been something between them once, and Attar well knew how fickle emotions could be.

He moved to the captain's side and let his demeanor soften a bit. He'd scared the fellow enough. Now for a bit of honey.

"These humans are different," he said confidentially. "They travel with apes."

The captain hesitated. He had no idea what such a

ridiculous statement meant, but he didn't like the sound of it. He let out an uneasy laugh.

Attar stiffened. "You find this amusing?"

His tone announced quite plainly that this miserable excuse for a worm had damned well better *not* find anything humorous about *anything* Commander Attar might choose to say to him.

The captain couldn't have gotten the message any more clearly if Attar had written it out, wadded up the paper, and rammed it down his throat.

He blanched. "No, sir."

Satisfied, Attar turned and inspected the perimeter of the camp, then looked up at the surrounding mountains.

"I'm assuming command," he said abruptly. "I will *personally* make sure this camp is prepared."

And more power to you, you son of a forgotten mother, the captain thought as Attar stomped away. *Then if this thing—whatever it is—blows up in our faces, you can assume command of the blame as well.*

He spat, and followed the new commander toward his tent.

At night, in the high mountain valleys, the air was clear and cold and still, and the stars were like thorns of light scratched against the velvet sky.

Two moons gamboled above the horizon like errant billiard balls. Davidson still couldn't get used to those moons.

But now, as he crouched near the natural stone corral where the apes penned their mounts, he was glad of their clear, limpid light, not so much for the illumination, but for the shadows it cast, large enough to conceal his entire party.

The crystalline mountain air magnified sounds. He could hear the low mutter of ape conversations in the distance, the clink and chink of plates and spoons, an occasional bark of raucous laughter.

Good. Let the monkeys settle in for the night. The greater the surprise, the more chance he had that this lunatic scheme would actually work.

He raised one hand and gentled the curving, graceful neck of the huge dun-colored stallion he'd spirited out of the corral. Thank God the apes felt secure enough not to post guards on their animals. Although why would they? Their camp was only a few yards away, and if they'd been told anything about their mission, they knew they had only humans to be concerned with.

Davidson had been here long enough to understand that, to apes, a pack of wild humans was no more worrisome than he would find a breakout of spider monkeys from the zoo. Irritating, possibly, but certainly not dangerous.

So let's see if I can't change their minds about that, Davidson thought. *Without, if at all possible, getting any of us killed . . .*

Which might be easier said than done. If he could hear the apes, they could certainly hear anything untoward from the humans busily pillaging their horses. And Daena and Ari were already hissing at each other again. What a relief it would be to just knock both of them in the head, stuff them in bags, and *haul* them to this Calima place.

Of course, if he tried that with Ari, Krull would knock *him* in the head, and he'd decided he wouldn't want Gunnar at his back if he popped Daena, either.

He glanced at the horse, who returned the favor with

a wall-eyed look. The beast seemed reasonably calm, though Davidson could tell that it was a little spooked by so much human scent in its nostrils.

He patted the stallion's neck one last time, then grabbed its long, flowing mane and used the leverage to vault onto the horse's bare back.

The horse started, did a couple of dancing steps, but then, to Davidson's relief, settled right down. He waited until he was sure nothing untoward would occur, then looked down at the circle of faces staring up at him in amazement. To the humans, seeing another human on horseback was as strange and unbelievable as seeing one riding an ape.

"Who's next?" Davidson asked.

Evidently, from the way they all took a couple of shuffling steps backward and began to carefully inspect the ground at their feet, nobody wanted to be next.

Davidson shrugged. It wasn't as if he'd actually invited everybody along on this party.

"Then I guess we're saying goodbye here," he hissed.

That was enough to send Ari stepping hesitantly forward. She looked up at Davidson, then cast an apprehensive glance toward the corral, where the rest of the horses milled quietly.

Daena sneered, "You can't go. You're afraid of water."

Stung, Ari turned and spat right back, "You can't go. You're afraid of horses."

Wonderful, Davidson thought.

He leaned forward, took a double handful of his horse's mane, then booted it gently in the ribs and urged it between the two females, effectively ending the latest confrontation.

He looked down at Daena. "You want to ride? Grab a fistful of mane and hold on."

Then he turned to Ari. "You want to cross the river?" He gave his mount a pat. "Horses are great swimmers. They'll carry you across."

Krull slipped out of the shadows, silent as a ghost. He kept his voice low, but Davidson could hear him clearly.

"You're assuming the soldiers won't tear you to pieces." Krull paused, then added, "I saw Thade's greatest warrior ride into the camp."

Davidson stared at him, surprised at the way he said it.

"Sounds like he scares you," he said, half joking.

But as usual, if Krull had a sense of humor, he was keeping it well under wraps.

"He does," he replied flatly. "I trained him myself."

Great, Davidson thought. *Another revelation about my buddy Krull, and another prophecy of doom to go along with it. Just what we all need.*

Evidently Limbo was impressed also. He uttered a sickly chuckle, then babbled, "Well, good luck, have a pleasant ride. Obviously I can't go, so if you don't mind . . ."

He rattled his chains, then held them up hopefully.

Davidson surprised everybody, even himself, by fishing in his pocket, finding the key, leaning over, and unlocking them.

Daena was shocked. "You're letting him *go*?"

Limbo's shackles fell to the ground with a muffled

clink. The chimp sighed, rubbed his chafed wrists in obvious pleasure, then looked up at Davidson.

"No," Davidson replied. "He'll ride with us."

Limbo took a hop backward, shaking his head emphatically. "There is *no* way . . ."

But Ari overrode him. "And if you try to get away, I will tell Thade we bribed you to help us."

Limbo stared at her in disbelief. But he didn't discount her threat. He knew she had connections, not just with her father, but with the general himself. And the general scared him to death. Well, maybe not that far, but far enough to make him rub stinky-smelling flowers all over his body.

"I'll deny it," he countered.

But then Krull shot an ugly grin over his mistress's shoulder and added, "A very *large* bribe . . ."

Limbo was trapped. He didn't understand *how* he'd gotten trapped—all he'd tried to do was reclaim his property, as any sane, intelligent ape would do, and now here he was in the middle of the mountains, at night, being falsely blackmailed by other so-called respectable apes, and it just wasn't *fair*!

He exploded. *"The whole thing's suicide! Ride through an army encampment? Only a human would think this could work!"*

Davidson knew the chimp hadn't intended it as a compliment. Nevertheless, there was something almost hilarious about the fuming slaver's helpless rage.

He grinned down at him and said, "Attitude is the first human freedom."

And with that, he reached into the messenger box that never left his side, and pulled out a flare gun.

* * *

The captain's tent, which Attar had temporarily appropriated for his own use, was small, dim, and clogged with thick blue clouds of smoky incense.

A few candles flickered dimly in the murk, illuminating the patterns of the small woven tapestry on which Attar knelt, his hands moving slowly over the incense, stirring the smoke, which rose in slow billows around a small icon of the First Ape, Semos.

Attar bowed before the image with a stiff intensity that made the depth of his belief and faith unmistakable. He was alone, having given explicit orders that his devotions not be disturbed for any reason.

All the more, then, was his shock when his silent prayers were interrupted by a sharp, rising, breathy whoosh, which was immediately followed by a glare so bright he thought for a moment that somehow the suns had risen again, but in the middle of the night.

He lurched to his feet, his heart pounding as he reached for his sword, and then rushed out of the tent to find the camp in total chaos.

Terrified troopers were gathered in clusters, pointing at the sky and moaning or shouting in fear. High above, a vast white star rained blinding white streamers of light down on them, hissing softly.

Attar glanced at this, and took in the rest of the disarray also, but he cocked his head and began to listen intently, for his sharp hearing had picked out a sound no one else had yet noticed: the thunderous clatter of horses' hooves pounding across the earth.

He didn't know what that hissing light in the sky was, but he *did* know what that sound meant. He turned toward its source, just in time to see his worst fears confirmed.

Careening out of the shadows of the stone corral came a stampede of frenzied beasts. That was bad enough, but these animals had riders.

Human riders!

The man he most wanted, the man his general had charged him with finding and capturing, rode a snorting, bucking stallion in the van. Right behind him were two more wild humans, the woman whose father he had fought, and Thade had killed, and a young boy Attar didn't recognize.

In a clump behind these, an even worse sight: more humans, but also Ari, Senator Sandar's daughter, and the great ape Krull, her servant and Attar's own military mentor from the misty past. Last came the chimp slaver, Limbo, a horrified expression on his face, holding on for dear life.

Krull was perhaps the biggest surprise, and certainly the least welcome. If *he* had gone over to the humans willingly . . .

Then his own training, learned at the relentless hands of the very ape now riding down on him, snapped him out of his momentary paralysis. He whipped into action with his usual decisiveness, though there wasn't much he could do right at the moment but gauge the extent of the damage.

The humans had freed the rest of the horses, and they were pounding right along with them, eyes wild, kicking and snorting, trampling anything unlucky enough to get in their way. Ape soldiers dove in every direction, or, if they weren't quick enough, found themselves stomped into bloody mush by their own steeds.

The humans whooped and screamed as they rode,

adding even more to the din and the confusion. Tents collapsed as horses foundered into them. Hooves crashed into campfires and sent sparks flying, as mounds of equipment were first scattered, then crushed beneath the irresistible onslaught.

Almost as soon as it appeared, the wild stampede roared through the camp and began to vanish on the other side. All Attar could do was turn and watch it go, seething with anger that he'd been so easily taken.

He saw that the last rider, the slave trader, was trying to pull up. It didn't take an expert to see the little ape was no horseman. He could barely control his steed, in fact had only managed to slow it somewhat, and turn it back in the general direction of the camp.

The troopers turned out to be better trained than he would have guessed from the nature of their leaders. Already, though stunned by the suddenness and ferocity of the assault, they were pulling themselves together and reaching for their weapons.

He saw a squad of men armed with fire throwers go rushing past, chasing after the rapidly disappearing riders, and a few moments later, another troop of spearmen pounded past.

The slaver was trying to drag his horse toward the soldiers, without a whole lot of luck. Attar started to run toward him. He could hear the chimp's voice crying with thin panic.

"Help, help, don't hurt me, I'm on your side!"

But the enraged troopers weren't having any of it. A volley of fireballs suddenly sizzled through the air toward the chimp. One nicked his arm, leaving a smoking patch, and nearly startling him off his mount. Then

the spearmen arrived and followed the salvo of fireballs with a charge of their own.

The slaver's horse had come to a confused, dancing
halt, jerking first one way, then the other, unable to figure out how to respond to threats of fire on one side,
shouting spearmen on the other, and a rider jerking
hard but ineffectually at his mane.

Limbo wailed in despair as he saw his own doom
approaching.

I should have known, he sobbed inwardly. *Nothing I
do turns out right . . .*

He heard the clatter of hooves behind him, and
turned in time to see Davidson riding hard toward him.
The big dun stallion looked wild, but Davidson was
controlling him easily. He missed Limbo by bare
inches, but as he rode past, he reached out and gave the
chimp's horse a tremendous whack on the flank.

It was enough to get the beast going again, and with
a kick and a snort, it set off after Davidson.

As a final insult and injury, as Davidson galloped
past a scattered fire, he reached down, snagged a burning log, and heaved it into one of the half-collapsed
tents. A few moments later the blaze, whipped by the
constant wind, began to spread like wildfire, and then
the entire encampment was burning. Attar saw an ape
run from a blazing tent, his fur on fire as he howled in
agony.

Davidson spared a single glance over his shoulder at
the chaos he'd left behind—the chaos he'd *caused*, he
thought, with a warm glow of revenge building in his
belly—and then he was riding hard for the river.

He quickly caught up with, and then passed, Limbo,
who was still clinging to his mount like a rag doll

glued in place. The river was dead ahead. In the flickering glowlight from the burning camp, he saw the
shadowy figures of his people, milling about in a pack
of riderless horses, trying desperately to control their
own mounts.

He galloped into the confusion, rode through it, and
pulled up on the bank of the river. In the mixed glint of
firelight, moonlight, and starlight, it flowed with a
cold, heavy power, deep and wide.

Around him, he could see Ari, Krull, and Limbo
staring at the rushing water with unconcealed fear. The
humans were still unsettled by the thought of actually
riding horses, but some of their unease was fading
away. Davidson grinned to himself. They were relieved
that none of the beasts had tried to eat them, and none
of them had fallen off, either.

In the distance, the apes were regrouping, led by a
huge, ominous figure he recognized—General Thade's
hatchet man, the one they called Attar.

He seemed to have his head about him, despite all
the chaos in the camp. He'd already marshaled several
small groups of soldiers into a larger force, and was
now at their front, urging them toward the river.

Suddenly a burst of fireballs arced up from the approaching soldiers, and though they fell short, Davidson could tell that wouldn't last much longer. Time to
go . . .

He circled back to the heaving horseflesh and confused riders, waving one arm above his head for attention.

"Drive them through!" he roared, then turned and
led the way back to the river.

Daena heard his cry and, with a fierce joy, slammed

her heels into her horse's ribs. The animal leaped forward with a surge of power that thrilled her to her bones. Why had she ever been so frightened of these beasts? It was almost as if they'd been *created* for humans to ride.

Just another ape lie, she thought bitterly, as her mount soared across the riverbank and splashed into the water, snorting and lunging deeper and deeper into the icy flood. She felt a moment of fear as the horse seemed to founder as the water grew too deep for it to keep its footing, but then it began to swim, bearing her weight easily, its bulky muscles writhing like great machines. And then they were across, the horse blowing and tossing its head as it scrambled up to solid ground.

Birn felt a similar rush of exhilarating power as he pulled hard on the mane of his own mount and leaned forward, shouting into its twitching ears. It responded almost immediately, wheeling and following Daena into the water. His grin grew until it extended nearly from one ear to the other. He felt no fear at all, and wondered if he'd be allowed to keep his steed. In just a few short minutes, he'd come to love the mighty animal.

Tival had no such exalting thoughts. He was scared witless, and if he'd had any alternative at all other than riding one of these devil beasts, he would have taken it. But that alien madman hadn't given him a choice in the matter, and now, with enraged chimps and gorillas racing toward him waving spears and fire throwers, his range of choice was even narrower. In fact, at this point, there was no choice at all.

Shivering, his fingers wrapped in his horse's mane tight enough to rip hair out by its roots, he closed his eyes and screamed as his mount followed the others into the water.

Krull was near the end of the line. His horse held no terrors for him. He'd been riding such animals all his life. In fact, he'd crept into the animal pens and selected his own. He weighed almost three hundred fifty pounds, far too much for most horses to bear for very long, and so he'd picked a monster, the biggest mount he could find. It felt strong and steady beneath him.

As a soldier, he *had* ridden horses across rivers before. But he'd never enjoyed the experience, and he wasn't looking forward to it now. Maybe it was this apprehension that led him to forget, if only for a few instants, what his real duty was. But when he finally sucked in a huge, breathy sigh, squeezed his squat legs around his mount's belly, and kicked it forward, he didn't check around himself to see where his mistress had gotten to. And by the time he realized his error, he was halfway across the water, riding a swimming horse, with no way to turn back.

Ari had none of Krull's advantages. She'd neither ridden much before, nor had anything at all to do with deep water, other than to acknowledge her own terror of it. And now she was perched precariously atop an unfamiliar beast, and faced with the prospect of somehow riding it across an expanse of water that frightened her nearly out of her mind.

She held back, trying to nerve herself, trying to fight her own building panic, lest it destroy her. Her attention was so concentrated on her own plight that she didn't notice the apes from the camp were approaching rapidly, with Attar leading them in the van.

But Attar spotted her, with the same facility a wolf will always spot the weakest of prey, the potential victims cut away from the herd, or the wounded, alone and unable to flee. Not that his discovery pleased him. He had broken bread with this woman in her own home, he knew her family, and he respected her father's position. Worst of all, he knew his own commander still had feelings for this female, though what they might be now he had no idea.

Yet in the end, none of it made any difference for him. At his very core, he was a devout servant of the empire and the world that Semos, Father of All, had created, and he knew his duty, both to his people and to Semos himself. Apes and humans together as equals were an abomination.

He didn't hesitate at all.

Somewhere in the chaos he'd picked up a bolo. Now he raised it over his head and began to whirl it. The whiplike ropes with their stony ends made a vicious, whirring sound as he brought them up to speed and then sent them flying toward Ari and her skittish, frightened mount.

The bolo wrapped itself around the forelegs of her horse as tight as a pair of shackles, catching the beast in mid-stride and sending it tumbling headfirst across the ground. Ari went flying with it, arching out over its neck and hitting the earth hard as she kept on rolling.

Davidson had waited until the end, to make sure all his people got across. But though he tried to keep watch on everything and everybody at once, with the shadowy bedlam going on all around him, he, like Krull, missed a few things. He didn't spot Ari until just a heartbeat before Attar brought her down.

Like the ape commander, he didn't hesitate, but jerked his horse around and rode hell-for-leather back to the fallen chimp . . . and an onrushing horde of frenzied, heavily armed apes.

Across the river, the rest of the party splashed and scrambled up the far bank. Krull, by far the best rider of them all, was the only one who lost his seat, tumbling out when his mount's front hooves slipped on a patch of mud. He leaped to his feet instantly, looked around for his mistress, and found that, as he'd feared, she hadn't come across. He turned back and rushed to the very edge of the water, where he stopped, defeated.

Ari was still back on the other side!

He could see her well enough. She'd lost her horse somewhere and was on foot now, scrambling toward a jumble of rocks that overlooked the riverbank several yards down from where everybody else had crossed.

Right behind her raced a pack of apes, led by his old trainee Attar. Every bone in his body vibrated with rage and frustration. He was *here*, and she was *there*, and *he couldn't protect her*!

Attar! If he could only get his hands on him, he'd break him like a twig! But he couldn't, and so he threw back his head and roared.

Across the river, Attar heard that cry, froze, and raised his head. For a moment, his eyes locked with the molten gaze of his old mentor, and for a moment, he hesitated.

Only for a moment, but it was enough for Ari to reach the rocks and scuttle up.

Davidson saw it, too, and kicked his horse across the field of fire, toward the stony jumble. There was no way he could ride his animal up into the rocks. It would break a leg within a stride or two.

He pulled back hard on the mane, yanking the dun stallion's head up and bringing it to a skidding halt. He threw himself from its back, landing running, and raced up into the rocks after Ari.

She was several feet ahead, panicked, bouncing from rock to rock as she fled the horrors she knew were coming behind her. It took Davidson some sweaty work before he caught her. He grabbed her hand just as they reached the pinnacle of the rocks overlooking the river flowing darkly below.

She jerked at his grip blindly, then realized it was him and calmed a bit. Down below, Attar and the ape soldiers reached the base of the rocky ridge and began to climb, roaring and growling threats.

He tugged her toward the brink. White rings showed around her eyes as she looked down on the thing she feared the most. Davidson could feel her muscles lock up like steel springs.

He leaned toward her. "You have to swim," he told her as gently, but firmly, as he could.

She shook her head. *"I can't!"* she wailed.

Davidson heard the clatter of falling rock. He turned and saw Attar clambering up, closer and closer, red-eyed with determination.

"I won't let go of you!" he promised. Then he jumped, dragging her with him, just as Attar and several monkeys came storming up.

They plummeted into the water, hit with a resounding splash, and vanished beneath the cold black surface as Attar, breathing hard, stood on the rocks and watched his prey disappear.

Several of his troops raised their fire throwers and

sent a volley of fireballs hissing uselessly after them. Attar growled, disgusted.

Very well. Let the river have her.

Krull stood at the edge of the riverbank, shaken to his core as he watched his mistress's horse—he'd picked it out for her himself—come scrambling up, riderless. Krull watched the horse gallop away, then turned back and stared at the water. A moment later, Limbo came bobbing into view, still holding on to his mount with fingers hooked into claws. Krull noted that the slaver was no more guiding his horse than he was the two moons overhead. But the horse didn't need any help. Blowing and snorting, it followed Ari's riderless steed up and out, but brought its hapless rider with it.

As soon as Limbo realized he was back on solid ground, he fell off his mount with a grateful sigh, numbly relieved to find his soaked, soggy self still in one piece, with a river between him and the apes who'd tried to barbecue him.

He looked at the burned patch in his fur, whimpered, and began to lick the wound. Krull watched this display of cowardice with distaste, then dismissed Limbo from his thoughts entirely and turned back to the river.

Behind him, Gunnar walked toward the fallen slaver with the shackles they'd used to bind him before. Limbo looked up, saw what he was about, and waved him away.

"No, no. Wait. There's no need now."

Gunnar's dour, glowering expression made his dislike of his former captor more than obvious. He kept on coming.

"Says who?" he replied, giving the shackles an ominous rattle.

Limbo raised one arm and pointed angrily at the soldier apes still howling at them from across the water.

"Says *them*! They tried to kill me . . ."

He looked down, touched the burn gingerly, winced. ". . . like I was nothing but a miserable . . ." He groped fruitlessly for a word sufficient to express his meaning, but couldn't come up with anything.

Daena looked down at him with a hard, glittering smile. "Human?" she supplied.

Gunnar scowled, took another step, and rattled the chains again.

"He's a liar and a coward!" he spat.

Limbo raised his head and stared at the two humans. Once, he'd thought them, and anybody like them, nothing more than beasts for branding, training, or sale. Animals whose sole reason for existence, as far as he was concerned, was as objects of profit. And he'd made a profit over the years, a huge one, trading in them.

But he'd seen Attar back there, and knew the gorilla had recognized him, too. And as soon as the ape commander reported back to his diabolical general, that would be the end of Limbo and his lucrative slave-trading business.

If that were all of it, he might still have had some chance of survival, but he was too smart to try to fool himself. It didn't matter to apes like Attar and Thade *how* he'd come to be with this band of wild rebels, only that he *was*. They'd do away with him as quickly now as they would this horrible human female glaring down at him.

He'd seen Attar throw his bolo at Ari, who was a senator's daughter. If a gorilla would do that to *her*, what would he do to him?

Probably string him up to the nearest tree and leave him with his guts dangling to his toes.

It was too much. By his lights, by everything he'd ever known or been taught, all that he'd done had been right and proper. But the truth he now faced was that he'd been wrong. Wrong about the teachings he'd accepted, wrong about these animals who weren't beasts at all. Wrong about everything.

All his bravado melted away. He looked up at his two tormentors, not at all missing the significance of the chain Gunnar held, the very same chain he'd once used to recapture the human with.

"Please," he said softly. "I've got nowhere else to go . . ."

His plea didn't seem to be having much effect on either Daena or Gunnar, but then Tival stepped between the other two humans, approached him, bent down, and helped him to his feet.

"Then you belong with us," he said. He stared calmly at Daena as he said it.

Gunnar twisted away, angry. He scanned their bedraggled little troupe.

"We're the only ones who made it. I say we should stick to our own kind!"

He stared hard at Daena, as if waiting for her to decide the issue. She stared back, nonplussed. Yes, with Davidson gone—and he was nowhere to be found, nor that wretched chimp female either, thank God—she was probably their leader now. But it was a mortally hard thing, and went against the grain of everything she'd ever known, to permit an ape like Limbo—a *slaver*—to join with them.

Yet she was both intelligent and sensitive enough to realize that Limbo must have gone through some enormous change of perception himself, in order even to ask them to accept him into their company.

But he was an ape, and a slaver. In her mind's eye, she could still see, with burning, unforgettable clarity, the dead expression on the face of that little girl's mother when her daughter had been handed like a lump of still-breathing meat into Thade's niece's arms. For a *pet* . . .

She glanced down at Limbo, his features soft with his hopeless plea, and then at Gunnar, who was stony with hatred and vengeance. And she didn't know. She just didn't know. Once, it would have been her father who made such a decision. Now the responsibility rested on her shoulders, and she didn't know what to do.

As she wrestled with it, another element intruded, as Krull forced his huge form into the little knot and stood silently, watching her, Gunnar, and Limbo. Unlike Limbo, there was nothing subservient about Krull, and she doubted that there ever would be with that old, battle-scarred gorilla. But even Krull seemed interested in what she decided, as if her decision might have greater meaning than even she understood.

What would my father have done? she wondered. Then, surprised, she found herself also wondering, *What would Davidson have done*?

She didn't know. And they were gone, and she was here. Perhaps inevitably, she fell back on the truths and understandings that had bulwarked her all her life.

Apes were evil. Apes were enemies. Apes and humans did not, and could not ever, mix. That was the way it had always been, and that was the way it would be. Forever and ever.

She looked over into Krull's waiting gaze, and said sadly, "It's no use. Nothing will ever change."

Krull said nothing, nor did he move, but she sensed from him a wave of sadness that equaled her own. It touched her in a strange and uncomfortable way, but before she could consider it further, a pale shape darted through their midst, sprinting full tilt back toward the riverbank.

Birn!

Everybody rushed after him, and arrived in time to see Davidson, with Ari glued to his back, her claws digging into his shoulder, stagger up out of the water and onto the shore.

Birn was young, his own beliefs, prejudices, and habits not yet fully formed, or hardened into bitterness by a lifetime of abuse and fear. So as he helped the couple—man and chimp—out of the water, the sight struck a slightly different chord deep in his heart than it did with the rest.

He *knew* how the world was supposed to be, with humans like him on one side, and apes like Ari on the other. But this knowledge had not yet—quite—hardened into the kind of steely blindness that rejected everything else, as it had with his elders.

And so he saw Davidson and Ari clinging to each other, helping each other, treating each other not just as equals, but as *people*, and though it contradicted everything he thought he knew, he was open to the idea that maybe things could change, maybe things could be different. Maybe it was possible for *both* apes and humans to change, to discard their ancient enmity, and live as equals with each other.

Daena watched Davidson set the exhausted Ari on the ground before settling back to catch his own breath. Krull, still stinging inwardly by what he judged his own betrayal of his mistress, hurried to her, knelt, and took her hand.

She stared into his face. They'd known each other since she was in the cradle, and they didn't need words. Silently, she stroked his fur as he bowed his head, perhaps to hide a tear. She knew what he must have felt, and she gave back to him what he had given to her so many times throughout her life. She comforted him.

The other humans were gathered around Davidson. She could see nothing more than the clear light of joy in Birn's young eyes. He was simply glad that his hero had survived. Some of the others, though . . .

Relief. That cut a little. They were glad Davidson had returned, relieved that he'd come back, because . . .

She had to say it, if only to herself. Because they thought he was a better leader than she was. Because he was a man. Because he had a box full of miracles.

Who *knew* the reason? Maybe all of them were true. But the fact remained, some of those she'd always thought of as *her* people would rather have this strange alien man lead them than the daughter of Karubi.

Oh yes, that burned.

Not to mention . . .

She stomped over to him, pushed the others away, and leaned over to examine his shoulders. There was blood leaking turgidly through the tattered remains of his shirt. That chimp female had claws, and she'd left her mark on him.

Was it really fear? Daena wondered. Or something like the branding irons Limbo used to mark his property?

"She hurt you," she told him, her voice flat.

Davidson glanced up at her, hearing something in her tone, but unable to figure out exactly what it meant. He was bone-tired, cold, drenched, and suffering from the hollow jitters of toxic adrenaline overload. What little strength he had left was not worth frittering away on trying to untangle the ins and outs of Daena's convoluted psyche.

"She was holding on pretty tight," he said.

Daena grunted and slapped a wad of wet leaves onto the wounds, then began to massage the mess with her strong fingers.

"I know," she said. "I've seen the way she looks at you . . ."

Davidson was pretty well fogged in by now, but that got through. He blinked, turned, peered up over his shoulder at her. There was no expression on her face, no more than if she'd just told him the suns rose in the morning.

He blinked again. "She's a *chimpanzee!*"

"A *female* chimpanzee," she replied.

Which was about the time Davidson noticed how *very* strong Daena's fingers were. She was kneading his shoulders so vigorously it felt as if his collarbone was trying to separate from his spinal cord.

"*Ouch!*"

Daena sniffed disdainfully and dug in harder. "These are Goma leaves."

Now it felt as if she were ripping a little bit wider each of the cuts Ari had inflicted on him, then pouring boiling acid into them.

"And they're supposed to help?" Davidson asked her plaintively.

Now Daena put her back into it. She looked like a baker making bread. A *strong* baker . . .

"First your body will tingle," she told him dreamily.

He winced.

"Then you'll feel very dizzy . . ."

Dizzy? Hell, he *already* felt dizzy. Probably because her ministrations to his health felt more like an attempt at strangulation.

He peered up at her, his confusion plain.

"And if you don't start growing fur everywhere . . . you'll be healed!"

She gave his shoulders a final, brutal twist and stepped away, laughing.

His face sagged and his mouth fell open as he realized the joke. His realization was helped along by the fact that everybody else was standing around him, also laughing their heads off.

His cheeks suddenly felt unnaturally warm, but he locked his gaze with her. She stopped laughing, but didn't look away, as something else crept into her expression. Something at the same time defiant—and almost yielding. Davidson's inner heat grew, and it wasn't all just his own embarrassment.

Whatever it was going on between them, it evidently sent out signals that were unmistakable, even to a female chimp.

Ari had been sitting with Krull, conversing quietly, but now she jumped up and bounded over to Davidson.

"The apes will head downriver till they find a crossing. We should keep moving."

Groaning, Davidson climbed to his feet, not noticing the way Daena locked her gaze with Ari, who didn't flinch away, either.

"*You've* recovered quickly," Daena said to her, her voice dripping with sarcasm.

Tival came loping up to Davidson, waving for his attention. When he had it, he pointed at the crest of cliffs that made up the valley wall on this side of the river.

It was hard to see in the dim light, but Davidson squinted hard and finally made them out: two human male faces, scrawled with intricate tribal tattoos, peering down at them.

As soon as the strangers realized Davidson had spotted them, they vanished. Davidson waited awhile, but when they didn't reappear, he told everybody to gather the horses.

It was time to ride to Calima.

9

The city of the apes had calmed somewhat from the earlier frenzy of panic over the escaped wild humans, though now it thrummed to a darker, more serious beat. Deep in its collective heart, the city trembled to the ominous pounding of the drums of war.

As always in such times, the streets were mostly clear of civilian traffic, as the females stayed home and kept their children inside, while the males either made ready for battle, or did what they could to help others prepare.

The focus of all this martial activity was a vast square in the center of the city, a parade ground surrounded by armories, facing the headquarters of the growing army's commanders. The troops had been gathering for days, riding in from the nearer outposts, or, as was the case with many grizzled veterans, digging out their armor and weapons from dusty, forgotten closets, strapping them on, and taking up their duty to defend the city of their people once again. Had Krull still been within the walls, and his loyalty without blemish, no doubt he would have returned, too, maybe even as a high officer to General Thade himself—if he could have found a way to settle his old score with the general.

But Krull was gone, and it was Attar who stood just inside the imposing doorway of the headquarters, facing the plaza where hundreds of soldiers were falling into rank after rank of formations—and more arriving every moment.

He was still watching them when Thade himself came into the building, saw him, and drew him along to talk privately as they walked.

"Where is he?" Thade asked.

Attar couldn't bring himself to look at his commander. The shame he felt at having failed him in so simple a matter as running down a handful of barbaric humans was overwhelming.

"They crossed the river," he finally managed.

If Thade's stride faltered a bit, it wasn't really noticeable. However, the intensity of his surprise did thicken his throat as he stared disbelievingly at Attar and said, "You didn't stop them?"

Attar hesitated, remembering the ludicrous scene in the mountain camp, and the way the man, Davidson, had so thoroughly outwitted him. Not just escaping, but destroying the ape camp in the process, and scattering all their horses as well.

Horses. That was the most unbelievable part.

"They were carried by horses," he told the general.

Thade made no reply, just glared at him. Attar knew that with some officers, ugly looks were meaningless, and could be ignored. But with Thade, glaring silence could mean the death of a man's career, maybe even worse: death itself.

"Horses?" Thade finally ground out.

Attar sighed. "Yes, sir. *Our* horses."

Once again, Thade went silent, but this time Attar actually felt a chill, because that silence held the same quality as the blinding emptiness after lightning, before the thunder crashed in, or that one momentary exhalation of stillness before a tornado touches down . . .

He started to turn, but Thade was gone.

They had reached a large, tapestry-covered room dominated by a huge chandelier suspended from the ceiling like a snowstorm of crystal.

Thade leaped across this room, hit the far wall, and kept right on going, his mouth working wordlessly, his fingers and toes curved into claw-tipped grappling hooks. He swarmed up the tapestry like a spider climbing a web, reached the top, and then launched himself out into space.

Attar shuddered back as Thade's flight ended with a jingling crash into the chandelier, where Thade hung by one hand, glass clashing and ringing all around him as he drew his sword.

He still had not yet made one sound, nor did he even when his arm flashed out, sending the razorlike blade of his weapon through the chandelier's supports, severing them as neatly as an executioner might lop off a head.

A hundred candles shivered as the whole thing came smashing down, Thade right along with it, his sword glittering like a poisoned tooth, everything landing at once in the center of the room. Candles flew every-where, popping and spitting, and then the whole thing went up in an eyebrow-scorching fireball.

Thade walked out of the blaze, hardly even singed, and seemingly unmindful of the paroxysm of unbri-dled rage he'd just unleashed.

He strode out, found his horse, and leaped nimbly onto its back, then waited calmly as a considerably un-nerved Commander Attar approached him with the same gingerly care he might approach a hissing fireball.

The only evidence that Thade was even aware of what he'd just done was the two or three deep breaths he took as Attar walked up to him. When his com-mander was close enough, Thade leaned down and looked into Attar's somewhat stunned gaze.

"Forgive me. I'm not angry at you. My father has been taken from me . . ."

Attar had already heard, but they hadn't spoken of it yet between themselves, and now his heart went out to his general. He reached up and the two apes embraced, each finding solace in the strength of the other, and in the strength of their mutual embrace of the iron dic-tates of duty. They were soldiers, but that didn't mean they couldn't be apes, either.

Attar said huskily, "He was a great leader. Your fam-ily are direct descendants of Semos." His voice grew stronger, became a clarion call to all the things they held both highest and dearest: duty, ape-hood, honor, friendship, and Semos himself.

"Now it is time for you to lead!" Attar thundered.

The two men stared at each other. Behind them, the fire crackled merrily. Beyond them, a different kind of fire was building, a fire in the hearts of the soldiers gathering in the great square, their weapons clashing as loud as their fangs.

Thade nodded.

"Form the divisions," he said.

Attar turned and hurried out into the square. His lieutenants were lined up there, awaiting word from the general.

"Form the divisions!" Attar barked, feeling the wild and furious exhilaration any true man of battle knows when the sword is finally drawn, and the blood is fresh for the tasting.

"Full battle ready. *Sound the call to march!*"

The trumpets blared back at him with a sound that set blood boiling and turned bones to ice. Higher and higher trilled the call, as Attar's lieutenants hurried among their men, forming them into squads, companies, battalions, and finally divisions.

The city stirred as the slow, heavy tread of the ape army on the move sent rhythmic shudders through stone and bone. The apes moved as one, chimps in jingling mail, their skulls topped with burnished pointed helms, gorillas lumbering along, ponderously graceful, their lowering foreheads protected by brazen helmets the size of washtubs, their massive chests encased in gold-chased iron breastplates a human couldn't lift, let alone wear.

Above the rumble of marching feet, and beneath the skirling shriek of the bugles, lived the sound of the drums, ruffles like a thousand heartbeats, flourishes that hammered the brain into a frenzy.

Inside the homes of the city, women, children, and old men crouched, silent and uneasy, listening to the tumult of war. The younger boys crowded the roofs and cheered them on, throwing flowers down like a cloud of colored snowflakes.

The army of the apes exited the city through the main gate, an endless river of fur and metal and strength, the heart's blood of the city setting out to defend the city, setting out with the sound of trumpets and drums and distant cheers, setting out beneath a thousand flaming torches, setting out to maul and crush and destroy.

At the head of the juggernaut rode Thade, the twisting gold embossments on his breastplate gleaming like burning coals. Gleaming like his eyes.

He was well-pleased.

Death to humans!

From a distance, the campfire was a lonely flicker in the vast darkness of the high plains. The wind shuffled constantly back and forth across low ridges of rock and dust, and stirred the ashes around the edge of the fire, sending up spinning little devil-whirlwinds that held only for a moment or two before dissolving.

It was a bleak time in a bleak place, and the humans and apes huddled around the fire were mostly silent, either numb with exhaustion or speechless from contemplating the uncertainty of their futures.

Krull had been the most silent of all, sitting hunkered close to the fire, his eyes hooded as he stared at the flames. He held a thin switch in one hand and occasionally poked at the embers, but in general he displayed as much animation as a fur-covered rock.

Now he suddenly grunted, stood up, and marched off to the perimeter of the little camp, where he took up a watchful post, looking out into the night.

Davidson and Ari watched him go.

"He'll stay like that all night," she murmured.

Davidson nodded. He'd known the type before. One more instance of the often startling similarities between apes and men. It seemed soldiers were more alike than not, whether their skins were naked or covered with fur.

"No question," he replied. "He's army."

Ari shifted slightly, trying to find a more comfortable position, one that didn't irritate her numerous scrapes and bruises quite so much. Davidson sympathized. His own body felt like he'd spent several hours on spin-dry with a load of rocks.

"A general," Ari went on. "Until he opposed Thade. After Thade ruined his career, my father took him in."

Davidson grunted, leaned back, and stared up at the sky, wondering what had come between Thade and Krull. The strange stars gleamed silently; if there were constellations, he recognized none of them. He'd been a pilot, and even in a time when the planes almost thought for themselves, pilots still learned the stars. But the glittering canopy overhead was a mystery. As much as anything, that made him realize how far away from home he was.

These random thoughts left him feeling vaguely saddened, and he turned his gaze back to more mundane things. Their camp was crude and makeshift, just a fire and a few folks gathered around it. The humans, as usual, had pulled away from the apes, and sat or reclined in a tight little cluster away from where Limbo sprawled and Krull had been sitting. Daena, Gunnar, Birn, even Tival, whose human loyalties were slowly reasserting themselves over his habitual sense of duty toward Ari, looked on first glance as if they were all a solid knot of dislike and contempt for all ape-hood. But Davidson could see cracks in the wall of prejudice. Tival seemed obviously uncomfortable that he was neglecting his mistress, and Birn kept casting longing glances at Davidson, as if he'd much rather be sitting with him, even if it meant sitting next to Ari as well. And something was going on with Daena, too, though Davidson wasn't at all sure what it meant. He thought it might have more to do with something female than any issues of human solidarity.

Only Gunnar, whose face never lost its sullen glower, still seemed to be partaking of the pure drafts of human-ape hatred.

God, what a messed up place this is, Davidson thought. The biggest thing he had going for him was that it wasn't his problem, that once he got to the other beacon that was still winking on his messenger, he'd get back to where he belonged, able to permanently forget about this topsy-turvy world and its weird troubles.

Ari saw what he was looking at, and perhaps read a little of his thoughts.

She tipped her head in the humans' direction and said, "They think you're going to save them. But tomorrow when you meet your friends, we'll never see you again."

Davidson noticed how she shifted from *them* to *we . . .*

But that, whatever the hell it was, wouldn't be his problem much longer, either.

"That's what I've been trying to tell them. I never promised them anything."

Ari looked up at the sky. "No, you just dropped in from the stars." She made it sound like it was something he should apologize for.

Davidson didn't know what to say to that, so he didn't say anything. After a moment, Ari broke off a dainty piece of the food Krull and the others had gathered earlier, popped it delicately into her mouth, and slowly began to chew. A crumb spilled; she paused to wipe it neatly away.

Across the fire, Daena watched her from the corner of her eye. The humans were eating, too, but the difference was startling. Daena was surprised she'd never noticed before. Gunnar and Birn shoveled it in with both hands, cramming their mouths as they squatted on their haunches, almost growling in their eagerness to shove the food down their throats.

The same way I do, Daena thought suddenly. Still covertly watching Ari, she used the back of her hand to wipe smears of grease away from her lips. The ape female was so measured, so precise. She didn't eat like a starving animal. Neither, she noticed, did Davidson.

Daena glanced thoughtfully down at the hunk she'd been gnawing on. Finally she used her other hand to break off a bite-sized piece. She popped it into her mouth and forced herself to chew slowly.

Not bad . . .

It made her feel almost . . . elegant.

Tival had been watching her. He smiled faintly.

"It's not the way she eats. It's the way she thinks that pleases him."

Daena's face colored. She dropped her food, stood abruptly, then turned and loped off into the dark.

Gunnar glanced at Tival with a sour grin. Birn was

watching, too, but he had no idea what was going on. Some sort of female stuff, he guessed. And while he found women interesting enough, what was really on his mind was Davidson, and dreams of glory. He'd never known anybody as brave, as resourceful, as commanding as the strange male who said he came from the stars. He saw himself striding beside Davidson, a mighty sword in his hand (or maybe even one of those amazing *guns* like the one Krull had smashed), slaying apes. Boy's dreams, but they were the best he'd ever had.

Out on the plain, Daena kept on running until she'd outdistanced her own embarrassment. The soft gurgle of water drew her attention and she slowed.

She found the tiny spring leaking down a rock face a few yards away. She went to it, stared at the limpid little trickle, thinking hard. She looked around, saw that she was alone.

She took out a small piece of cloth, folded it, then touched it to the water until it was soaked through. Then she quickly took off all her clothes and began to run the wet cloth over her gleaming body.

Though the following two days and nights on the high plains were cool, almost frigid, the worst part of the day could be like the breath of a huge oven, and so Davidson had made some changes.

When the heat became unbearable during the day, they would find shade, stop, make a camp, take care of the horses and let them rest a bit, too, and then take up the march again in the middle of the night.

The night's chill was still with them, painting the rocks with a gleaming coat of dew, when, two days later, dawn exploded above the mountains just as they clambered up to the crest of a low ridge.

As nearly as Davidson could determine, from crude estimates and the little knowledge he could glean from both the apes and the humans, his goal and this Calima place must be very close together, if not actually the same spot. And today, if his calculations were correct, was the day they would reach the place.

The old adrenaline rush of hope was fueling him now, quickening him as he rode along, so that every new ridge seemed like it might be the final one, and he would cross and see his goal at last.

When the heat of dawn light struck the powdery plains, it always stirred up a thin haze of dust and evaporating dew, and this obscured his view when he trotted up to the top of the ridge and looked out over another long vista of ancient, rolling stone.

He pulled up, stared, then shaded his eyes. Something out there, something that wasn't just a rock formation . . .

Krull came up behind him, noted the direction in which Davidson was staring, and grunted.

"Calima," he said.

Davidson leaped down from his mount, electricity pulsing in his veins. He faced the distant shadowy vision, squatted, and opened his box. It took him a few moments to get the messenger set up, and, as usual, when he finally got it going, he heard the customary gasps of awe from the techno-primitives gathered around him.

Once again, he watched intently as the sweep line began to flash back and forth across the little screen. The two flashing dots reappeared, and the beeping that marked each sweep was the loudest he'd heard yet. When he'd started his journey, they'd been far apart. Now they were so close together they had almost merged into a single blinking beacon, and the beeping was nearly a continuous piping tone.

He looked up.

Damn it, if not for the dust, I could probably see them . . .

He couldn't control himself any longer. He'd been waiting for, *fighting* for, this moment almost since he'd arrived on this planet. Now it was upon him, and he would wait no longer.

He gathered the messenger unit under one arm and vaulted back onto his horse, dug in his heels, and set off toward Calima at a full gallop.

As he rode, with the wind whipping through his hair, he kept on checking the messenger's screen. The two dots grew closer, closer still, the farther he rode.

The messenger was making a single high-pitched whine, as if it shared his excitement. Slowly, the veil of haze before him parted, and at last he saw the culmination of his journey.

Calima spread before him—

Silent. Cold. Empty.

He jerked his horse to a halt, dismounted, and waited for the others to catch up to him. The thunder of their approaching hooves echoed the thudding of his own heart.

He stared at the sere bones of Calima, trying to still the tsunami of despair that threatened to drown all his hopes. The messenger was still beeping, a seamless electronic shriek that echoed in his ears loud enough to wake the dead.

Which is what it will take, he thought. *That isn't a city. It's a cemetery.*

And where is the pod?

He held up the little instrument and stared at its screen. It *said* a pod was there. Or at least *something* from the *Oberon* broadcasting from an identification beacon. There could be no mistake. There was nothing on this benighted technological pesthole of a planet that could duplicate that signal. He was no box-and-wire jock, but he did know enough to understand that signals like these were digitally encrypted, to prevent any mistake about source identification. Even if these apes had been able to discover electricity and then build some sort of crude radio, they were hundreds of years away from the computer knowledge it would take to properly encode the signal.

No, if the messenger was picking up a signal at all, it *had* to be what it said it was: one of *Oberon*'s identification beacons. There was just no other alternative.

But there was also *no pod*. He stared at the ruins of Calima. Maybe they'd landed beyond the city, someplace he couldn't see them yet . . .

The others arrived, their puzzlement at why he'd reined up obvious. They stared about them, looking for a reason, but the only thing in all this vast wasteland was Calima.

Davidson was still holding up the messenger, staring at it as if he could *will* it into making the *Oberon*'s emissary visible. It was still beeping like a demented alarm clock. Davidson gave it a shake. Its stunted digital brain was telling him as loudly as it could that *there was a damned pod* around here someplace.

But *where*?

Gunnar, of all people, maybe because of his deeply inbred pessimism, was the first to correctly read the news written on Davidson's face.

He stared at him, at first in disbelief, then in anger.

"They're not here," he said softly.

When Davidson didn't reply, that was all the answer the rest of them needed. Every one of them had hopes or dreams of some kind tied up in the stories Davidson had told them. And now they could see the disappointment written clearly on his slack features, and it stunned them into silence.

Gunnar's face grew redder and redder as the full implications sank in. Suddenly he exploded.

"They were never here!" he roared.

Daena pushed in, her expression a study in dismay. Her voice shook as she spoke.

"But . . . you said they'd come for you." She sounded like a child promised a favorite toy for her birthday, only to be disappointed.

Ari, Krull, and Limbo, riding apart from the others, as usual, watched Davidson in silence. Suddenly Limbo raised his head and let go with a mockingly exaggerated sniff.

"I know this smell." He sniffed again. "Right. It's a catastrophe."

Davidson, his eyes a study in agony, suddenly turned and ran full tilt into a stone passageway that led into Calima, Semos's ruined city, and now, to him at least, the city of murdered hope.

Calima was strange. There was something bizarrely familiar about the even arrangement of its crumbled stone spires, all tilted in the same direction, but Davidson couldn't quite figure out what it reminded him of.

The rocks around the ruins were cracked and tilted, as if some ancient volcanic force had been at work here. Davidson noted all this only in passing. All his concentration was still reserved for his messenger unit, which was still cheerfully assuring him that there was a beacon from the *Oberon* broadcasting *right here*.

He hadn't found it yet. But he'd tuned the unit to alter its volume with the distance between its own location and that of the mysterious signal, turning it into a crude sort of directional signal locator.

The variations in tone had led him here, to the mouth of the cave he stood before, holding the messenger in his hand and staring at the darkness beyond. If he understood what the messenger was trying to tell him at all, it was that the beacon was *inside* this cave somewhere.

He took a deep breath, squared his shoulders, stepped past the cave mouth, and found himself heading down a dark, stone-crusted tunnel.

Within a short time, he had to slow his progress. The footing was uncertain, and though some sunlight filtered in, what illumination there was was dim and murky. The faint glow cast by the messenger's screen didn't help much, either.

The tunnel abruptly made a sharp downward turn, a feature that would have also struck Davidson as bizarre, if he'd bothered to think about it. Natural underground caves were mostly caused by running water, and water didn't of its own accord decide to suddenly dig nearly vertical corridors . . .

But he didn't really notice. Every fiber of his being was concentrated on the messenger, and the mysterious messages it was announcing with ever louder beeps. Amazing as it seemed, whatever it was sensing was buried down here, or at least the messenger thought it was.

He descended in a shower of scattered pebbles, mini-avalanches that accompanied him all the way to the bottom. He stumbled slightly at the end, and as he paused to dust himself off, he could hear muttered imprecations and more gravel-like flurries as the rest of them followed him down.

He didn't care. They meant nothing to him now. He ignored the sounds they made and plodded on, only noticing that the tunnel had widened into a larger chamber here, one that sent back faint echoes of his own passage.

And then he grunted, struggling to catch himself as his foot plowed painfully into something half-buried in the tunnel floor. He looked down and saw a small round shape that gleamed white in the light cast by his screen. Something familiar about that shape . . .

He dropped to his knees and began to dig in the dirt around the form until he had it free. Then he stood, brushing bits and pieces of detritus away, to find that he was holding a skull.

A human skull.

His mind lurched, gave a sudden yawning tilt as everything he thought he knew slipped and slid away from him, leaving him teetering over an abyss of incomprehension.

A *human* skull? But that was impossible . . .

Thunderstruck, he dropped the ancient artifact and

gazed slowly around the chamber. Now that he knew what he was looking for, he saw them: a half-buried rib cage, a pelvis, assorted tangles of other bones, even a spidery hand peeping up from the dirt.

All human.

He hadn't been wrong when he thought of Calima as a graveyard, but never in his wildest nightmares had he suspected that it was a *human* burial ground.

In the dim light, the chamber walls slowly became visible to his bulging eyes, and once again he experienced that bizarre, impossible sensation of *familiarity*.

Déjà vu. The deepest part of his mind was telling him: *you've been here before*.

But he hadn't. He'd *never* been here. What was happening? For the first time, he began to fear he was losing his mind.

Then his eye caught a familiar pattern. He stumbled closer to the nearest wall, snatched up a rock, and began to hack at the soft stone. He worked with frantic, maniacal intensity. Stone and gravel flew.

Something was under the rock!

Then his makeshift scrape made a different sound, hollow and sharp, as it bounced off some new substance. Something metal?

He pitched the stone and began to claw at the loosened stone matrix, ripping large chunks of it away with his bare hands. Bit by bit, the pattern that had first caught his eye as only a ripple in calcified limestone now revealed itself.

Something in the back of his mind had already recognized that pattern, but his conscious mind refused to accept what he knew, until, with a final gasping heave, he tore away a broad swath of stone and saw what even his waking mind could no longer deny.

The pattern. Oh yes, he *knew* that pattern. How could he not? He'd been looking at it dead on just a few days before.

It was the large emblem that was the symbolic representation of the *Oberon*. And not a copy, either. It was the exact same one he'd seen on the wall before the bridge.

His mind reeled. He let out a soft whimper. "No . . . no . . ."

But it was still there, no hallucination, but hard, cold reality emblazoned on enduring steel. And as he stared at it in horrified disbelief, his subconscious mind, still rummaging busily in the more obscure depths of memory, found another terrifying, inexplicable little shard, and cast it up for his horrified inspection.

Slowly, he stripped up his shirt and exposed the brand that Limbo's handlers had seared into his flesh. The scab had cracked away in places, exposing the bright pink glisten of healing scar tissue, but the shape was plain enough. *Too plain . . .*

The two were the same. Not precisely, but the resemblance was undeniable. The brand was only a section of the *Oberon*'s full emblem, but there could be no doubt at all as to its source.

Because the *Oberon*'s emblem had a purpose more specific than simple decoration. Every ship in the fleet had a different sigil, each one designed by computers to be unique, and to serve as a visual identifier of each vessel. That a planet full of apes could stumble on even part of that shape by accident was . . . well, it was impossible.

But so was everything else.

For a long moment, his mind simply shut down for extensive recalibration. When he awakened, he was more or less sane again, though no happier. But at least it was better than just standing there pointing at a pattern on a wall and screaming silently.

He turned, lurched away from the emblem, and put his shirt back into place. But now that he was seeing with new eyes, *everything* looked familiar.

He even knew which way to go.

He found the animal cages right where he remembered them to be. They'd been crusted over, and took a bit of chipping to see clearly, but there they were, coated with a thick layer of limestone, and beneath that, metal bars smelted to last in pristine purity a thousand years, now rusted and pitted with corrosion.

On a nearby wall, a warning sign still peeped through, or at least part of it did. He'd seen it fresh and bright not long ago, in the animal labs as he held Pericles's trusting hand.

CAUTION: LIVE ANIMALS, that sign had read, in bright, clear letters. Now, after God knew how many years, much of its message had been scoured away, or obscured by the slow growth of stone across its face.

Only a few of the original letters were still visible. They spelled out a single word: CA . . . LI . . . MA.

Calima. The city of the First Ape. For the monkeys, the city of the creator, literally the city of Semos.

He didn't want to think about the implications, in fact, he *refused* to think about them, at least not until he'd seen the rest, not until he'd confirmed that his hopes were as dusty and dead as the wreckage he now knew surrounded him.

He left the cavern that had once been the animal labs and headed back past the emblem he'd excavated from the cavern wall. Not far away was a wide, smooth expanse of stone, but thin here, barely coating the familiar shapes he could make out beneath.

He found what he was looking for and chipped away the rocky carapace that covered it, to reveal the *Oberon*'s bridge lock control mechanism, and the hand reader that activated it.

Trembling, he extended one hand over the identification plate and waited.

Nothing happened. He let out a long breath. Why should anything happen? The *Oberon* had been designed for the ages, made with impossibly obdurate steel alloys, powered by a source that had no moving parts and should last for millennia, but *how long had it been?*

Evidently too long.

A deep hum filled the chamber, as if a long-buried, deeply hidden giant had begun to grumble up out of slumber. He knew that hum.

He sensed a building tension, a strain, as if some secret power strained against invisible chains. Then, with a sharp crack, the thin layer of stone on the wall before him shivered, cracked, and fell away, revealing the wide glass barrier of the bridge itself. Beyond that wall, light began to glow.

Then the whole thing was sliding open. A billow of stale, dead air blew out into his face, as a thick layer of dust, undisturbed for centuries, swirled up in a hundred spreading clouds.

Hacking and wheezing, half blinded by the acrid dust, Captain Leo Davidson staggered on through into the entombed bridge of the vessel he'd departed in such hope and valor only a few days before.

Behind him, Daena and Ari, for once together without fighting, moved carefully across the outer chamber toward the glow of light they saw behind the strange transparent shield. They both noticed the emblem that had been partly revealed on the wall, but neither spoke of it. Ari knew that it represented Semos, and Daena hated the other things it represented to her.

They crept through the opening onto the bridge, and saw Davidson standing in the center of the vast room, staring silently, deep in thought. He looked as frozen as everything else around there.

The two females also looked around, understanding nothing of what they saw, but knowing that it must be very important to Davidson.

Daena was the first to speak. She took a hesitant step toward him, paused, then said, "What is it?"

Davidson gave a start. He hadn't even noticed their arrival. He shook his head, as if he still couldn't believe it. "It's my *ship*," he replied.

Ari was lost. Apes feared water, and shipbuilding was not one of their primary interests. And even so, the few ships Ari had ever heard described—crude log rafts, mostly—bore no resemblance to this amazing, intricate chamber.

"But these ruins are thousands of years old," she protested, noting with some worry the wild, strange glint that had begun to gleam in Davidson's eyes.

Davidson started to laugh, but caught himself just before it could belch out in some kind of hysterical cackle. "I was here, just a few days ago."

Neither Ari nor Daena could make any sense of *that*,

and Davidson was in no mood to try to enlighten them. He wasn't sure he could enlighten himself, as far as it went. Though the few moments of intense thought he'd experienced before the females arrived had given him a few ideas . . .

None of which, of course, he could meaningfully explain in a culture where human-drawn slave carts were considered a pinnacle of technological achievement. He sighed and left them to their puzzlement as he turned and headed for the main control boards. These had been primarily Commander Vasich's domain, though Davidson, as a pilot, was as familiar with the control sets on the bridge as he was with all the rest aboard the *Oberon* and its pods.

The touchpads and keyboards were covered with dust and a thin scattering of soil, but no stone had ever grown here. It took only a few moments of frantic dusting before he had a workable operation in front of him. The ship might now be thousands of years old, but his piloting reflexes were still fresh as new-picked petunias. He ran his fingers across one board with the skill of a concert pianist, and then began to press a complicated series of keys.

The boards themselves began to light, and above them the screens, untouched except for some dust, also flared into brightness. Davidson punched one key and glanced at the nearest screen.

A series of bright digital numbers began to scroll through a long, rising series, finally dialing to a halt on the figures: 5021.946.

Fifty twenty-one, Davidson thought. Three thousand years. They sure knew how to build stuff back then . . .

Okay. So they had power, and working controls. Let's see what else they had.

He played a few more practiced arpeggios, heard Ari and Daena gasp as the bridge lights began to flash on, section by section. His lips quirked. Outside of sunlight, this was no doubt the brightest light they'd ever seen, surely the brightest indoor light. These were thousand-candlepower shielded overhead fixtures, designed to light up the bridge like an operating room, which, in a sense, was exactly what it was.

After he had the light he needed powered up, Davidson hesitated a moment over the next control board he turned to. What he wanted would require the ship's computers, which were considerably more complicated—and delicate—than the remote subsystems that powered such things as the digital screens and the automatic clocks built into them.

Well, there was only one way to find out . . .

He tapped a few more keys, then reached over and pushed the red ship's tracking lever all the way forward. Immediately the main screen lit up, as the ship's systems swung into action and began to seek any remote beacon sources. Davidson watched a huge version of the tracking line sweep across the screen, and noted the single beacon point it illuminated.

He sighed and glanced at the two goggle-eyed females. "This is what my messenger was picking up. The *Oberon.*" He made a gesture that said, *This place. Right here.*

He found the lid to another control box and forced it open. He activated the boards inside and began punching in new codes.

Ari moved closer, some of her confused stupefaction ebbing away, to be replaced by a lively, growing interest. "What are you doing?" she asked him.

Davidson didn't look up. "Accessing the database," he mumbled. "Every ship keeps a visual log."

Daena wasn't about to let Ari hog all the attention, even if she didn't know what to say. She could always say *something*. "I don't understand," she said.

He shrugged off her ignorance. "A way for them to tell their own story."

Ari knew no more about what Davidson was doing than Daena did, but at least her questions seemed more sophisticated.

"Will it work?" she asked.

Good question, Davidson thought. He gave her the easiest answer.

"This ship has a nuclear power source with a half-life of forever."

Maybe *he* thought that was a sufficient answer, but given that the words *nuclear*, *power source*, and *half-life* had no meaning whatsoever for Ari, all she could do was shrug and try to look as if she had some idea of what he was talking about.

On board all USAF ships, the log was automatically classified top secret, and so it took Davidson several moments of trial-and-error code punching before he came up with the correct unlock sequence. Once that was started, he knew it would take a while for the ship's computers, if they were still functioning properly, to sort things out and find the correct sections to display. He spent the time dusting off the huge primary digital screen.

He'd just finished when the screen emitted a static-clogged hum and exploded with a flare of blinding white light. Davidson slammed his eyes closed, but not fast enough to prevent an after-wash of white stars across his vision, as he worried that he'd somehow managed to fry all the screen's circuits. But when he looked again, the light had subsided, and it looked as if he apparently had full viewer capability.

He returned to the controls and, with one eye on the screen, began to scroll backward through the visual log. As he did so, the date-and-time telltale in the lower corner of the screen also began to roll back. On the screen itself, a fractured jumble of pictures flashed past, interspersed with jagged interruptions of naked binary code, which wasn't the best of indicators. It shouldn't have been there at all, and Davidson wondered just how trustworthy the log would be after all these years.

Suddenly he saw Commander Vasich's face, but different than he remembered. Somehow the man's face had become disfigured with prominent burn scars, and looked much older besides. The scars were like faded purple worm tracks across his face.

Abruptly the sound of his voice filled the bridge. It was tremulous and weak, as if he were making some kind of deathbed speech.

"We were searching for a pilot lost in an electromagnetic storm," Vasich whispered.

Davidson pointed at himself and raised his eyebrows at Daena and Ari.

"When we got close, our guidance systems went haywire," Vasich went on, before dissolving in another burst of visual and aural static.

"They couldn't find me," Davidson said. "Because I was punched forward through time."

Vasich reappeared, evidently speaking at a later date. "We've received no communications since we crash-landed. This planet is uncharted and uninhabited." He coughed. "We're trying to make the best of it. The apes we brought along have been helpful. They're stronger and smarter than we ever imagined . . ."

Davidson remembered Pericles and his bag of treats. *I bet they were still lousy pilots, though*, he thought.

The screen blanked out again, wave after wave of static, and strange, blooping sounds from the speakers. Davidson went to work on the controls, looking for undamaged fragments of the log.

He kept on working, trying one search after another, but with no luck for a long time. Then, suddenly, he struck pay dirt again when Lieutenant Colonel Grace Alexander's face suddenly appeared on the screen above their heads.

Davidson stared at the woman, shocked by what he saw. Vasich had been bad enough, but, even knowing what had happened, to see the woman he remembered as youthful and vibrant now shrunken and desiccated by age was a weirder thing than he wanted to deal with.

Her hair was long, dull, and silvered, her eyes flat and dim with weariness. But some shreds of her previous determination still remained with her, and she faced the recording cameras with tough-minded stubbornness. The recorders were picking up ominous sounds issuing from somewhere behind her, a heavy, continuous thudding, as if something massive was trying to batter down the hatch into her compartment.

"The others have fled into the mountains," she said, her voice dry and husky with tension. "The apes are out of control. One male named Semos, who I raised my-self, has taken over the pack. He's extremely brutal."

Suddenly her voice broke.

"We have some weapons, but I don't know how much longer we'll last."

She glanced over her shoulder at something off-camera. The thudding sound was rising to a crescendo now. Alexander stared for a moment, then turned back.

"Maybe I saw the truth when they were young and wouldn't admit it. We taught them too well. They were apt pupils—"

She broke off again as a thunderous crash sounded behind her. Her face blurred into a mask of horror. She raised one arm, trying to shield herself, but then four huge apes bounded into the picture and overwhelmed her. The largest—Semos himself, Davidson guessed—suddenly looked directly at the camera. He bared his fangs in a ferocious snarl. The last thing Davidson saw was a huge ape hand reach toward him, blocking everything . . .

And then nothing. Static.

He watched to make sure nothing else would appear, but in his heart he knew it wouldn't. He'd just seen, not the last of Semos's victories, but the first. Pupil had replaced teacher in the most brutally final way possible, and in so doing, one of the pupils had made himself a god.

He wondered if they'd eaten Alexander after they finished killing her, then shuddered at the thought.

Finally he reached for the controls and made the static go away. He wished he could make the memories of what he'd just seen vanish so easily.

10

The sounds on the bridge were subdued, as the two females tried to absorb what they'd seen on the screen.

Davidson was scrolling through the crew lists on the screen, until he found his own name and froze the page.

Captain Leo Davidson.

Missing in action.

He didn't know whether to laugh or cry, although laughter seemed the more obvious reaction. He wasn't missing. *They* were . . .

Nonetheless, he realized his eyes were stinging. For them, partly, even Vasich, and for himself as well. Because he really was missing, in one very essential way. He was still alive, yes, but now he knew he was marooned on a world he'd never imagined could exist.

I found me, he thought. *I just don't like* where *I found me . . .*

Ari seemed to sense his mood, and knelt beside him.

Davidson looked down at her. "The crash, their deaths. They're all dead because they were looking for me."

It was harsh, but he'd never been one to shy away from the truth, whether it hurt or not.

Her eyes gleamed at him. "But we're all alive because of you."

He didn't know how to answer her, because what he felt at that moment—that he wished he'd never seen her planet—would only have crushed her. Instead, he turned away, fiddled meaninglessly with the controls. One of the digital gauges caught his eye.

He paused, stared. Could it be . . . ?

"There's a little power left in one of the fuel rods . . ." he muttered, his fingers beginning to dance on the boards with real purpose again.

Daena watched him, saw the change. "You're trying to find a way to leave us," she said suddenly.

Davidson looked up, gazed around the bridge with something very much like hunger.

"I've been away from home for thousands of years," he said softly.

Davidson, Ari, and Daena emerged from the mouth of the tunnel into the haze-softened light of Calima. A few moments later, the rest came straggling out, their expressions shifting among various flavors of confusion, dismay, or just simple shock.

Calima was not a large city. In fact, it wasn't even a city at all, in any real sense. Now that Davidson knew what it really was, he saw it in a new light. Those bizarrely tilted spires were nothing more than the *Oberon*'s drive tubes, scarred with scorch marks and encrusted with millennia of rocky accumulation. It was obvious that the earliest apes, those led by Semos himself, had done some crude building here. And over the years either his descendants, or, once actual knowledge of his existence had faded into divinity, his acolytes and worshippers had also built modest structures here and there. Religion aside, though, it was really nothing more than a long-forgotten crash site.

As he wandered aimlessly out from under the shadows of those tall blast tubes, Davidson almost laughed. The apes had no idea what was really here. For one thing, they had a functional nuclear reactor. They also had electricity, radio, probably weapons, the ship's library, and probably a hundred other things he hadn't even thought of. If the apes understood what the ship was and began to exploit it properly, they could probably develop a high-tech civilization in only a few hundred years, and maybe even faster. Of course, he wouldn't be around to see it . . .

Depression battered at Davidson's psychic defenses. There was going to be no rescue. His potential rescuers had been dead and dust for nearly a hundred generations, and now he was alone on a planet ruled absolutely by hostile monkeys. It was fairly difficult to see much of a future for himself in that.

So he didn't really notice the strangers until he almost stumbled over them as they emerged out of the haze in a wide, loose circle surrounding Calima.

He stopped and stared at them, already numb, and incapable of feeling much more surprise. They halted as well, and stared at him, too.

Humans. Lots of them. Men, women, children, most of the males marked with those tribal tattoos he now realized incorporated elements of the *Oberon's* identification emblem. The human legacy had spread far and wide, and the humans here didn't even know what it was.

Many of them, men and women alike, were loaded down with huge packs. The men carried weapons, handmade spears with stone points, or sharp tips carved and then hardened in fire. Also clubs, and stone knives, even a few pieces of honed metal they'd scrounged from who knows where.

Closest to the ruins were two he recognized. He'd seen them peering down at him from the cliffs at the river where the apes had camped. This time, they didn't run when they saw him staring at them. They stood stolidly, as scores more of their people material- ized out of the dust to join them.

His own people were standing with him now, and for once, he was glad of it. Playing odd man out with a hundred barbarians of whose intentions he knew noth- ing about was not a game he relished.

"Who the hell are they?" he asked of no one in particular.

Tival stepped closer. "Your story is spreading through the villages. They all want to see this human who defies apes."

As the implications of that notion flashed through Davidson's mind, he felt a sudden surge of almost un- bearable weariness.

"Send them back," he said.

"Back where?" Daena flared. "They've left their homes to be with you."

Oh, *great,* Davidson thought, as he watched more of

them appear. Lots more of them. Hundreds. All seeing him as their savior, maybe. Their human Semos.

He wanted to scream at them: *I'm no god, and neither was Semos. He was an escaped monkey, and I'm only a marooned space pilot.*

But gods and saviors existed as much in the eyes of their beholders as they did in reality. And he could see their eyes . . .

They cheered him as he moved through the motley crowd, pushed close to him, touched his strange, ragged garments in wonder. He felt hemmed in, oppressed by their adoration, stifled by the hope they laid on his back like a great stone. But he couldn't turn away. If he was stuck here forever, these were his people. And he *did* know a few things, the most important of which was that the apes weren't inherently superior to humans. Maybe it was time he taught that to these humans, as well.

Limbo appeared out of the crowd, close behind him, talking rapidly. "See if you can talk your space friends into taking me. Because whichever way this goes, I'm out of business."

What space friends? Davidson wanted to yell at him, but he settled for simply walking away from him, and plunging deeper into the crowd. He'd had it with monkeys for the time being, especially not very reliably reformed chimpanzee ex-slavers with fast feet and faster tongues.

Ari materialized next to him, and that worried him a little. These humans might be as degraded and beaten down as any he'd seen, but they outnumbered the three apes fifty to one. And he doubted any of them had much use for apes. Live ones, at least. Most of them glared at Ari, although nobody made any overt attack.

Not yet, Davidson thought.

Ari didn't seem to notice, though, and kept on walking with him, staring in wonder at the joyous expressions on the faces around her.

Then one face jumped out of the crowd. A small woman of Asian ancestry, hesitantly pushing forward a little blond girl. Davidson stared at her, trying to remember. Bon, that was her name. Ari's old servant. And the girl was the one they'd rescued from Thade's niece. The *pet*.

Ari leaped toward her and the two females, human and ape, embraced. Suddenly they both burst into tears. The little girl, shy and frightened, hid behind Bon, but then Ari dropped to her knees and coaxed her out. Ari lifted her and cuddled her, and after a long moment, the child relaxed and smiled up at her.

Davidson was touched. *I guess that's about as hopeful as anything I've seen today*, he thought. But then a darker memory intruded. He doubted if General Thade would agree with him.

At dusk, Davidson stood on the top of the cliffs that ringed the Plain of Calima and the most spectacular sunset he'd ever seen. What with the perpetual haze, and the high clear air above, the setting of the dual suns touched off a blood-crimson and gold riot of light across the fading sky.

It should have been a moment of peace and repose, but Davidson's face was creased with deep lines of worry. Down below, the camp near the city was still growing as more and more wild humans gravitated toward the holy city of the apes, and the mighty human hero that rumor told them was waiting for them here. Many fires had been kindled, adding to the haze, and even from his high vantage point, he could hear the distant murmuring hum of their chatter, like the hollow whisper of some faraway sea.

They thought they were coming to find salvation, Davidson knew. But from what he could see, all they were doing was turning themselves into the biggest target on the planet.

And what was he supposed to do about *that*?

Far away across the plain, where the shadows had deepened into night, Birn rode in silence and solitude, his thoughts also wrinkled with worry. Not the same worries that Davidson struggled with. Birn still felt the same youthful confidence in the alien man that he always had. But his sharp ears had detected an ominous thunder, still far, far away, but moving closer.

A range of wind-scoured hills thrust up from the plains nearby. He kicked his horse and galloped quickly up until he topped the crest.

From this height, the horizon was a long way away, and in the dim light, he probably wouldn't have been able to see it at all. But the distant line was etched with flickering fire. Hundreds of torches, he guessed. He didn't have to guess who would be carrying them in such disciplined lines, and he didn't have to be a genius to know that the distant, muted thunder he heard was the *thud-thud-thud* of battle drums.

He watched for a while longer, then grabbed his horse's mane, wheeled, and galloped back down with the wind streaming in his hair.

Davidson had returned to his own camp in the ruins of Calima when Birn came racing up, yanked his mount to a halt, and threw himself down. He ran to Davidson and, still breathing hard, blurted, *"I saw them!"*

Before Davidson could say anything, Krull looked up at the boy and growled, "How many?"

Birn spread his arms wide. "As far as I could see."

Krull raised his thick eyebrows in surprise. Then he thought about it a moment before he turned to Davidson and said, "Thade has brought all his legions. That means the senate has capitulated. He answers to no one now."

Davidson didn't need any manuals of military strategy to understand what *that* meant. He turned to Daena, who was listening anxiously.

"Get your people away from here," he told her. "They can go to the mountains, hide. While there's still a chance."

Daena shook her head. "They won't listen to me."

Davidson started to argue, then stopped. She was probably right. Most of them out there didn't know her. Why would they pay any attention to her? There was only one they would all listen to . . .

"Okay," he said. "If they came here to follow me, I'll let them follow."

The word had gone out among the humans encamped around Calima that the strange, wild human would speak to them. Since rumors were running rampant that a huge army of apes was also bearing down on them, and would arrive at any moment, when Davidson climbed onto his horse and rode out to face the crowd, everybody was there waiting for him to speak.

His appearance was greeted with more cheers, until he waved his arms for silence.

"This is a fight we can't win," he shouted. He waved toward the mountains that edged the plain. "Break up and scatter! I'll draw them off. I'm the one they want!"

A low mutter of fear ran through the crowd. Men raised their fists, watching him.

"Let's go!" he cried, and kicked his horse away from the camp.

He got several hundred yards before he realized his was alone. Nobody was following him. He turned, looked back, and saw Daena and the rest, standing silent with the rest of the humans, staring at him.

There was nothing else to do. He turned around and rode back, clattered up to Daena, stopped, and dismounted.

"They don't understand," he told her urgently. "It's over. *Finished*. There's no help coming!"

Her eyes were luminous. She reached up, stroked his cheek.

"You came . . ." she whispered.

Then she kissed him.

The haze above the plain persisted even after darkness fell; over the huge camp of the ape army, it hung like a foggy reflecting shield, reflecting the dull glow of a thousand campfires.

Near the edge of the camp, a huge shape slipped through the flickering shadows toward Attar, who stood and stared silently out over the plain.

Suddenly Attar looked up. Something moving out there, coming toward him. "Stop!" he barked.

No reply.

Attar went tense, his nostrils widening along with his eyes. He strained with every sense, as the hairs at the base of his spine rose straight up. Something . . . there!

"Come closer and identify yourself!"

The shadow paused, moved toward him, then solidified into a gorilla even bigger than he was.

Krull.

Attar stared at his old mentor in disbelief. "You dare show your face here?" he rasped.

Krull spread his hands. "It was not my decision."

Then he moved aside, to reveal the one who'd been hiding behind him. Ari looked at Attar.

"I wish to speak to Thade," she said.

It took Attar a moment to gather his wits. He'd not expected to see either of these apes again, unless it was at the tip of his sword.

He shook his head. "Impossible. You have betrayed your race."

Krull snarled softly. "And *you* have betrayed everything I taught you."

That stung. Attar glowered at him. "I could have you killed on the spot."

Krull moved forward a step, shielding Ari. He lowered his arms and flexed the immense muscles that corded his back. His lips pulled back to reveal a great expanse of yellow fang. A growl bubbled low in his throat.

"You could try," he told Attar.

Ari quickly stepped between the two gorillas. She

placed a light hand on Krull's chest, restraining him, as she spoke to Attar.

"Don't you ever think we apes have lost our way? Don't you ever have any doubts?"

Attar almost laughed. What did this female think he was doing, standing out here on the edge of nowhere, staring off into the distance? Thinking about breakfast? Oh yes, he had doubts. Although he had no intention of letting her see them.

Then he realized she saw them anyway. Saw something, at least. *Am I that obvious?* he wondered.

He stared at her while she waited. Finally, he nodded. And led her into the camp.

The inside of Thade's tent was no palace, but it was larger than that of an ordinary officer, littered with maps, armor, weapons, clothing.

Ari stood just inside the door, her head down, waiting. Krull and Attar remained outside, trying to ignore each other, as both cocked their heads to listen.

Thade looked Ari up and down, as if he'd found something painful and repulsive stuck to the bottom of his foot.

"Why have you come?" he said at last.

She looked up at him. "To be with you. Isn't that what you want?"

Thade stalked toward her, then circled her in silence, as if he were inspecting a piece of goods offered to him for sale.

He snorted in disdain. "A trade? That's what you're proposing. Yourself for the humans."

He looked away suddenly. "Even when you were young, you took in stray humans. Your family always indulged your every whim."

Suddenly his hand lashed out, and Ari flinched. But Thade only smiled as he picked a fleck of dirt from her fur.

"Now look at what you've become." His voice was thick with disgust, and . . . something else.

Or at least Ari thought she heard something else, and it was to that she launched her final appeal. She let herself relax into a position of submission whose meaning and intent would be unmistakable to any male ape.

Thade froze.

"It's what you want, isn't it?" she whispered. "I will be with you."

And in that instant she saw him waver, his iron will close to breaking . . .

He pulled back. Physically stepped back, turned away from her, from what she offered.

"I have no feelings for you now," he said thickly.

He reached into a pile of clothes, pulled out a colorful scarf. Ari recognized it. It was the one he'd taken from her in her bedroom.

He let it flutter as he went to his fire. He gave it a final stroke, then dropped it into the flames.

Thade watched it spark as it burned, his gaze hooded and thoughtful. Suddenly he reached into the fire and withdrew a branding iron. He spun, catching her hand with his one free hand as he plunged the searing metal into her flesh. The smell of burning hair filled the tent. Ari uttered a sharp moan of agony.

"You want to be human?" Thade snarled. *"Then wear their mark!"*

The tent shook as Krull sprang through the door,

snarling, closely followed by Attar, his own fangs wide. The two gorillas faced each other.

Thade looked at them, then dropped Ari's wounded hand and gestured at Attar to calm himself.

"Let them return," he told his commander. "Tomorrow they will die with the humans."

Slowly Attar relaxed, nodded. He stepped back from Krull. The old gorilla touched Ari, who seemed stunned, and gently led her out.

Thade followed them outside the door of his tent and stood, watching them walk away. After a long moment, he turned to go back inside, but before he let the tent flap fall, he cast one final glance over his shoulder at her, just before she vanished in the shadows.

She didn't see. He was glad. He felt as if he'd just fought the greatest battle of his life. He didn't want her to know how close the final outcome had been.

With the ruins of Calima at his back, Davidson stood beneath the hazy stars with Daena and the rest of the humans closest to him.

"There's one possibility. One shot, but it's worth taking," he told them.

He gestured at the ruins. "We've got to draw them in close. Put all those people behind the ship. But don't hide them. I want them seen."

Daena looked puzzled. "What about us?"

"You'll be on horseback. In front of the ship. Waiting for my signal." His gaze swept them. "*Absolutely* still." He paused. "You're the bait."

Birn looked eager as a puppy. "I won't move until you say so!" he said stoutly.

Davidson glanced at him. "You won't even be out there."

"But—"

Davidson shook his head. "That's enough."

Birn wilted immediately, although anybody who knew the boy well might have seen the hint of stubbornness remaining on his smooth features.

Inside the *Oberon*'s bridge, Davidson blew a thick layer of dust off another bank of controls. He had the messenger box with him as he began to tap the keyboard tentatively, watching the nuclear fuel gauge as he did so.

He was still intent on his work when Limbo came creeping up behind him.

"Whatever you're planning," the slaver said, "don't tell me. The anticipation will kill me before Thade does." He paused, waiting for Davidson to respond, but when Davidson ignored him, he burst out, "I can't stand it! You *gotta* tell me!"

Davidson grinned a little, then looked away from what he was doing. "We can't stop them . . . but we can *scare* them. Scramble up their monkey minds."

Limbo had never met Pericles. He puffed out his chest and said pompously, "We apes don't scare easily."

Davidson nodded. "But when you do, it's out of control. You start running and never look back."

Limbo started to protest, then stopped. He had his own memories. Maybe this wild human was on to something . . .

The third dawn of Calima was just blooming over the distant mountains as Davidson, astride his horse, looked down on the coming battlefield. The ape camp was just beginning to stir and morning cook fires flickered alight in constellations brighter than the fading stars overhead.

The apes seemed to cover half the plain. His own people, the humans, were clustered around Calima, and seemed to him a pathetic force with which to oppose the armed might of the monkeys.

How did they all come to be *his* responsibility? He didn't know. Things had just happened, one after the other, and somehow he'd gone along for the ride.

But they might all die today. And he might die with them. For a moment he thought of how much things had changed for him in just a few short days, how he'd gone from a confident young USAF pilot to rebel leader on a planet he'd never even known existed.

What had happened to him? Bad luck? Stupidity? Fate?

He didn't know. But somehow, this didn't feel bad. What had happened on this world was stupid, and evil, and wrong. Maybe he could help fix it.

That would be enough.

He kicked his horse and rode back down to the plain, dawn light reflecting in his eyes.

As Davidson rode back to Calima, the ape camp stirred like an angry beehive. The rosy blush of dawn hardened into the hazy light of early morning, as prebattle breakfasts were finished and cook fires banked.

Officers ran about, shouting orders, forming their men into squads and companies. Near the center of the camp, Attar stood before his general's tent, waiting. Suddenly the tent flap flew wide, and General Thade strode out, resplendent in gold-chased armor, a mighty sword buckled at his waist, his golden helmet under one arm.

Thade's eyes gleamed with martial lust. He stopped as a hostler brought up his armored charger, then nodded.

Attar's welling emotions finally got the better of him. He bared his fangs, threw back his head, and *roared*.

The sound of Attar's roar echoed across the length and breadth of the camp, where the soldiers, now arrayed in divisional ranks, heard it with quickening hearts and a narrowing of their eyes.

They threw it back, a fearsome mass thunder that shook the earth as Thade picked his way through them to the van. As he took up his position, the buglers began their wild skirling, a steely counterpoint of sound to the apes' continuous roars.

General Thade gave a final inspection to the irresistible force arrayed behind him, and then, well-satisfied, nodded at the line of mounted officers at his rear. He raised his right arm, held a moment, then brought it forward, as he slammed his heels into his charger's ribs.

As one, the army of the apes marched on Calima in the morning sun, screaming for human blood.

The humans hidden throughout the jagged, rocky crevices of the ruined city heard the blood-roar of the apes long before they saw the army.

Davidson could see a few of their faces from where he stood. They were all strangers to him, but they shared a kinship, and even on this strange planet, he knew human fear, and the stubborn bravery that conquered it, when he saw it.

Nevertheless, with the bloodcurdling thunder rumbling from beyond the horizon, he could smell panic in the air, and hoped they would hold until things began to play out. If they broke and ran at the wrong time, they would all die.

He held the messenger in his hands, open and activated, and scanned its screen as he waited. A sudden scrabble in the rocks behind him interrupted his concentration, and he turned to see Krull and Ari scrambling toward him.

Davidson didn't think the old warrior gorilla looked especially happy, but he took a place among the rest of the humans, and made ready to fight.

From above, where Tival had been keeping watch on the highest pinnacle of Calima, came a cry: *"I can see them!"*

Davidson shaded his eyes. The horizon was smudged with haze, and for a moment he couldn't make anything out. Then the distant line grew thicker and seemed to waver as the van of the ape juggernaut slowly trod into view.

He could see glints of light from the dark, shimmering line, as sunlight struck bright flashes off the officers' armor.

Closer they drew, and closer still, until Davidson could make out Thade himself, riding in the front, and a line of armored cavalry behind him. The size of the force shook him. He'd expected an army, but not a flood.

Well, it was too late to turn back now. There was no place left to hide.

Suddenly, trumpets blared across the distant host. The infantry behind the officers dropped from their upright marching position and surged forward, running on all four of their limbs with frightening speed.

It was like watching a blood-colored tsunami surge across a shore toward them, destroying everything in its path. Davidson watched a few moments longer, then ran for his horse.

Gunnar, Krull, Daena, and several others mounted themselves and followed him out onto the plain a good distance from the spires of Calima, toward the onrushing wave of apes. As they waited, Ari came galloping up and took a place next to Daena. Daena glared at Ari, then saw the brand on her hand.

The horses smelled the blood lust, and began to prance and skitter about. The humans, who had small experience with controlling frightened horses, were having trouble keeping them in hand.

Davidson yelled, "Hold them . . . *hold them*! As long as you can!"

Suddenly, out of nowhere, Birn came galloping up. Daena knew Davidson had told him to stay back with the others hiding around the city, and hailed him.

"What are you doing here?" she yelled.

Birn set his jaw stubbornly. "I'm part of this!"

She shook him off. Hundreds of bloodthirsty apes were now almost on top of them. She didn't have time to argue with an obstinate brat.

"Wait with the others like he told you!" she ordered, but by then, it was too late.

The apes came loping up, howling at the top of their lungs, the rattle of their armor like the sound of a thousand clanking chains, and Davidson shouted, *"Now!"*

The group of riders split in half, and each part rode full-tilt toward one side or the other of Calima, swirling around the city in a wide pincer movement, to join again on the other side.

The apes, enraged at the near escape of their prey, surged forward even faster, uttering savage roars as they came.

Davidson had already reached his old position when he looked back and saw Birn, riding hard, but only a few yards in front of the first wave of apes.

Come on, he urged the boy silently. *Go! Go!*

But then Birn's mount stumbled, tumbled, and hit the ground, kicking and stunned, with Birn trapped underneath.

Davidson ran out onto the plain, knees pumping like pistons, gauging the distance between the boy and the first of the monkeys. With a little luck, he just might make it . . .

He slid in beside the boy, slid in and slammed his shoulder against the horse. It shied away from the blow and somehow managed to get itself righted again. Moving like a monkey himself, Birn leaped up onto its back. Davidson slapped the horse's flank and sent it galloping away.

He turned to see Thade, his sword out and gleaming in the morning light, riding hard toward him.

He turned and ran for his life.

Thade watched him go, did a quick calculation, and realized he wouldn't be able to catch Davidson before the human reached the relative safety of the rocks. He pulled up, but the troops pounded on. The rocks held no fear for them, as they had no horses whose legs could break on the treacherous footing.

Davidson, breathing furiously, reached the messenger again, only a few paces in front of the apes. Behind him, humans peered out of the rocks, their eyes bulging, their mouths gaping, terrified at the onrushing swell of doom about to crash over them.

Davidson grabbed the messenger and punched in a few quick commands. Nothing happened. He tried again.

Still nothing. In despair, he turned to face the charge of the ape army.

Deep inside the rocks of Calima, a light came on in the bridge. The fuel monitor flickered, flickered again, then burst into a strong, steady light.

The rocks began to vibrate.

Outside, Davidson felt the sudden jolt, and looked up at the strangely angled spires, which were the *Oberon*'s partly fossilized drive tubes.

An eerie, piercing hum filled the air. Watching the apes, Davidson slowly began to smile.

The monkeys were in full battle frenzy. Only a few noticed the strange new sound, and of those, even fewer paid it any attention. They were still pounding forward, claws outstretched, when white fire belched from the spires and spilled out over them like a blast furnace.

They never knew what hit them. The first wave was simply vaporized where they stood. The ranks behind them were blasted off their feet, their coats singed away, and the naked flesh beneath barbecued into charcoal. Bits and pieces of ape, even whole carcasses, rained down on the staggered survivors, who immediately broke ranks and began to run for their lives.

Farther back, General Thade watched the inexplicable destruction of his finest troops. Somehow he managed to throttle the blind rage that threatened to send him sweeping out to his own death in those awesome flames, and forced himself to watch and think.

Suddenly the roaring thunder died, and the heat that had blasted across the plain faded away. Thade squinted. Where the front of his army had been was now a huge, dusty cloud his vision couldn't penetrate. Out of the cloud staggered a few broken troops, hideously burned, wandering aimlessly.

Thade closed his eyes. That was that, then. He'd probably just lost most of his best soldiers to that wild human beast. He had no idea what the man had done, or whether he could do it again.

He looked over his shoulder. He still had the rest of his army, though, and he didn't need his best troops to hunt down and kill vermin.

On the other side of the cloud, Davidson gazed in awe at what he'd done. The wind was stronger here, whipping away some of the murk. He could see a few wounded apes staggering about. The humans in the rocks could see them, too, and they rushed out and surrounded the nearest pair of apes, waving their makeshift weapons.

But these were no soft city apes. They were two of Thade's finest, hardened in battle, confident of their superiority over even a hundred times their number of humans. After all, did an ape fear a thousand ants?

They wheeled on their attackers, growling fiercely, and waited for the humans to run away.

And the humans did stop. Three thousand years of submission was bred into their bones, their muscles. They stopped . . . but they didn't run.

The apes stared, shocked at the unexpected turn. They raised their mighty arms, showed their fearsome claws, and growled again.

The nearest humans flinched, took a step back, then stopped again. Suddenly one of them, a man whose eyes were slitted with rage, growled back! Then the rest of them were growling, too!

Behind them, the rest of the humans began to shout. The roars built until the sound was nearly physical, a great upwelling of rage finally loosed on those who had tormented them for all their history.

The apes quailed, rings of white suddenly showing at the rims of their eyes. Then the humans rolled over them, and they vanished.

Thade saw all this, and contemplated the ruin of his duty and of his dreams. Attar came pounding up. "How can there be such a weapon?" he gasped. "We cannot defeat them."

Thade didn't reply immediately. He sat, his face like iron, as the wind whipped about him, and the shattered remnants of his van lurched past. Farther back, the rest of his force began to break ranks as the first hints of panic set in.

He wheeled on Attar. "We will attack!" he snapped.

"But sir! He can destroy us all!"

Thade drew his sword.

"We will see," Thade replied, then turned and galloped straight toward the swirling dust cloud. As Thade rushed forward, he glanced back and saw Attar leading the rest of his army after him. His fangs glinted once. Then he was in.

Davidson lifted his head, listening to the distant

sound of hooves. Everything had depended on the ape
army panicking. But if they hadn't . . .

The dust cloud had pulled back, exposing the battlefield on this side. Ape bodies littered the earth. A few
humans were still beating the survivors. Otherwise, all
was still.

General Thade galloped out of the cloud and pulled
up his horse. His eyes found Davidson as if the two
could sense each other. Davidson stared back at him,
his heart sinking.

Thade opened his mouth and roared his hatred and
defiance at the filthy human who thought to defeat him.

Limbo, beside Davidson, shuddered, and whispered, "By Semos, we're done."

Now Attar appeared out of the smoke, followed by
hundreds more apes. He rode quickly to his general's
side.

Thade waited for him, then lifted his sword and
pointed it at Davidson. "I am tired of this human."

He raised his voice. *"Attack!"*

Spurred by his command, the apes rushed toward
the enemy, and were met by an answering roar from
the humans. Thade spurred forward. Then the wind
shifted, and the dust cloud rolled over all.

For Davidson and the rest of them, what followed
was a blur, as battles always are, a jagged frenzy of
fragmented action and disjointed memory.

Davidson found himself surrounded by milling,
roaring apes and shrieking humans. One ape jabbed at
him with a long spear, growling ferociously. Davidson
dodged, rolled under the spear, then grabbed the
weapon and twisted it from the hands of the startled

ape. He kept on going, straight into the path of another monkey wielding a net like a man catching fish. The ape saw him, made ready to cast, but Davidson, still running, scooped up a handful of dusty earth and threw it into the ape's eyes. As the ape struggled to clear his vision, Davidson rammed his spear into the monk's belly. He wrenched the net from the ape soldier's flaccid fingers and headed for the next confrontation.

High above, Tival still manned his lookout. He was trying to watch the battle, but couldn't see much through the dust. Even the sounds seemed muffled and far away. As he strained forward, a sharper sound intruded. A rattle of gravel . . .

He turned and found himself facing a huge gorilla. The gorilla turned its head back and forth, fangs slavering, as if trying to decide whether Tival was good to eat.

Numb with terror, Tival raised quaking hands and backed away . . . straight into the arms of the second ape.

They threw him off the spire and laughed as he screamed all the way down.

Daena charged her horse straight through the center of the battle, slashing her weapon one way, then the other, as her mount's hooves added to the deadly work. Thade saw her coming, unlimbered his bolo, set it whizzing above his head, and spurred toward her.

She saw him coming and kicked her mount just as he let fly. The bolo whipped past her, the ropes just barely missing, but one of the stone weights clipped her head, stunning her, and she tumbled to the ground.

From some distance away, Ari saw Daena fall. She grabbed the mane of a riderless horse, swung herself up, and galloped into the battle.

Daena had barely managed to stagger to her feet when Ari arrived. The chimp, clinging to her mount with her strong thighs wrapped around its middle, leaned out, grabbed Daena, and with a single mighty heave, flipped her up onto her mount. Then she wheeled to retreat, but her horse screamed and reared, its path blocked by an advancing phalanx of apes clashing their weapons fiercely.

Ari cast a despairing glance at Daena, who sat behind her, pale and shaken. There was no way out. The apes growled in triumph and charged toward them. Ari took a deep breath—

A thunderous roar crushed the other sounds of the battlefield, as Krull, in full fury, sprang at the charging apes, scattering them like bowling pins. Some few dodged his assault and, preferring easier prey, leaped at Ari and Daena, while the rest picked themselves up and closed in a ring around the gigantic old ape.

Ari tried to ride out of trouble, but one of the monkey spearmen got in a lucky thrust and laid open Daena's shoulder to the bone. Once again the human nearly lost her seat, but then Ari grabbed her and steadied her with one hand as she guided their mount with the other.

The apes who outnumbered Krull got a nasty surprise as they piled onto him. His hands were like vises, twisting and crushing everything he touched. His claws were still sharp, as sharp as his fangs, and he knew how to use both. In moments, his gray coat was splotched with fresh blood, and the field around him was littered with crippled apes either moaning in pain or choking on their final breaths.

He'd almost fought his way free of them when a shadow fell on him, and he looked up.

Attar stared back at him. He'd lost his horse somewhere and was on foot. It didn't make him any smaller.

The two, once teacher and student, then friends, and now mortal enemies, faced off against each other. Krull raised his sword as Attar drew his own blade.

They launched themselves at each other in a flurry of whirling steel. Attar had the advantage of his youthful strength and speed, but Krull was a wily old swordsman, whose skill with edged weapons gave him parity. They clashed, clashed again, and somehow in the third collision, both swords went spinning away.

Neither ape hesitated. They went at it again, with tooth and claw, in a spinning blur of blood and fur and dust. But Krull, despite his strength and skill, was old, and in the end, it was enough; Attar, slashing and gouging, his endurance seemingly inexhaustible, inexorably began to wear his teacher down. He sank his claws into Krull's throat and bent him back, back . . .

Not far away, Limbo, trying to sneak across the battlefield and escape, suddenly found himself flanked by a pair of armored apes who snarled and rushed him at the same time.

Limbo was carrying a spear, but he didn't think to use it, didn't think at *all*, in fact, just leaped straight up into the air at the last moment, leaving the two soldiers to crash headfirst into each other and then stagger off, dazed, as he landed again. The little chimp stifled a shiver and kept on running.

Deep inside the *Oberon*, as the battle raged above, the bridge was silent. The only movement was the back-and-forth swish of the main tracking screen. The glowing line moved slowly from one side to the other, undisturbed, a ticking metronome of light.

Then, abruptly, as the locator line passed the center of the screen, a single glowing dot bloomed in its wake near the bottom of the screen.

Ping . . .

General Thade, his sword nicked and dripping with blood, swept across the battlefield like a plague, reached the far edge, and wheeled back again, his mind in flames.

The battle fury was on him now, leaving him nothing but a rage to kill, maim, destroy. He wanted the wild human. He should have killed him when he'd first seen him, that night at Senator Sandar's house. It had been a mistake to let him live, but the time had come to rectify the error. He'd seen him once, early in the battle, but hadn't been able to find him again in the frantic, bleeding scrum the plain had become.

But a quick glance showed him it would be over soon. Most of the humans were down. Some were already being led away by his men, chained up properly, as animals should be.

Only near the center was some fighting still going on. He caught a glimpse of Attar, his mighty fists hammering his armored chest in triumph. Beyond him, a horse carrying two riders fled rapidly in the other direction. And a bit to the side of that . . .

Yes.

Thade's fangs gaped wide. He jerked on his reins and sent his charger careening back onto the field.

Davidson raced toward a pair of apes, spear in one

hand, net in the other, but before he could reach them, strong fingers leaped out of nowhere, grabbed him, and dragged him down. He twisted onto his back and saw a huge monkey standing astride him, eyes glittering, a great, crimson-smeared sword raised high over his head.

Davidson reflexively closed his eyes, heard a wet, punching sound, realized it wasn't the sound of his own skull splitting, and looked up to see the soldier still there, but now looking down in disbelief at a bright spear tip that had somehow appeared, sticking out of his battle mail. Limbo put one foot against the ape's side and yanked the spear out. The wound belched a gout of blood, and the ape fell over. Limbo nodded at Davidson and continued to back toward the spot where the humans were clustering to make their final stand. Davidson clambered to his feet and ran after him.

Ari rode right into the center of the last of the human fighters. Birn and Davidson helped Daena down. She had an ugly lump on her skull, her shoulder was bleeding freely, and her face was ghost-pale from the loss of blood. They tried to settle her down, but she pushed them away, snatched up a weapon, and dashed back toward the fighting.

Davidson wiped sweat and blood off his face, and looked around. There were so few of them left. And the apes surrounded them in an unbroken ring of fangs and steel.

As he watched, the ring split apart, just enough to allow a huge warhorse to ride through.

Thade.

In triumph.

* * *

On the *Oberon*'s bridge, the locator screen was flashing brightly. The glowing dot moved closer and closer to the center of the screen.

Ping ping ping ping ping . . .

Out on the battlefield, something glittered high above the haze, but nobody noticed.

11

As Davidson stepped forward, Thade charged him. Davidson dodged, parried with his spear, as Thade thundered past.

The field had grown quiet. Most of the fighting had died away, as if everybody could sense that this was the final confrontation, the ape general against the human hero.

Even Thade felt it as he wheeled his horse, then pulled up, staring intently at Davidson, who waited for his next charge.

Thade was many things, but he was no coward. And what would his men think, what sort of story would it make, for him to slay vermin from the safety of horseback?

He cantered slowly forward, then slipped down from his horse and faced Davidson on foot. A long, breathless moment as the two stared at each other. Then they closed with a rush.

Davidson was drained nearly empty, Thade less so, but it wouldn't have made much difference if they'd both been fresh. Thade was still twice as strong and twice as fast as any human.

He met Davidson's charge with a buffeting blow to the head that knocked the human sprawling. Davidson absorbed the force of the blow by rolling away, and then sprang back to his feet, only to be met by another flurry that ended with a bone-crunching strike that left him dazed and helpless.

Grinning, Thade flexed his long fingers and moved in for the kill . . .

The heavens split wide open.

The sound was ear-splitting, skull-cracking, unlike anything ever heard on this world before. Thade froze, then looked up. All across the plain, people and apes crouched, yelled in terror, pointed at the sky.

It streaked across the heavens in a blazing line, impossibly fast. Davidson shook the fog from his brain and stared at it.

Could it be . . . ?

Then the contrail popped out, scintillating like a hundred tiny rainbows, casting shards of light across the upturned faces below. And Davidson knew.

In the distance, he could hear his messenger beacon beeping wildly.

The craft swooped lower, lower, and now the wild wind of its passage split the dust cloud like an angel parting the murk of hell—or like the ancient pictures of Semos stepping down from ape heaven—and the pod appeared in all its glory. Its turbulent wake scoured away the haze as the pod settled in on a pillar of fire, then finally skidded to a halt in a storm of

dust and light right on the edge of the rocks of Calima.

Thade recovered quickly. He didn't know what this
was, but he didn't like it. Some kind of human trickery,
no doubt. He spun around, glanced across the battlefield, and saw that, trickery or no, it was having an effect on his army.

They'd already been battered by the fire weapon
Davidson had used on them in the beginning. And now
this, this impossible flying *thing* smashing down from
the sky. His troops seemed unable to move, frozen by
terror and confusion.

He turned back to the pod. Its superheated flanks
steamed in the morning light. Its hull gave off sharp,
creaking sounds, as the metal cooled.

The hatch on the pod suddenly popped open. Light
poured out. Davidson, staring in disbelief—he *knew*
what must have happened, he just couldn't quite make
himself *accept* it—felt a shiver as a single hand appeared
in the opening, reached out, and groped around until its
long fingers closed on the top rung of the escape ladder.

The hand was covered with thick, silky hair.

Then a face slowly rose into the opening, eyes huge,
peering about uncertainly. At the sight, a deep, perva-
sive murmur of awe whispered across the battlefield.
Pericles, the chimp pilot Davidson had left behind only
a few days before, or thousands of years ago, depending on your viewpoint, heard the exhalation, but didn't
know what to make of it. He looked lost, and confused
by the sight of so many apes. Then his gaze found
Davidson. As soon as he spotted his old friend, Pericles seemed to relax. He pulled himself the rest of the
way out and made his way to the ground.

What with the heat still steaming from the pod's shields, the dust beginning to settle back, and the clear light of the two suns illuminating everything like dual spotlights, the chimp looked a lot like he was descending to Earth from clouds of immortal splendor.

Attar sank slowly to his knees, his eyes wide and brimming with wonder. *"Semos,"* he whispered.

Those nearest him heard what he said, and within instants the name was spreading in an irresistible tide across the gathered ape troopers. Then the whispers became roars, as word of the miraculous return reached even those too far away to see.

The army became a mob, hands outstretched, pressing forward.

"Semos!" they howled. *"Semos! Semos!"*

Jaw hanging, Davidson utterly forgotten, Thade stared at this impossible apparition, a chimp who flew down from the sky in a steel chariot, and appeared before them wreathed in glory, wearing garments the likes of which none of them had ever seen before.

Pericles stood at the bottom of the pod's ladder, staring about uncertainly as the thunder from the apes rolled over him in waves of ear-bursting sound.

Attar rose to his feet and ran to Thade. "Sir!" he cried. "The prophecy is true! *Semos has returned to us*!"

The humans watched all of this in stunned silence. Some of them used the opportunity to pick themselves up from the ground and slowly retreat back toward the rocks. The thunderstruck apes paid them no attention. Every simian eye was riveted on what they believed to be the Second Coming of their Creator.

So everybody saw Davidson run across the field to Pericles, pick him up, and give him a heartfelt hug. The chimp looked up at him, spread his rubbery teeth in a wide smile, then looked down at his hand. He thought a moment, then picked out his right thumb, glanced at Davidson, and offered him a perfect thumbs-up sign.

Now the humans began to cheer. They still didn't understand what they were seeing, but they could see that the relationship between this ape from the sky and their strange human hero was unlike anything they'd ever known. To them, after the disaster of the battle, it seemed a sign of hope.

Davidson heard them cheering. He grinned at Pericles, and returned the thumbs-up.

"Okay, Pericles," he said. "Let's go explain evolution to the monkeys."

Pericles clung to him happily, as Davidson carried the chimp out into a world now utterly changed from what it had been only a few moments before.

For both of us . . . Davidson thought.

For the apes, too, as it turned out.

They were simple soldiers, but devout in their belief, and unshakable in their view of their world. They had marched out behind their general, ready to fight and die in the cause of slaughtering human vermin, just as Semos commanded.

And now Semos had returned. But not to lead them to victory. No, their God now approached them *in the arms of a human*!

The process was called cognitive disassociation. If God commanded them to kill humans, but God didn't kill humans, He hugged them, then did God lie? But God had told them He would return to them, and they could see with their own eyes that He had. But if God didn't hate humans, then why did His church preach that they must do so? But if the church preached . . .

The mutual contradictions whirled faster and faster in each ape's brain. They could not be processed, could not make sense, because each part was irreconcilable with any other part. Either their church was wrong, or their God was wrong, or *they* were wrong, and—

And still the impossible pair of God and man walked toward them!

They were simple apes, sturdy and brave. They did the only thing they could. They howled in fear and despair, threw down their weapons, and ran.

The sight of his army dissolving before his very eyes finally jerked General Thade from his stunned paralysis. He rushed at his retreating troops, screaming, *"Stop him!"*

He grabbed a couple of soldiers, tried to drag them toward Davidson and Pericles, but they just pushed him away, their eyes wild, and joined their fellows.

"Go back!" Thade screeched. "I order you! Hold your positions!" He began to rave, spit flying from his pink tongue. *"Cowards!"*

The surviving humans began to cheer again, as they watched their would-be killers fleeing the field en masse. None of them had ever thought they would live to see apes flee from a human. Especially a human carrying another ape as if they were old friends.

Attar watched his retreating troops, watched his raving general, watched Davidson and Pericles. His head swiveled back and forth, back and forth. He was an ape seeing everything he'd held high and sacred crumbling before his eyes, and he didn't know what to do.

Thade uttered a low, groaning growl, snapped his fangs together like a trap, and launched himself at Davidson. He landed in front of the pair and backhanded Pericles so hard that he sent the shocked chimp flying ten feet away, and knocked loose the standard survival pack the monkey had been wearing on his shoulders. "Wherever you come from," Thade snarled at Davidson, "you're still just a wretched human."

Attar and the few apes who had not yet run away gasped in shock at the sacrilege.

Thade didn't care. He grabbed Davidson next, lifted him over his head, then tossed him away like a bag of garbage. Davidson landed hard, groaned, tried to rise. Several feet away, Pericles's backpack had rolled to a stop near the cavelike entrance of the tunnel that led down to *Oberon*'s bridge.

Davidson stood, faced Thade again, and the general, now beyond rage into a sort of red-foaming insanity, leaped at him and threw him again.

Landing the second time was like being run over by a car. Davidson didn't know if he could get back up, but at least Thade had thrown him in the right direction. Pericles's backpack was only a few inches beyond his hand.

Furtively, he tried to reach inside without Thade seeing what he was doing, but Thade was too quick. Davidson had to settle for grabbing the pack and staggering into the tunnel as Thade charged a third time.

The narrowness of the tunnel constricted the ape general's movements, so instead of picking up Davidson and heaving him again, he just punched him as hard as he could.

Davidson felt something crack in his chest—a couple of ribs, maybe—as he went flying backward. He landed right before the tunnel's sharp downturn, and when he tried to get up, Thade hit him again, and knocked him over the edge.

He landed in a heap at the bottom of the decline, and looked up to see Thade grinning malevolently down at him from the top.

Davidson scooted backward, got his feet under him and lurched on, hearing the soft thud of Thade's landing behind him. He made it almost all the way to the bridge before Thade caught up to him again and heaved him bodily through the doorway. Davidson crashed into the edge of one of the consoles, felt more ribs go, and landed on the steel deck. Thade swaggered over and looked down at him a moment, then, judging Davidson harmless, looked around the strange environs of the bridge. He seemed unimpressed.

"I will bury your remains." He spat into the dust. "So they can be forgotten like the rest of your race."

The moment he took to gloat was his mistake, because it gave Davidson a chance to finally get his hand inside Pericles's survival pack. Now he pulled it out, and aimed the standard-issue handgun at Thade's face.

Thade immediately froze, then abruptly stepped back, one hand coming up fearfully.

Davidson stared at him, then at the gun. He looked at Thade and suddenly understood. "You know what this is . . ." he said, shocked at the realization.

How? How could he know*?*

But Thade obviously did know that what Davidson held was a weapon, and a very dangerous one, from the way his eyes were bulging.

Groaning, Davidson climbed slowly to his feet,

making sure the barrel of the gun never wavered from Thade's chest. He'd almost gotten himself upright when Ari came running into the chamber, saw him, and tried to swerve around Thade.

She never made it. Thade wrapped her up on the way past, pulled her close, and used her as a shield. It all happened so quickly Davidson never had a shot, and when it was over, Thade had one hand wrapped around Ari's throat like a vise while he leered triumphantly over her shoulder at him.

Davidson set himself and pointed the gun at Thade's head. But he couldn't risk it. "Let her go," he said huskily.

Thade shook his head. "I'm willing to die," he replied. He gave Ari a little shake, then shot Davidson an evil grin. "Are you willing to see her die?"

Davidson stared at Thade, then at Ari and the terrified look on her face. He could risk a shot, but . . .

He set the gun down on the floor, and kicked it in Thade's direction. The gun spun across the steel deck toward Thade, who leaned down to catch it. But it never reached him. A huge, black-furred hand reached out, snagged the weapon, and lifted it.

Attar eyed the thing curiously, but gingerly. He'd overheard the conversation, and knew the thing was a dangerous weapon, he just didn't know how or why.

"With that weapon they are no longer the weaker race. We can't allow it."

"Look around," Davidson broke in. "This is who you really are. We brought you here. We lived in peace . . . until Semos murdered everyone."

His voice rang with the conviction of truth, and Attar heard it.

"*No . . .*" he murmured, shocked. He turned to Thade. "Can it be true?"

Thade sneered. "They'd make us their slaves." He glanced at Davidson. "*Bring me the gun,*" he roared suddenly.

Attar twitched uncertainly. He looked at Davidson, then at the gun, then at Thade and the terrified chimp Thade still pinioned. Finally, he gave in to his confusion and fear, and responded to the ape on whom he'd depended ever since Krull had vanished from his life.

Slowly, he moved toward the general, extended his hand, and gave him the weapon. Thade took it, wrapped his hand around the butt, slid one long finger across the trigger. He pushed Ari away.

He said to Attar, "Does it really make a difference how we arrived here? We are the only ones who will survive."

Ari twisted in his grasp, her gaze on Davidson, who stood with his shoulders slumped. "Please don't hurt him," she pleaded.

Thade gave a low, bitter chuckle. Her sincerity was as undeniable as the fact that her first concern was for the life of a filthy human, and not for her own. He looked at her with disgust.

"I was always less than a human to you . . ."

He raised the gun and pointed it at Davidson. His fangs flashed. "Someday," he said, "if humans are even remembered, they will be known for what they really are. Weak . . . and stupid."

He pulled the trigger. The sound was small and sharp in the silence. Click.

But nothing else. Thade stared at the thing in his hand, shook it, pointed it, and pulled the trigger again.

Click. Click click click!

Davidson shrugged. "Stupid people, smart guns."

Thade whirled, glared at Attar. "Kill them!"

Attar didn't move, just stared back at him, deeply thoughtful. Looking at him. Looking at Ari. Considering . . .

Spit flew from Thade's lips. *"I'm your commander! Obey me!"*

Attar finally shifted, as if some weight had risen from his massive shoulders, and began to speak. "Everything I have believed in . . ."

He paused, shook his head. ". . . is a lie. You and your family have betrayed us. I will not follow you anymore."

He folded his arms across his chest and fell silent.

Davidson had been moving slowly, a step at a time, enough to keep Thade's attention without alarming him. Thade tracked him with the weapon, even though he knew it was useless. He didn't care. He'd already come close to ripping the human apart with his bare hands. It would be a pleasure to finish the job.

He threw the gun aside, intending to do just that, but Davidson had finally maneuvered him into the position he wanted. Thade laughed at him.

"When you're dead and this place is buried beneath the rocks, no one will know the truth." He stretched out his arms, flexed his fingers, and began to move forward.

Davidson took one last step and said, "You will. *Forever* . . ."

With that, he pressed hard on one particular section of the wall. The move was so strange that Thade paused a moment, trying to understand. In the interval, Davidson grabbed Ari and quickly yanked her out of the control room. Behind him, the thick glass security door began to slide shut, faster and faster.

Thade threw himself at it, but the gap was already too narrow for him to squeeze through. He let out a roar, grabbed the edge of the door with both hands, and exerted every ounce of his strength against it.

The door stopped in its tracks, groaned, and then, inch by inch, began to slide open again.

Thade's roar grew into a bellow of triumph. Until another set of hands closed on his wrists. Big hands. Covered with black fur.

Thade stared up into Attar's pitying, but uncompromising, gaze.

"Help me," he gasped. "My friend."

Attar said nothing.

"I command you!" Thade screamed.

Attar looked down. "I will pray for you," he said softly, regretfully. Then he ripped Thade's hands away from the door and shoved him backward. Before Thade could recover, the door slid shut with a solid, echoing thud.

Thade crashed into the thick glass, but even his force was not enough to make more than a quiet thump. He pounded with his fists until the glass was streaked with blood. Attar watched him silently, then turned and walked away.

Thade sank slowly down the glass, his features both wild and crumpled at the same time. Suddenly he sprang up, turned, and leaped at the control panel. But he knew nothing of it, only enough to guess it might help him, if he only knew how. But he didn't. He slammed his fists down on it and splattered more of his blood across the keys.

In the end, he sank slowly to the floor, weeping in rage and terror. He, who'd intended to bury the evidence of his crimes beneath the earth, now buried himself. For all eternity.

Davidson thought it was fitting. He took Ari's hand and led her back to the tunnels. In the dim light, he saw a few sticky red splotches leading off in a different direction.

Ari saw them, too. "What . . . ?"

Davidson looked at her. "Pericles."

She didn't understand, but she followed him anyway. They ended up in the animal lab, where the corroded sign that read CA . . . LI . . . MA still hung on the wall. Pericles was near the far wall, his fur streaked with blood, working his way along as if he were searching for something.

Ari started to speak, but Davidson touched her shoulder and she fell silent. They both watched as Pericles found a small, limestone-crusted cave, sniffed, then slowly climbed inside.

Davidson led her over. Pericles was curled up inside his old cage, the only home he'd ever known. He looked up, gave Davidson a sleepy smile, his rasping breath slowing, growing soft.

Davidson reached in, took his hand, held it, smiling down at him. Pericles uttered a sigh, and slowly lay his head down.

The ape army was long gone, scattered before the winds that now swept the battlefield clean. Near the outskirts of the ruins, Attar knelt beside a mound of stone. He lifted the last stone as Ari came up. On it was written one name: Krull. He brushed it off, placed it on top of the pile.

Ari touched the grave gently, as if afraid to disturb the mighty ape who slept beneath the rock. "All the years you put up with me," she murmured softly. "This time, I wish I could have protected you."

Attar glanced at her, but said nothing.

Davidson approached, hanging on to Pericles's hand. The chimp gamboled next to him like a kid.

He handed the monkey into Ari's arms. Pericles seemed happy enough to be there.

"Take good care of him," Davidson said.

Ari sniffed at him. "I can promise you I won't put him in a cage." She spoke tartly, but there was a suspicious gleam of moisture in her eyes.

Attar turned, stared out across the battlefield. "We will leave the graves here unmarked," he said slowly. "No one who comes here will be able to tell ape from human. They will be mourned together . . . as it should be from now on."

Davidson nodded. It seemed fitting.

A loud beeping erupted from the hatch of the pod behind him. Davidson gave a start. "It's found the co-ordinates of the storm that brought me here!" he said, his excitement suddenly at a fever pitch.

Ari moved toward him, trying to look unconcerned, and failing badly. "It would mean a great deal to everyone if you would stay." She paused, looked up at him. "It would mean a great deal to me . . ."

Davidson looked torn, but his voice was firm. "I *have* to leave now. I have to take a chance that it can get me back."

Ari reached out, touched him, stroked him gently. Finally she nodded, accepting. "One day they'll tell a story about a human who came from the stars and changed our world. Some will say that it was a fairy tale, that he was never real."

Her voice broke as her tears welled over.

"But I'll know the truth."

Davidson looked down into her eyes, then took her hand and squeezed it. The beeping grew louder, more insistent.

He turned and sprinted for the pod. As he reached it, he saw a small figure leap down from the hatch. He stood, waiting, until Limbo turned around, spotted him, and twitched, nearly dropping the thing he held in his hands.

"You gonna sell that?" Davidson asked him.

Limbo had the grace to look sheepish, but his reply was as insouciant—and dishonest—as ever. "No, I wanted something to remember you by," he said.

Davidson was amazed. Limbo sounded sincere.

Slowly, he extended a plaque embossed with *Oberon*'s full identification pattern, but gleaming shiny and new. Davidson pressed it back into his hands and grinned faintly. "Make sure you get a good price," he said.

The delay allowed enough time for Daena to catch him before he entered the pod. She stood off to the side, her shoulders back, her chin tilted proudly. As if she didn't care he was going.

Davidson went to her, and as he approached, her charade collapsed. She moved forward and wrapped her arms around him, as if she intended to hold him forever.